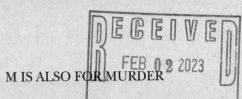
M IS ALSO FOR MURDER

I waited a good minute before knocking again, this time harder. When Joe still didn't answer, I made my way back to my van, grabbed a Post-it out of the glove compartment, and scrawled him a note to let him know I'd stopped by. I returned to the stoop, opened the storm door, and slapped the note in place.

The front door creaked open.

I froze as a chill washed down my spine that caused me to shiver despite the warm day.

"Hello?" I called. There was no answer. "Joe? It's Liz Denton of Furever Pets. I'm here with Sheamus, your new cat. Are you here?"

Still, no one answered.

I debated on pulling the door closed and walking away, but something about how it had been left unlatched bothered me.

"Joe?" I pushed the door open a little farther. "Mr. Hitchcock?"

Feeling like an intruder, which I supposed I was, I entered the house . . .

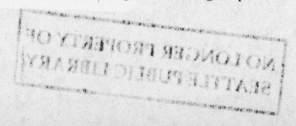

Books by Alex Erickson

Bookstore Café Mysteries
DEATH BY COFFEE
DEATH BY TEA
DEATH BY PUMPKIN SPICE
DEATH BY VANILLA LATTE
DEATH BY EGGNOG
DEATH BY ESPRESSO
DEATH BY CAFÉ MOCHA
DEATH BY FRENCH ROAST
DEATH BY HOT APPLE CIDER

Furever Pets Mysteries
THE POMERANIAN ALWAYS BARKS TWICE
DIAL 'M' FOR MAINE COON

Published by Kensington Publishing Corp.

ALEX ERICKSON

Dial 'M' For Maine Coon

KENSINGTON
PUBLISHING CORP.

www.kensingtonbooks.com

KENSINGTON BOOKS are published by

Kensington Publishing Corp.
119 West 40th Street
New York, NY 10018

All Kensington titles, imprints, and distributed lines are available at special quantity discounts for bulk purchases for sales promotion, premiums, fund-raising, and educational or institutional use.

Special book excerpts or customized printings can also be created to fit specific needs. For details, write or phone the office of the Kensington Sales Manager: Kensington Publishing Corp., 119 West 40th Street, New York, NY 10018. Attn. Sales Department. Phone: 1-800-221-2647.

The K logo is a trademark of Kensington Publishing Corp.

First Kensington Books Mass Market Paperback Printing: September 2021

ISBN-13: 978-1-4967-3171-5
ISBN-10: 1-4967-3171-9

ISBN-13: 978-1-4967-3089-3 (ebook)
ISBN-10: 1-4967-3089-5 (ebook)

10 9 8 7 6 5 4 3 2

Printed in the United States of America

1

Eyes followed me as I made my way across the room. The small dog carrier sat in the corner, next to the dryer. Most cats didn't need the bigger carrier, but Sheamus wasn't like most cats. The eighteen-pound Maine Coon looked bigger than a lot of dogs, thanks to his long tail and fur. And while he wasn't overweight, there was still a lot of meat beneath all the fluff.

I glanced back at Sheamus, giving him my best innocent smile. He was seated by the closed door that led into the rest of my house. His tail was curled around his clodhopper front paws, and his ears were slowly pinning back as the tabby's greenish eyes moved from me to the carrier.

"It has to be done," I said. "If you want to get home, you have to go in."

A meow outside the door caught Sheamus's attention long enough for me to snatch up the carrier without him seeing me do it. My calico, Wheels, was anxious to play with her newest friend one last time before the Maine Coon was whisked off to his furever home. I could hear her wheels rolling on the hardwood floor as she paced back and forth in front of the door.

I set the carrier down in the middle of the room and took off its top half. There was no way I was going to get the big cat through the doors. When I'd picked him up from an abandoned farmhouse over two weeks ago, I'd tried to do just that. He'd become all legs and claws, and I had the battle scars to prove it.

"It's a necessary evil," I told the cat as his gaze swiveled back my way. "Once this is over, you won't have to look at another cat carrier again." Or, at least, one of mine. With his health issues, Sheamus was going to need quite a few vet visits over the years, but he didn't need to know that.

I took a step toward him, hands spread wide. All I needed was to get my hands on him, and gently lower him into the carrier. After that, it would be a quick ride in my van, and then freedom.

"Here, Sheamus," I said, slowly reaching down for him.

That's when disaster struck.

The door opened and my son, Ben, stuck his head into the room. "Hey, Mom—"

"Ben! The cat!"

Sheamus might be big, but he could move when he wanted to. The Maine Coon leapt to his feet and bolted for the doorway. By the time Ben realized what was happening, eighteen pounds of feline had already slammed into his shins and around him.

"Whoa!" Ben managed to keep his balance as Sheamus careened off of him and into the house. Wheels merrily gave chase, moving just as quickly as the bigger cat, despite her harness and wheels. The two of them were gone in seconds.

I closed my eyes and groaned.

"Sorry," Ben said, flipping his hair out of his eyes. His grin said he wasn't *too* sorry; he was amused. "Forgot about that."

I'm not sure why, but the Maine Coon was terrified of carriers. Once you got him inside, he calmed down well enough, but before that, it was a fight.

"It's all right," I said. "It just means *you* get to catch him again."

Ben winced and rubbed at his arm, which still had a Band-Aid on it. He'd taken Sheamus to the vet for his last checkup, and had been forced to retrieve the cat from behind the washing machine.

It hadn't gone well.

"Wish I could," Ben said. "But I can't. I have to go."

"Go? But we've got to take Sheamus to his new home."

"Yeah, I know." Ben rubbed the back of his neck. He might be in his early twenties now, but he still acted like a teenager sometimes.

"Is it important?" I asked him.

"It is." He shot me a crooked smile.

I narrowed my eyes at him. I knew that smile for what it was. "Is there a woman involved?"

He pressed his hands over his heart. "Mom! I'm offended." His grin widened. "But, yeah. A respectable young lady will be accompanying me in my endeavor on this fine day."

"Do I know this respectable young lady?" Knowing Ben, I doubted it. It seemed like he had a new girlfriend every other week.

"No," he said, confirming my suspicions. "But this

isn't a date or anything. I actually do have an appointment. I didn't want to go alone, so, well . . ." He shrugged.

"All right," I said, resigned. "Go. Have fun."

"Thanks." He stepped into the room and gave me a hug. "I'll help out next time."

"You'd better."

Ben left the room, whistling under his breath. I looked at the carrier at my feet, and then, with a sigh, picked it up and lugged it into the dining room, where I set it down.

"Hey, Liz." My husband, Manny, was sitting at the dining room table, a newspaper in front of him, and a glass of orange juice in hand. His brown eyes swiveled up from his paper to me when I entered. "Did I see Sheamus go tearing through here?"

"You did." I moved to the foot of the stairs and raised my voice. "Amelia!"

"She's not going to hear you."

"I know, but it was worth a try."

Manny chuckled and went back to his paper. "Good luck."

Feeling only mildly stressed out, I tromped up the stairs to Amelia's bedroom.

I'd had concerns about finding a home for Sheamus from the moment I'd taken him in, and was still worried that the plans would fall through. The first person I'd contacted was happy to take on the cat until she saw how big he really was. Turns out, she'd wanted a lap kitty, and was afraid the bigger cat might be too much for her to handle.

And then when she heard about his health issues, well, she sadly had to turn me down.

But this is what I do. My rescue, Furever Pets, specializes in animals that many deem unadoptable. I make sure to find each and every one of them a loving home. Whether the dog or cat is ill, or simply too old for most people, there's a place for them out there.

Amelia's bedroom door was closed. I could hear faint music coming from inside. Knocking would be pointless, so I pushed open the door, gave it a couple of seconds for her to react, and then poked my head inside.

Amelia was sitting cross-legged on her bed, earbuds in her ears. She was flipping through her phone, blue-tipped hair falling down around her face, so she didn't see me. A pair of books sat on the bed next to her, but I couldn't read the spines from where I stood to see what they were about. They looked bigger than her usual novels.

"Amelia!" She didn't budge. "Amelia!" I reached into her room and flipped her light on.

Her head snapped up, eyes going wide. "Mom!" Her voice was loud as she tried to shout over her music. "Don't do that!"

I mimed pulling earbuds out of my ear. Chagrined, Amelia tapped her phone, and then removed her earbuds so she could hear.

"I need your help," I said. "Ben's gone and I need to take Sheamus to his new home."

Amelia's gaze jerked to the books beside her. I knew they weren't college texts—she was on summer break—so my next best guess was they were gifts from her mentor—and private investigator—Chester Chudzinski.

Her next words proved me right.

"I can't go," she said. "I've got to get these back to Chester." She rested a hand atop the books.

"Can it wait?" I asked with just a hint of pleading in my voice.

"Not really." She reddened slightly. Even though Manny and I supported her desire to become an investigator, she was still embarrassed by it. "He's working on something really important and needs them back today. I'm kind of helping him out."

"Oh." My heart sank a little, but it wasn't the end of the world. I didn't actually *need* one of my children with me; I'd only wanted the company.

"I mean, if you need help packing everything, I can do that."

"Actually"—I grinned—"I could use help getting Sheamus into his carrier. That is, if you can find him."

Amelia groaned, but rose from her bed. "Fine. Where is he?"

"That's the mystery!" I slung an arm around her shoulder and squeezed.

We headed downstairs together.

"It lives!" Manny said from his place at the table as we entered the dining room.

"Ha ha." Amelia rolled her eyes. "So, where's the cat?" A series of sneezes came from the living room. "Never mind." She tromped off in that direction.

"Do you have the information I gave you?" Manny asked.

"I do. It's with the paperwork." Sheamus had a couple of upper respiratory ailments that caused the poor kitty to go on regular sneezing fits. He also spent most of his time sniffling and sounding like he had a bad cold, but it was nothing that would hurt his quality of life.

His teeth, however, would need constant monitoring. A variety of oral diseases meant his chompers were under constant attack from his body. As long as his new owner kept his teeth clean, and made sure to take him to the vet regularly, Sheamus *should* still have most of his teeth by the time he was ten.

"I gave him his vaccines, but his new owner is going to want to bring him in every few months to have him checked out."

Manny was a veterinarian and took care of every rescue I took in. It meant that I often got to see the animals again, long after I'd found them new homes.

It was probably the only reason why I didn't break down into heaving sobs every time I had to let one of them go.

"You sure you don't want to come with me?" I asked. It was Manny's day off and I knew he wanted to sit at home and vegetate. His dark hair hadn't been brushed, and I doubted he planned on working a comb through his curls, but I was hopeful. "Both Ben and Amelia have begged off."

"If you want me to, I can . . ." He looked down at his slippers with an expression of such longing, I broke immediately.

"Oh, all right." I laughed. "Stay home. Enjoy being lazy."

"Well, if you insist . . ." He stretched and leaned back in his chair.

"Ew!" Amelia strode into the room with Sheamus held out at arm's length. "He sneezed on me!"

"It won't hurt you." I hurried and pulled the top off the carrier. Amelia eased Sheamus down into it. He tried to fight, but with the two of us working together, he stood no chance. We managed to get him safely inside with nary a scratch on either of us.

"There," I said, snapping the lid back into place. "That wasn't so bad, was it?"

Sheamus meowed his displeasure. Amelia kept her arms out in front of her as she headed for the kitchen. "I need soap. And sanitizer. And maybe another shower."

Wheels rolled into the room and bumped up against my leg. Her stunted back legs were kept off the floor by the harness that held her wheels. She wasn't slowed in the slightest by her deformity, and although she couldn't jump onto things like a normal cat, I often wondered if she even realized there was anything different about her.

"He's got to go home now," I said, running a hand down Wheels's back. "I know you like him. We all do."

She meowed at me, then rubbed up against the carrier. Inside, Sheamus sneezed.

I hoisted the carrier up with a grunt, grabbed the paperwork, and with a goodbye to my family, I headed outside with Sheamus in tow.

My van sat in the driveway with *Furever Pets* sprayed on the side, along with the rescue's slogan, *Purrfectly Defective*. I wondered if I should spruce up the artwork on the side a bit, add something that really would make it stand out, and then decided against it. I'd let my work stand for itself.

I loaded Sheamus into the back, climbed into the front seat, and then we were off.

Grey Falls, Ohio, wasn't a large city by anyone's standards, but it would take me fifteen to twenty minutes to reach Sheamus's new home, and that was if I avoided downtown. Because the town was once a farming village, it was spread out rather than up, which often meant longer travel times if I had to transport an animal from one side of town to the other.

I pulled my phone from the cupholder where I always left it—though I was trying to remember to

keep it with me more often, in case of emergency—
and gave Sheamus's new owner a ring to let him
know we were on the way. No one answered, however. I tried once more, just in case he hadn't heard
it the first time, and when no one picked up, I set my
phone aside and turned my full attention to the
road.

Joe Hitchcock lived on Ash Road, in a small home
set behind a line of trees that gave the property some
privacy. As I neared, I noticed the field across the
street from Joe's property was speckled with a dozen
or so tents, but no one was within sight.

I turned into Joe's driveway, vaguely wondering if
the local Boy Scouts troop had camped out last
night. My van shuddered over the gravel drive that
was bare in quite a few places. I was forced to slow to
a crawl to keep from bouncing my teeth from my
head.

A stack of wood sat by the front stoop, though no
smoke curled from the chimney. Not that I expected
there to be any, mind you. It was going to be in the
mid-eighties by the afternoon. A fire would be
overkill.

I pulled up behind a red-and-blue pickup that
looked to have been pieced together by quite a few
other vehicles. Rust lined the bottom of the truck,
and one of the tires was dangerously low.

But despite the downtrodden look of the truck and
driveway, the house itself looked nice from the outside. It was a single floor, but appeared big enough for
a man like Joe Hitchcock to live comfortably alone
with his cat.

The door didn't open, nor did a curtain part as I
came to a stop. Since Joe hadn't answered his phone,
I was worried he'd forgotten our appointment and

wasn't home. Just because there was a truck in the driveway, didn't mean he didn't have another mode of transportation.

I left the engine running to keep the air flowing so Sheamus would stay cool until I saw whether or not Joe was home. There was no sense in dragging the cat out into the heat if I was going to have to bundle him right back up again.

A woodpecker was hammering away at a tree somewhere out back. A mower was running in the distance. The air smelled of nature. It was peaceful. I could already tell Sheamus was going to be happy here.

I stepped up onto the front stoop, and since there was no doorbell, I knocked on the outer storm door. The bang seemed out of place in the serene atmosphere. The woodpecker paused in his hammering, and then continued on.

I waited a good minute before knocking again, this time harder. When Joe still didn't answer, I made my way back to my van, grabbed a Post-it out of the glove compartment, and scrawled him a note to let him know I'd stopped by. I returned to the stoop, opened the storm door, and slapped the note in place.

The front door creaked open.

I froze as a chill washed down my spine that caused me to shiver despite the warm day.

"Hello?" I called. There was no answer. "Joe? It's Liz Denton of Furever Pets. I'm here with Sheamus, your new cat. Are you here?"

Still, no one answered.

I debated on pulling the door closed and walking away, but something about how it had been left un-latched bothered me. I'd met Joe a couple of times when we'd discussed Sheamus. He seemed like a genuinely nice black man. His clothing might have been a little outdated, and his shoes were scuffed and worn, but that meant little. You didn't need to have a ton of money to be a good pet parent.

"Joe?" I pushed the door open a little farther. "Mr. Hitchcock?"

Feeling like an intruder, which I supposed I was, I entered the house. A pair of muddy boots sat by the door on a small dirty mat. I could see into the living room and kitchen from where I stood. A hallway ran between them, down to what I assumed were the bedrooms and bathroom. There was no dining room.

"Joe?" I eased farther into the house. The place was quiet, orderly. There weren't a lot of furnishings, but there was enough for a single man. There were no photographs on the wall, which I found a little odd, but not entirely uncommon.

A mild worry worked through me. What if he'd had a heart attack or a stroke or something? Joe Hitchcock wasn't too terribly old—maybe in his fifties or sixties—but that didn't mean he didn't suffer from some underlying illness.

Determined to make sure he was all right, and feeling like I was overreacting all the while, I moved to the hallway. There were three doors down there. The one at the end of the hall was open a crack, revealing Joe's bedroom. To the right was the bathroom. It was small, and contained only the toilet, the sink, and a standup shower. No baths for Joe Hitchcock, apparently.

"Joe? It's Liz." I licked my lips, which had gone dry. Something in the air felt off. It wasn't so much a smell as an ominous feeling. It was as if I knew what I was going to find when I opened the door to my left.

The door, like the front door itself, was hanging slightly ajar. I pushed it open with my foot, hands held at the ready, and glanced inside.

At first, I wasn't sure what I was looking at. Folders and papers lay scattered on the floor. A corkboard hung on the wall immediately inside the room. Photographs were pinned in place, and lines of yarn connected them. A few papers were tacked beneath that. Writing was scrawled across many of them, but I couldn't read it.

It looked like something you'd see on a cop drama, but Joe Hitchcock wasn't a cop as far as I knew. I had no idea what any of it meant, or why he would have something like this in his house.

Across the room sat a desk. More papers were scattered atop it. It appeared as if that was where the rest of the pages that were now lying on the floor had come from. A computer monitor was facedown atop the desk, but the computer tower itself was missing.

And behind the desk, with eyes open and staring, lay Joe Hitchcock, in a puddle of his own life's blood.

2

Flashing lights filled my vision. A pair of police cruisers sat in Joe Hitchcock's driveway, as did an ambulance. I knew for a fact the paramedics wouldn't be able to do anything for Joe, but still, I prayed that, somehow, I was wrong, and he was still alive.

My arms were wrapped tight around my chest as I leaned against the front bumper of my van. I'd refused to be looked at by the paramedics when they'd first arrived—I wasn't the one who needed attention —yet I felt cold, despite the heat of the day.

Sheamus was still in his carrier in the van, but he would be fine since the air was running. Still, I wanted to get him back home as soon as possible. I would have left already if they'd have let me, but since I'd found Joe's body, I was required to stick around to answer a few questions.

While I waited for someone to come out to talk to me, I mentally played over everything I'd seen, over and over again. Had I seen a car leaving the area? A person running or walking away? Did I hear anything out of place?

I was pretty sure the answer to all those questions was no, but was I positive? It wasn't like I'd been paying that much attention when I'd arrived. Who expects to walk into a house and find a dead body?

The crunch of gravel brought my head up. A grim-faced Detective Emmitt Cavanaugh approached. His hair was still buzzed short, but I noted he appeared to have lost a little weight since the last time I'd seen him. He still looked like a former football lineman who'd let himself go, but he seemed to be on the right track to a healthier lifestyle.

"Mrs. Denton," Cavanaugh said as he came to a stop in front of me. "How you holding up?"

"Okay, I guess." I shivered. "Is he really . . . ?"

Cavanaugh nodded. "Shot once. Death was likely instantaneous, so he didn't suffer."

"That's good." I took a shuddering breath. "About him not suffering, I mean."

"Did you know him?"

"Not well," I said. "We talked a couple of times. Mr. Hitchcock was going to adopt Sheamus." I jerked a thumb back toward the van. "Sheamus is a cat, if you're wondering."

Cavanaugh's expression turned confused. "Mr. Hitchcock?"

"Yeah, Joe Hitchcock."

"One second." Cavanaugh spun and marched back to the house. He was inside for another five minutes before he came back out. He didn't look happy.

"What's going on?" I asked.

"Are you sure the man you saw in there was Joe Hitchcock?"

"Yeah, I am."

"Have you met him before today?"

A creeping dread spread from my toes, upward. "Once or twice when we discussed Sheamus."

"And you're sure the man you met those times is the same man you found today?"

I stood straighter. "Detective, what is this about?"

Cavanaugh paced back and forth in front of me a moment. He rubbed at his jaw, brow furrowed, as if he was trying to work through a rather difficult problem.

I waited him out, heart hammering. What had I walked in on?

Cavanaugh stopped pacing and turned to face me. His expression was dead serious. "I'll need confirmation, but the man whose body you found wasn't named Joe Hitchcock."

"He's not? Then who was he?"

There was a moment when it looked like Cavanaugh might not answer me. His mouth firmed, his eyes went briefly hard, before he softened. "His name was Joseph—Joe—Danvers. He . . . well, from what I know of the situation, he wasn't someone you would want to hang around, if you get what I mean?"

"You think he was dangerous?"

Cavanaugh nodded. "Walking into that man's house on your own could have led to you getting hurt."

Even as he spoke, I was shaking my head. "That can't be. I looked into him."

Cavanaugh's eyebrows rose.

"I vet any prospective pet adopters. There was nothing sinister about Joe Hitchcock when I looked him up. And I sure didn't find anything about anyone named Joseph Danvers either."

"I doubt you would." Cavanaugh took a deep

breath and let it out in a huff. "Mrs. Denton, did you see or hear anything when you arrived? Anything that stands out in your mind that might not have appeared important at first?"

I swallowed a lump that had grown in my throat. Could I have been wrong about Joe? "I don't recall seeing anything out of place other than those tents." I jerked a thumb over my shoulder. "I tried calling, but Joe didn't answer. And then when I put a note on the door, it opened. Did you see the note?" I knew I was starting to panic a little and forced myself to breathe slowly lest I hyperventilate.

"I did." Cavanaugh reached out a meaty hand and put it on my shoulder. "You aren't in trouble here, Liz." I was surprised he used my first name, but it helped calm my nerves somewhat. That had probably been the intent. "We have a pretty good idea why Mr. Danvers was killed."

"Was it that board in his office?" All those photographs and pages connected by yarn had to mean something. "Was there something on it that caused his death?"

"I can't comment on that now."

A well-dressed older man poked his head out of the house and called Cavanaugh's name. His voice sounded angry. I could barely see him through the tears that were pooling in my eyes, though I got the impression I'd seen him somewhere before.

Detective Cavanaugh glanced back toward the house and motioned to the man that he'd be a moment before he turned back to me. "Go ahead and go home. Get some rest. We'll do what we have to do here, and then, if I need a more comprehensive statement from you, I'll stop by."

"But . . ." I had no idea what I was objecting to. A

part of me felt responsible for Joe's death, despite how insane it sounded. What if I'd shown up a little earlier? What if I'd been more aware of my surroundings coming in? Could I have done something to save him?

"Go." Cavanaugh urged me around to the side of my van. "You can't do anything more here. Get the kitty somewhere cool."

"My van's cool," I said, but it wasn't much of an argument. I climbed into the driver's seat, barely cognizant I was doing so. Cavanaugh closed the door for me.

I stared dumbly at the steering wheel for a moment, unsure what to do. A man was dead; a man I was supposed to meet. I saw his body. I never wanted to see another dead man again.

The van was already running, yet I tried to turn the key anyway. The engine complained, causing me to jerk back like it had shocked me. I closed my eyes, took a couple deep breaths, and centered myself.

Everything was going to be okay. *I* was okay.

Cavanaugh watched me back up and pull out of the driveway before he turned and joined the others inside the house.

I'm not sure how long I'd been driving before I realized someone was following me. One minute I was tooling along, mentally churning over anything I might have seen for Detective Cavanaugh, and then, the next moment, my paranoia was through the roof.

The car was a small brown sedan. I vaguely recalled seeing it when I'd turned off Ash Road to go home, but it hadn't really registered on my conscious mind. I saw it again when I'd turned down a quiet side road that kept me from having to navigate a busier part of Grey Falls.

Now, I was nearing my house and the car was still

there. I tried to recall if I'd ever seen it before, either when I was heading to Joe's house, or sometime earlier, like at the police station, back when I'd first dealt with a murder. Could Cavanaugh have sent someone to watch me—for my protection or otherwise?

Or could it be Joe's killer?

My mind raced as I tried to decide what to do. If it was a cop and I tried to shake him, he might think I had something to do with the murder, and take me in for questioning. If I pulled into my driveway and it turned out to be the killer—and if he thought I saw something while I was in the house—then he might come after not just me, but my entire family.

Or maybe you're just being paranoid, Liz.

Paranoid or not, as I approached my house, I made the snap decision to coast on by it. I turned left a block away so I could circle back around and see if I could gauge the driver's reaction. The car was far enough back that I lost it when I turned onto the next street over, but by the time I took another left to turn back onto my street, I saw it again, drifting slowly behind me.

"Okay, now what?" I muttered. I couldn't drive around forever, and while I could call the police, how stupid would I feel if it turned out it was an officer simply keeping an eye on me?

With tense shoulders and a lump in my throat, I pulled into my driveway, figuring I'd see what would happen and could improvise from there.

The brown sedan didn't slow. It drove by my house like it hadn't been following me for the last twenty minutes. Would a cop do that?

I got out of the van and checked down the street. The car was gone, having turned off somewhere. I waited a couple of minutes to make sure it didn't double back, before I retrieved Sheamus from the back of my van. I was about to carry him inside when a voice stopped me.

"I swear, I don't understand why you insist on parking that thing here."

I groaned and closed my eyes briefly, before turning to face my neighbor. "Joanne," I said. "We've been through this. There's nowhere else to park it."

"I know." She made it sound like I was parking in my own driveway just to spite her. "But you told me you might get a garage, and honestly, I don't know why you've waited so long. Look down the street. No one else has such a"—she frowned as she fluttered a hand toward my van—"such an eyesore parked in front of their home."

"I'm sorry you feel that way, Joanne. But it can't be helped. If you'll excuse me, I need to get Sheamus inside."

"Did you tell your husband about the shingles?" she asked, hurrying to catch up with me. "They're looking worse than ever. If we have a bad storm— and you know how the summer storms can get around here—they might blow off. I don't want to have to pick them up out of my yard. And imagine what everyone would think?"

"I'll tell him." I strode quickly to the front door, desperate to get inside and away from her. After the day I'd just had, I wasn't so sure I could keep my cool if she kept complaining at me. "I've got to go." But before I could open the door, Joanne moved to stand in the way.

"Really, Liz," she said, hand on her hip. She was wearing one of her favorite tracksuits, a lime green monstrosity that was probably a size too big for her frame. It was a wonder she wasn't sweating through the fabric, yet, somehow, she wasn't. Joanne wasn't exactly a small woman.

"Yes, Joanne?"

"You need to take me seriously here. Do you know how difficult it is to keep up appearances in this day and age? Sometimes, that's all we have. You're bringing down the value of our neighborhood with your neglect. All it will take is a little extra work on your part and we wouldn't be having these conversations."

The urge to scream at her was so strong, I opened my mouth to do just that, but I managed to hold it in check. Barely. This was who Joanne was. From what I've been told, all the neighbors went through it, yet I was pretty sure I suffered her the most.

"I do take you seriously," I said. "But sometimes, things can't be helped. Manny and I work hard and we do whatever we can to make our home a pleasant place, just as everyone does. Now, please, Sheamus is getting hot. I need to get him inside."

Joanne huffed, but thankfully stepped aside.

I opened the door just enough to slide both me and the carrier in. I made sure to close the door before Joanne could stick her nose in with us.

"That looked fun," Manny said from his seat at the table. I'm not sure he'd moved since I'd left. "If I'd seen her coming, I would have warned you." He paused and frowned. "Is Sheamus in there?"

"He is." I set the carrier down and opened the gate. The Maine Coon bolted from it with a sneeze. A few seconds later, I could hear him storming around the house, a pair of wheels whirring behind him.

"What happened?" Manny asked. "Didn't Mr. Hitchcock want him?"

"I don't know." I made my way to the table and sat heavily down into one of the chairs. "He wasn't able to tell me."

"Liz?" Manny stood and then eased down onto the chair closest to me. "Did something happen?"

I nodded, not quite sure I could tell him. I mean it was bad enough when Ben got into trouble for a murder he didn't commit. I'd been a wreck, while Manny had tucked his feelings away and tried to keep a strong face.

But we didn't know Joe Hitchcock. Heck, I wasn't even sure that was his real name anymore. How could I have been so wrong about him? The man I'd vetted had seemed kind, friendly, yet Cavanaugh had implied Joe was a dangerous criminal. How could I have missed that?

Manny rested a hand on my arm, causing me to start. I could feel tears threatening, but I refused to let them fall. I knew I was in some sort of shock, knew that my emotional reaction had more to do with finding a dead body than who that body belonged to. I mean, what did I really know about the man?

Apparently, nothing.

"Tell me."

I took a deep breath, held it until I felt close to bursting, and then, I did.

It didn't take long because there wasn't much to tell. By the time I was done, Manny had scooted his chair up next to me and had his arm around me. When I fell silent, he kissed the top of my head and pulled me close.

"Are you sure the car was following you?" he asked.

"I think so." I squeezed my eyes closed. "I don't

know. It *felt* like it was. I mean, it was behind me all the way from Joe's, and it followed me around the block."

Manny glanced toward the door. "You should talk to the detective about it," he said. "Just in case."

"I will." My voice cracked. "I keep thinking I could have done something, Manny."

"Don't be hard on yourself," he said. "You did nothing wrong."

"Didn't I? I should have known about him before I ever agreed to take Sheamus to him. What if he planned on hurting him? Or what if he has bodies buried in his yard? How could I have missed such a thing?"

"You can't be sure Detective Cavanaugh is right about him. Maybe it's one of those mistaken identity situations that'll get worked out in the end."

"Do you really believe that?" I asked, kind of hoping he did, because if he believed it, then maybe I'd find a way to do so myself.

"Anything is possible, Liz. The police will work it out. You did what you could and that's all anyone can expect out of you."

Did I? I rose, causing Manny's arms to fall from my shoulder. "I have to check."

"Check what?" Manny stood with me, concern in his eye.

"If his real name truly is Joseph Danvers, I need to figure out how I missed it. I vetted him, Manny. I looked into his life." Not deeply, granted, but I felt like I should have seen something that didn't add up if he'd indeed given me a fake name.

"Liz, are you sure you should?"

"What if this happens again?" I asked. "I need to

figure out what I did wrong so I can make sure I never walk in on something like that again."

Deep down, I knew it was unlikely I'd ever find another dead body, but right then, I felt as if every door I opened might contain one.

"If you think it's best, I won't stop you," Manny said. "But, please, Liz, don't blame yourself for this."

I forced a smile, despite how I was trembling. "I won't."

"If you're sure . . ." His eyes were filled with concern.

"I am."

He didn't look convinced, but he was willing to let me go. It was one of the things I loved about him. Manny would never try to stop me from doing what I thought was best, even if he didn't agree with my assessment.

I turned away and headed for my laptop. Somewhere in my brief look into Joe Hitchcock's life, there had to be a hint of the man, Joe Danvers. I was determined to find it so that I could move on, prove to myself that I hadn't missed something, and that none of this was my fault.

3

Joe Hitchcock seemed like a perfectly decent human. Admittedly, there wasn't much to go on, but normally, that's a good thing. I couldn't find his name attached to news articles reporting crimes. Nothing was listed about him abusing animals.

But there were no Facebook pages, no Twitter accounts. No websites at all. For a man his age, it wasn't unheard of, but these days, it's become more and more uncommon for people *not* to have some sort of online presence.

When I first looked into him, I only scratched the surface, looking to make sure he wasn't a violent man prone to hurting people or animals. I made sure his living conditions were adequate, and that he could afford to feed and care for Sheamus. Nothing else had mattered.

It appeared I might have been wrong.

While Joe Hitchcock appeared to be a good man, Joe Danvers wasn't.

As soon as I typed in his name, an article popped

up titled "Murder in a Small Town!" My heart just about stopped in my chest upon seeing it. I'd had lunch with the man, had talked to him. He was friendly, courteous, and showed no signs of being violent.

Yet, according to the article, he was accused of killing his wife thirty years ago. He'd denied it, of course. But after only a few weeks into the investigation, he'd vanished. No one, including law enforcement, could find him. It appeared as if Joseph Danvers had dropped off the face of the earth.

That's because Joe Hitchcock took his place.

The photograph accompanying the article was black and white and grainy, but I could see Joe in Joseph's dark eyes. When I checked another article, there was a color photograph showing a thin, dark-skinned man who smiled as he stood next to a pretty woman. I assumed it to be Christine Danvers—Joseph's murdered wife.

Joseph's skin tone was the same as Joe's, but his face was thinner, hair darker. The Joe I'd known was a bigger man. Joseph was rail thin. Thirty years did a lot to change a person, but while there were plenty of similarities, a part of me hoped that, somehow, Detective Cavanaugh was wrong, and my friendly Joe wasn't the killer Joe.

I probably should have taken the time to dig into the articles, but I found myself skimming just the important parts. My eyes kept returning to the photographs, trying to spot something that would prove that Joe and Joseph were two completely different people.

Yet, the more I looked, the more convinced I became that, indeed, Joe Hitchcock *was* Joe Danvers.

I should have known.

Nothing in either article I skimmed said *why* Joseph killed Christine. There was speculation, of course. Some claimed she had cheated on him, or that he cheated on her and she'd found out. The articles didn't even delve into how she'd died, either. They just claimed that Grey Falls had a killer who needed to be caught, and left it at that.

"Liz?" Manny poked his head into the room. "Do you need anything?"

"A better vetting method would be nice," I said, closing the laptop. I rubbed at my eyes and considered finding a dark room to take a long nap. Maybe after a few hours of rest, things would be clearer.

"Did you find something?"

"Maybe." I sighed. "It appears as if nice Joe Hitchcock was indeed Joseph Danvers, an accused wife killer."

"Accused? Weren't they able to prove anything?"

I stood and stretched. My back popped in three places. "He vanished before they could. I'm not sure if they dropped the case once he left, or if they'd hit a dead end, but the little I've read says he was accused, but not convicted of the crime."

"And he came back here?" Manny scratched the back of his neck. "I wonder why."

"It happened thirty years ago," I said. "Maybe he thought people would have forgotten about it by now."

"They do say killers often return to the scene of the crime. Maybe he wanted to, I don't know, revel in the fact that he'd gotten away with it."

"But after thirty years?" I shook my head. "It seems a bit much, don't you think?" I paced back and forth, trying to make sense of it. "I suppose Joe seemed a little lonely and sad when I talked to him."

"Remorse?"

"Could be. I thought he'd come to me because he needed a companion; hence Sheamus. Sometimes, a cat is all anyone ever needs to help them get through the day."

"Did he ever mention a wife?" Manny asked. "Or a girlfriend?"

"No. He told me he was a widower, and we left it at that. He didn't sound like he was happy about it, but I suppose he could have been playing a part. He never mentioned a new girlfriend, but a man his age, it's not like it's uncommon for him not to remarry."

"He *was* younger thirty years ago."

"True." I made a frustrated sound. "And not many people like being single for very long if they can help it."

"Like Ben."

"Ugh, don't remind me."

Manny laughed. Before he could say anything else, there was a knock at the door.

Manny and I shared a look before we both headed to the front door. When he opened it, I was surprised to find Detective Cavanaugh on our front stoop.

"Mr. Denton. Mrs. Denton." He shook Manny's hand and bowed his head to me. "Mind if I come in for a minute?"

"Sure." Manny stepped aside. "And please, call me Manny."

Cavanaugh nodded once and then entered the house. We led him to the dining room, which seemed a safe enough space to talk. He declined sitting.

"I won't be long," he said. "I just wanted to stop by to see how you were doing and whether or not you've remembered anything since we last spoke."

"I don't recall seeing anything out of place at the house," I said, "but a brown sedan *did* follow me home."

Cavanaugh's eyes hardened. "A brown sedan?" He pulled a notebook and pen from his pocket. "Are you sure?"

"Yeah. Do you know it?"

He shook his head. "What can you tell me about it?"

"That it was a brown sedan and that it followed me."

He gave me a flat look. "Plate? Description of the driver?"

"Sorry," I said with an inward wince. "I didn't think to look. I don't even know if it was a Chevy or Toyota."

Cavanaugh stared at his blank page a moment before flipping his notebook closed and stuffing it, along with his pen, back into his pocket. "All right. I'll see what I can find out, but it's not much."

"Thank you."

Cavanaugh's mien lightened. "When you spoke to Mr. Danvers last, did he say anything about his house being broken into?"

I shook my head. "Not that I recall. Why?"

Cavanaugh hesitated only briefly before he told me. "There's evidence that he might have been robbed at some point recently, but there's no police report about it. There was a busted window he'd blocked off, and scrapes on the doorframe. There were other robberies reported over the last few months in the area, so it's not like it's a complete surprise."

"Do you think Joe walked in on someone looting his house?"

Cavanaugh spread his hands. "It's one possibility."

"And the other?"

His smile told me that was information for him to know.

It frustrated me that he couldn't tell me more, but I understood.

"Well, if you think of anything, please, don't hesitate to call me." Cavanaugh made as if he might leave.

"Detective," I said. "I have a few questions, if that's all right?"

He paused, then nodded.

I took a moment to gather my thoughts before speaking. "Once I got home, I looked into Joe Danvers. Are you positive he and Joe Hitchcock are the same man?" Even though I was pretty sure they were, I needed to hear it from him again.

He put his hands behind his back. "I am."

"I read he killed his wife. Is that true?"

Cavanaugh's face went carefully blank. "He was accused of the crime."

"Did you investigate it back then?"

"No. That was before my time."

"I'm curious," I said, trying my best to play it off as idle curiosity. "How did he kill her? The articles I looked at didn't say."

Cavanaugh glanced at Manny, who merely shrugged, before the detective turned back to me. "I don't have that information."

"What do you mean?" I asked. "You knew who he was, so you must know what he did."

A frown crept across Cavanaugh's features. He did his best to hide it, but it was clear something about my questions bothered him.

"Please, Detective. I need to know. Was I truly in danger?"

Another glance at Manny, like Cavanaugh hoped my husband would be able to rein me in. Manny, for his part, just looked on. He wasn't about to get in my way.

Cavanaugh's sigh was put-upon. "I don't believe so, Mrs. Denton."

"Liz, please."

"Fine. Liz. I do not believe Mr. Danvers had any ill intent toward you."

"Then why did he come back here?" It was a question I couldn't seem to answer. If he killed his wife in Grey Falls, why return thirty years later? She likely had family here, friends who still remembered. There was no way they'd let him off the hook if they knew he was back.

He changed his name. While that might work for some, I seriously doubted it would fool anyone who was close to the couple back then. Joe himself likely had family who would know him by sight. And even if they didn't live here, someone would eventually recognize him. Cavanaugh did. Other cops would as well.

So why come back?

"I can't answer that," Cavanaugh said. "I wish I could. If I'd known Danvers was back in town, I would have gone to see him. We still have questions for him."

"Such as?"

"You know I can't answer that."

"Why not?" I asked. "He's dead. Maybe he told me something that seemed innocent at the time, but could shed light onto the investigation somehow."

"I seriously doubt that."

"Why's that?" I asked, hand finding my hip. I was starting to get annoyed. "You don't know what we talked about."

Cavanaugh crossed his arms. "Did he talk about his wife?"

"Well, no."

"Did he tell you anything at all about his past?"

I dropped my eyes. "No."

"Then it's unlikely he said anything to you that would help. I truly wish he would have. If nothing else, Mrs. Danvers deserves to rest peacefully."

Something by the way he said it caught my attention, an inflection that made it sound like there was indeed more to this story.

"What do you mean by that?" I asked.

Cavanaugh grimaced, as if he realized he'd said too much, before a resigned look came over his face. "You'll probably find out on your own anyway. It's not like it's a secret."

"What's not?"

"Christine Danvers's body was never found."

I blinked at him. "But the articles said he killed her."

"It's widely believed to be true." By Cavanaugh's expression, I wondered if he counted himself amongst the believers. "There was ample enough evidence against Joseph Danvers, but nothing that the detective assigned to his case could pin on him directly."

"Circumstantial evidence, you mean?" Manny said.

Cavanaugh's nod was harsh. "Danvers always proclaimed his innocence, but I'm not sure many people believed him at the time. Even now, if you were to ask anyone who'd known the two of them back then, they'd tell you they think he did it. Why else would he leave town if he didn't have something to do with the crime?"

"Persecution," I said. I could only imagine what Joe had gone through. If the majority of Grey Falls believed him to be a killer, I doubted he could so much as get gas without being harassed.

"That very well may be," Cavanaugh said. "But

running off like that did him no favors. When he left, it cemented everyone's opinion of him. People still talk about it. Mostly, everyone wants to know where he buried the body. Christine Danvers deserves a proper burial."

I tried to imagine what it would be like if someone I loved came up missing. How would I feel knowing they might never be found? That I couldn't visit their grave when I missed them the most?

It wasn't a pleasant thought.

"I'm guessing he didn't move back into his old house, did he?" I said.

"No, he did not. As far as I was aware, no one knew Joe was back in town."

"Someone must have figured it out," I said. I mean, I saw no other reason as to why someone would kill Joe Danvers. I suppose it was possible it was a robbery gone bad, or he might have sparred with someone he'd recently met and that it had nothing to do with his missing wife, but I doubted it; not with his history.

"It's possible someone did learn of Joe's return," Cavanaugh said. "If that's the case, they made a mistake and mentioned it to someone. Until we know more, there's not much else we can do." He looked to me, then Manny. "If you do remember anything, call."

"We will," Manny said.

"And if you see the car again, call someone immediately. Be it me direct, or someone at the station. If it's the killer and they think you saw something, you could be in danger."

My heart skipped a beat. "Do you really think they'd come after me?"

His eyes flickered toward my back door, and the window that had once been broken when a would-be intruder had tried to break in. "I think you should be careful, just in case."

Cavanaugh left a few minutes later, after handing me a card with his personal cell number scrawled across it. As soon as he was gone, I sank down onto the couch, my entire body giving out. Manny joined me, a concerned look on his face.

"What are you going to do?" he asked.

I considered it for only a moment. What else could I do? As I said before, I wasn't a cop. My part in this was done.

Well, almost.

Despite how my brain was screaming at me that a murderer might be at large, and that I should do something about it, I forced myself to stand. There *was* one thing I could do, and, darn it, it was something I was good at.

"I'm going to find Sheamus a new home."

4

Finding a good home for a cat with an incurable illness isn't always easy. You have to find someone willing to care for the animal, and then make sure they have the funds to cover the medical expenses. Not everyone is willing—or able—to do that.

I don't hold it against anyone when they say they can't take on that sort of responsibility. It's hard to deal with. And while Sheamus wasn't suffering, he did go on sneezing fits that seemed to last forever, and he often sounded like his nose was completely plugged. As I said, not everyone can deal with that.

I spent an hour slowly going through the names of prospective adopters, but struggled to find someone I liked. They were all good candidates, and if it hadn't been for Joe Hitchcock, I would have allowed any one of them to take the Maine Coon home. He *was* a beautiful cat. And while they're difficult to find sometimes, there *are* tons of people out there who are willing to deal with his health issues.

But every time I looked someone up, I began to

question whether or not I was making a good choice. Was the forty-year-old single woman really a banker? Or did she have a deep, dark secret that would put not just her, but Sheamus, in harm's way? What about the retired couple looking for a companion? Were they on the run, hiding from a trained assassin?

I pushed my laptop away and rubbed my eyes. I was definitely overthinking this, but it was hard not to. What would have happened if I'd dropped Sheamus off the day before? Would Joseph's killer have left the cat alone? Kicked him out of the house to fend for himself? With his respiratory issues, I doubted he'd last long outside with all the pollen and allergens floating around.

"I need a day away," I muttered, eyeing my laptop. One day to get away from the murder, from worrying about my vetting methods, and then perhaps I'd start to see things much clearer.

Sheamus was curled in a cat bed across the room, snoozing wetly away. He and Wheels had played for a good forty minutes before both of them crashed, exhausted.

"Looks like you'll be staying here for a few more days," I said, rising. I pressed on the small of my back and was rewarded with a series of pops that helped bleed some of the tension from my body.

Of course, it ratcheted right back up when the front door slammed open and Amelia rushed in, voice raised to a near shout. "Mom!"

"What? What happened?" Sheamus looked up, and then went right back to sleep as I hurried to the front door. "Are you all right?" Manny had taken my van to the car wash twenty minutes ago in an effort to help me out—the van was in desperate need of a cleaning—but now I was wishing he was home to help me deal with whatever latest disaster had befallen my family.

"I'm fine," Amelia said. Her face was flushed and I noted that she looked excited, not scared. "I heard about it on the news."

"Heard about what?" Though I already knew. As much as I'd like to, I couldn't keep every bad thing from my children, no matter their age.

"The murder. Joseph Danvers." She walked across the room and took me by the hands. "Do you know who that is?"

"I do. I met him." When she gave me a curious look, I said, "He was going by the name Joe Hitchcock. He's the man who was going to take Sheamus."

"That's what I thought! I wonder if . . ." She shook her head. "Never mind. Wait! Did you find his body?"

"I did." I shuddered. That was an experience I never wanted to repeat.

"Oh." Some of her excitement dissipated. "I'm sorry you had to go through that."

"It wasn't fun," I said. "Why are you so excited about this?"

Amelia grinned. "It's a case. You know, to investigate."

I was shaking my head even before she was done. "No, Amelia, you're not to get involved. You might be getting mentored by Chester, but that doesn't make you a private investigator."

"That's not what I mean." She paced in front of me, a bundle of energy. I'm not sure I'd ever seen her so animated before. "Well, I guess it is, a little."

"You should probably explain." I moved to the dining room table. "And sit. You're making me nervous."

Amelia dropped into a chair, but her leg kept jiggling up and down. "Chester. It's his case."

"He's looking into who killed Joe?"

"No. Well, yes. Kind of." She made a frustrated sound. "He worked on the Danvers case years ago."

"His wife's murder." I scrambled to come up with her name. "Christine, wasn't it?"

"Yeah, that's it." Amelia snapped her fingers. "The police said Joseph killed her, but because there wasn't enough evidence, Chester got involved. He worked on it back then and did what he could to prove his client's innocence."

"He worked for Joe?" I asked, somewhat surprised. I would have thought Chester would have worked for the police on a case like that. Or maybe the victim's parents, but the accused? I supposed it made sense, especially if Joe wasn't the bad man everyone made him out to be.

"Joseph hired him to figure out what really happened. I don't know the details yet. We'd just gotten started looking into old files when we heard about Joe. Chester had new information and was hoping to share it with him."

"Wait. Back up. Was he still working on the case?" I asked.

"Of course. I mean, he stopped for a long time, but something caught Chester's attention recently and he'd started working on it again. It's why I had all those books. Chester hadn't given me all the details, so I didn't put it together until recently. I guess the whole thing is kind of personal for him, like he feels responsible somehow."

My mind raced. What was it that got Chester interested again? Joe's return? A new development?

And, of course, did it somehow lead to Joe's murder?

"You need to talk to him," Amelia said. "You found the body, right? He'll want to know what you saw."

"Amelia, I didn't see anything." But was that actually true? I found the door ajar. I saw the room with the photographs and files. I even saw the body, though I'd mentally blocked that out as best as I could.

"He'll want to know." Amelia scooted closer. "Mom, please. You really should talk to him. I'm not saying you go poking around like you did when Ben was in trouble, but if you could help Chester with his case, don't you think you should at least try?"

There was such a gleam of hopefulness in Amelia's eyes, I honestly don't think I could have turned her down, even if I'd wanted to. I mean, if I could help, why not tell the PI everything I knew?

"All right," I said. "I'll talk to him."

Amelia leapt to her feet and clapped her hands. "Great! I'll call him. We should go right now. He'll still be in the office." She whipped out her cell and hurried from the room to make the call.

My head was spinning as I prepared to leave. I made sure the cats had water and some dry food, and made a quick pass through the house to make sure everything was put away. By the time I had my purse in hand, Amelia was waiting for me by the front door.

"Ready?" she asked in a voice reminiscent of all the times she'd impatiently waited for Manny and me as we readied for a trip to the zoo. Boy, did I miss those innocent times.

"As ready as I'll ever be," I said.

"Awesome! I'll drive." And she was out the door.

"Fantastic." With a resigned sigh, I followed after her.

* * *

The ride downtown wasn't as terrible as I'd imagined it would be. Normally, Amelia blasted her music so loud, you could hear it from blocks away, but today she kept it at a less ear-splitting volume. I couldn't make out many of the words, but I suppose that wasn't a surprise, considering most of the lyrics were in German.

Amelia pulled up in front of Chester's office and parked. The building was a small, brick structure that looked tiny compared to the mansion-sized buildings around it. The street was full of old houses turned into businesses, and Chester's office was no different.

I got out of Amelia's car and waited for her to join me on the sidewalk. She led the way up a short flight of stairs, to Chester's office door.

From the street, I hadn't been able to see a sign, but up close, I saw a small plaque on the door. **C. Chudzinski. Private Investigator.** No other names adorned the plaque. I wondered if Amelia hoped to have her own added there someday.

Amelia opened the door without knocking. A bell that sounded as if it had survived a cave-in or two, clanked above our heads as we entered. The entryway was cool and spacious, if not on the run-down side. A coatrack sat just inside the door. There were no coats on it, just a newsboy cap hanging from the top. The dust on it made it appear as if it had been there for years.

A pair of desks sat in the front room, but no one was sitting at them. There *were* papers atop the desks, and one closed file folder. Amelia walked straight past the two desks without a glance, to a door on the far side of the room. The top half of the door was of frosted glass with one word, **CHUDZINSKI,** in the center.

"Chester?" Amelia rapped on the glass. "It's Amelia. I have my mom with me."

A surprisingly soft voice came from the other side of the door. "Please, come on in."

Amelia opened the door to Chester's office, and with a look of pride on her face, allowed me to enter first.

The room was tidy, with a trio of bookcases along the back wall, filled with books I could only assume were legal texts. A small love seat sat near a window, and a pair of comfy-looking chairs faced the desk where Chester Chudzinski sat, glasses perched at the end of his nose as he perused a file.

Chester looked to be about sixty, if not a few years older. His hair was thinning, and had long ago gone to gray. His suit was brown, and looked as if he'd worn it for at least a decade. Fine threads trailed from his wrists where it was beginning to fray, and the elbows were faded near white.

He closed the file as we entered and set it aside before plucking his glasses from his nose and tossing them onto his desk. When Amelia entered behind me, his eyes lit up, and I noted a genuine fondness in his gaze that was more grandpa than dirty old man.

"Mrs. Denton," he said, rising and reaching out a hand. "I've heard so much about you. I'm thrilled you have found the time to stop by."

I shook his hand. His grip was firm, if not a little rough, as if he'd never used moisturizer in his life. "Call me Liz. I'm glad to be here. Amelia speaks highly of you."

Chester sat back down and gestured toward the

two chairs. I took one, Amelia the other. "Good to hear it. She's got a sharp mind in that head of hers. You can only imagine my good fortune when she told me her interest in the field and wished to mentor under me."

Amelia ducked her head, embarrassed by the compliment.

"She's a good one, that's for sure." I managed to resist reaching out and mussing her hair, but just barely.

"So, Liz"—Chester folded his hands on the desk in front of him—"Amelia was vague about why she wanted to bring you when she called. I assume it has something to do with Joe Danvers?"

Before I could speak, Amelia piped up.

"She was the one who discovered his body."

Chester sat back as if Amelia's words were a blow. "You were there?"

"I wish I hadn't been, but yes, I was."

Chester lowered his head briefly, as if in silent prayer, before he looked up. "Joe was a good man. I've worked with him for years. Well, not straight through, mind you. And not always for pay. But his case always intrigued me, and I regret I never was able to find out what happened to Christine."

"Amelia said you worked the case when his wife disappeared."

"I did. It was a horrible thing. Christine, by all accounts, was a good woman. I never got the chance to meet her, since, well . . ." His smile was sad.

"You were hired by Joe?" I asked.

"I was. When Christine came up missing, all eyes immediately turned to Joe. There were prejudices at the time, you see. And, well, people see what they want to see. The couple never fought, never had reason to hate one another, let alone resort to murder. Yet"—he spread his hands—"here we are."

I didn't need to ask what prejudices Chester was referring to. "You don't believe he killed her."

"No, I don't," Chester said. "It didn't help Joe's case when he vanished like he did, but I couldn't really blame him for doing it. All the police had to go on was a missing woman who hadn't taken a thing with her but the clothes on her back. There was no blood, no defensive wounds on Joe. The only supposed witness, a man named Harry Davis, had it in for the both of them from the start."

"He saw what happened?" I asked.

"He claims he did, but his story has never been consistent. He claimed he saw Joe carrying the body out into the woods, a shovel dragging behind him, but he couldn't decide if it happened in the early morning or during the late evening. Then, later, he said Joe was dragging Christine's body and the shovel was on his shoulder. It's small differences, but they do mean a lot. I think he just wanted to see both Joe and Christine out of town any way he could manage."

I wondered if that meant he'd resort to murder to get his way.

"I've spent years, decades even, on this thing," Chester said. "Even after Joe was gone, I couldn't get the case off my mind. I'd look into it here and there, check to see if any new information popped up somewhere. I feel like I've let Joe down by never finding Christine for him. And now, he's dead too."

"I'm sorry," I said. "This has to be hard."

"It is. When I learned Joe was back in town, I contacted him right away. I hadn't discovered much of use in the years since he'd left town, but I thought he'd like to know the tidbits I did uncover. Turns out, he'd been working on it on his own all this time." Chester leaned forward. "And I honestly believe he was getting somewhere."

My mind flashed back to the photographs and files. "I saw a room," I said. "The room he died in. There were files all over the place, photographs on the wall." I wished I would have taken the time to look at them better because now, I couldn't bring a single one to mind. "And his computer was gone."

"I was afraid of that," Chester said, voice going somber. "I warned him to be careful. He was obsessed, convinced that someone here in town knew what happened to Christine. He said he went to talk to some people he trusted not to turn him in, despite me warning him against it. Just because I accepted him, didn't mean anyone else would."

"I wish I'd seen something," I said. "No one was there when I got to his house, and nothing seemed out of place. He seemed like a nice man."

"Trust me, he was just as friendly as he seemed. Even if someone had killed Christine and then admitted to it, I don't think Joe would have hurt them. He would have been angry, sure, but he'd have let the police dispense the justice."

None of this was making me feel any better about what had happened. Sure, it eased my mind about my vetting process somewhat, but a man was still dead. You couldn't feel good about that, no matter what.

"Do you think the person who killed Christine killed Joe?" I asked. "If he confronted the killer, it would make sense, right?" I hoped he'd left detailed notes if that was the case. It would make it easier for the police to catch his killer.

If the notes haven't already been destroyed.

Chester folded his hands onto the desk in front of him. When he spoke, he looked me directly in the eye. "No, Mrs. Denton, I don't believe the person who killed Joe Danvers killed Christine." He paused, glanced at Amelia, before turning back to me. "In fact, I believe that Christine Danvers might still be alive."

5

"Proof," Chester said, "is tough to come by in a case like this."

Amelia and I sat side by side, each absorbing Chester's words like gospel. He had a magnetism about him that was hard to ignore. It wasn't his looks, or even the tone of his voice. I think it had more to do with the confidence with which he spoke, the certainty that what he was saying was the absolute truth.

"The police believe Christine Danvers dead. They have a witness claiming he saw Joe with the body and a shovel, but the witness is suspect at best. What else do they have?"

He looked at us, though I knew he wasn't expecting an answer.

"A missing woman," he said, smacking the top of his desk. "That's it."

"But Joe fled town," I said. "You can't ignore that."

Chester pointed at me, as if I was making a good point in *his* favor. "He did leave town. I, for one, believe that to be a mistake on his part, but it was understandable. He was being hounded by the people of Grey Falls, watched by the police. He was being labeled a murderer. His wife was gone, presumed dead. Let me ask you, Mrs. Denton, would you not also want to get away?"

I didn't have to think about it for long. "I suppose I would."

"And that's what Joe did. He left town to get away from the constant pressure building up around him. He hid, changed his name so that no one could find him."

"But he came back," Amelia said.

"That he did." Chester looked to Amelia as he might a prized student. "He came back because he knew Christine was still out there. He came back because he thought it was the only way he could find her again. He hoped no one involved in the old case would recognize him, but I did. And it seems someone else must have."

I truly wanted to believe what Chester was saying, but it was hard. So far, all he'd given me was his belief with nothing to back it up. "What makes you think Christine is still alive?" I asked. "Do you have any sort of proof?"

Chester's face fell at my question. "Unfortunately, no. I have a *lack* of proof when it comes to the popular belief of Joe's guilt. I have doubts that a man like Joe would have killed his wife for any reason. I have the fact that there is no hard evidence of him hurting her, *or* that she was harmed at all." He leaned forward, met my eye. "And I have rumors."

"Rumors?" There was a healthy dose of skepticism in my voice.

"I know it's not much," he allowed. "But sometimes rumors do pan out."

"Sometimes it's all you have to go on," Amelia said.

I knew that all too well, just as I knew that often, rumors could lead you down the wrong path and obscure the truth.

"What kind of rumors have you heard?" I asked.

"That while Joe was looking for his missing wife, Christine was, in turn, looking for him."

I raised my eyebrows at that. "Did she tell you that?"

Chester laughed. "How easy would my job be if she had? No, I have nothing so grand as a letter from her. But when you spend as much time on a case as I have, you hear a lot of things. A lot of it is bunk. But sometimes, there's something that stands out, especially when you hear it from more than one source."

"Yet, you haven't been able to confirm anything?"

"Sadly, no. But, if nothing else, I hope Joe's death will somehow draw out the truth."

Amelia and I left a short time later. I wasn't completely convinced of Joe's innocence, but I did feel better about the whole mess. If he didn't kill his wife, and she was still out there somewhere, then perhaps there'd be some form of justice for him.

"What do you think?" Amelia asked on the way home.

"I think we need to be careful," I said. "If Chester's wrong, we could be defending a guilty man."

"He's not." The confidence in her voice didn't surprise me. Chester had made a pretty good argument, despite his lack of proof.

Amelia dropped me off at the house and immediately took off again. I wondered if she was heading back to Chester Chudzinski's office to look into Joe's case some more. My chest tightened at the thought— I didn't want my daughter to put herself in harm's way—but there was nothing I could do about it. She was an adult, able to make her own choices.

Still, it was hard. They never stopped being your children, no matter how old they got.

Manny had yet to return with the van, and Ben was still out doing whatever he was doing, which left me to my own devices. I headed inside, checked on Sheamus and Wheels, and then grabbed the keys to Manny's car. There might have been a murder, and I had a cat to find a home for, but I still had shopping to do.

I tried not to think about Joseph and Christine Danvers as I made my way through the grocery, but it was hard. I kept coming back to what Chester had said about Christine possibly being alive, and wondered if there was any chance he was right after all these years. Did she know about his death? Could she have come back to town and killed her husband herself? If so, why?

I simply didn't know enough about their relationship to form any concrete hypotheses. Could I really trust Chester's view, considering he worked for Joe? That had to create a bias.

"It'll be two hundred dollars and forty-five cents, ma'am." I startled back to the present and shoved my card into the reader. The clerk was giving me a worried look, as if he'd told me my total more than once.

I wheeled the groceries to Manny's car, knowing I had likely forgotten a few important items in my haze. I packed everything away—rebagging the bread and other squishables that were bagged with sharp, heavy objects as I did—and then climbed into the driver's seat.

It took only a few seconds for me to realize I was being followed once again.

The sedan pulled out of a space a few cars down in the same aisle where I'd parked. In fact, I'd walked right by it when I'd taken my groceries to the car, but hadn't noticed it in the sea of vehicles.

The car stayed back, but always in sight as I pulled out of the lot, and onto the main drag.

"Christine?" I wondered aloud. If she truly was alive and had come back to kill her husband, who did she think I was? A mistress? A witness of some kind?

My first instinct was to drive straight to the police station and tell Cavanaugh about my tail. Of course, I doubted the driver would follow me all the way to the station. Even if I called ahead, it was likely they'd vanish in traffic before I got anywhere close to where Cavanaugh would be.

I didn't want my stalker to vanish; not entirely. If the driver was the killer, or perhaps if they knew who killed Joe, I needed to talk to them. Or, at least, the police did.

One thing was for sure; I wasn't about to lead my tail home again. Once was enough.

Jacking up the cold air so my ice cream would stand a chance, I turned away from downtown Grey Falls, and headed for a series of roads off the beaten path that I was familiar with. Here, there was more than one dead end road, but enough people around so I didn't have to worry about my safety.

The brown sedan followed from a distance, but follow it did. I drove with one eye on the road, the other on my rearview mirror. If the sedan were to break off, I wanted to know exactly where it did, and then, perhaps, I could turn the tables on my pursuer and follow *them* instead.

The car was still behind me as I turned onto a

bumpy, pothole-ridden street. It forced me to slow
more than I liked, and I feared the sedan might decide to cruise on past, but after a few long seconds, it
turned slowly onto the road.

"Got ya," I muttered, weaving around the worst of
the craters in the road. It looked like a meteor shower
had struck, but no matter how many times the city
tried to repair the road, it ended up looking like this
after only a few months. Farm equipment tended to
do that.

I continued on for five more minutes, and then
made another turn onto a dead-end street. The sign
had been knocked over years ago and no one had
bothered to right it again. I was counting on my
stalker not to know the area well enough to realize
what I was doing.

Sure enough, after a few moments, the sedan pulled
onto the road, though I noted they weren't following
me as quickly as before. Nerves? Or had they had
enough of the wild-goose chase?

Either way, this was it. If I waited much longer, I
feared they'd give up the chase and I'd miss my
chance.

The cul-de-sac was just up ahead. As I sped up and
made the turn quickly, I could *feel* the tires on the
driver's side want to lift from the road. I was facing
the sedan a second later, hoping the driver wouldn't
realize what was happening until it was too late.

Brake lights flared. The sedan came to an abrupt
halt, just past a driveway that led to a house that
looked to have been left abandoned.

I slammed on the gas and shot forward, heart
pounding in my ears. My eyes were locked on the
sedan. The driver was sitting bolt upright, but the

sun was reflecting off the windshield, making it hard to see them clearly.

The sedan started backing up, so I pressed the gas clear to the floor.

"No you don't," I muttered. My entire body was tense, and I feared that if I pressed it too much, Manny's car would stall. It was already shaking more than it should.

The sedan backed into the driveway, and stopped. I assumed the driver planned on gunning it and speeding away before I could get close.

Unfortunately for him, it was too late.

A dark, wide-eyed face stared back at me from the driver's seat as I shot past. But instead of a female face, like I expected, I saw the short hair and the well-trimmed beard of a man who couldn't be far into his thirties.

And then I was past. I hit my brakes and jammed the car into reverse, but I was too slow. The sedan's tires threw gravel as the driver shot out of the driveway and flew around me. I tried to get my car back into gear and give chase, but by the time I reached the end of the street, the car was gone.

This time, I didn't hesitate to make for the police station. Now that I had a description of my stalker, I had something to give Detective Cavanaugh.

The Grey Falls police station sat downtown, just across the street from the courthouse. I pulled into the lot and headed for the large plate-glass doors out front. My heart had slowed its rapid hammering, but I still felt jazzed up from the chase. No wonder some people became adrenaline junkies. It was exhilarating, if not terrifying.

I went straight through the metal detectors without setting them off. I had a feeling they didn't bother turning them on most of the time; it wasn't like Grey Falls was rife with crime. I made for the front desk and the officer who was sitting there.

"Hello, Officer Mohr," I said by way of greeting.

"Oh!" The young cop blinked and, for a moment, looked frightened by my appearance. "Hi! Mrs. Dyson, right?"

"Denton, but call me Liz."

He winced. "Right, right. Liz." Officer Mohr's face reddened. I kind of felt bad for him. He'd made a mistake or two during a recent investigation and it appeared as if it had earned him permanent front desk duty. He now had a nameplate sitting atop the desk, which hadn't been there before. The poor guy looked miserable.

Of course, his mistake nearly caused my son to be charged with murder, so I wasn't entirely sympathetic.

"What can I do for you, Liz?" he asked. "I hope there's nothing wrong."

"Not really." I glanced at the room behind him. Other cops were at work, but I didn't recognize any of them. "Do you know if Detective Cavanaugh is in? I have some information for him."

Mohr paled at Cavanaugh's name. "I . . . I'm not sure. Let me check." He rose, and nearly tripped over his own two feet as he scurried off somewhere into the back of the station.

I wandered away from the desk, to the red plastic chairs set against the wall. No one was currently sitting in them, and I decided I didn't want to change that. I had bad memories of this place, and those chairs. The last time I was here, I'd hoped it would be, well, the last.

Yet, here I was. I really didn't want to make this a habit.

"You wanted to see me, Mrs. Denton?" Cavanaugh approached, alone. Officer Mohr was back at his desk, head down, furiously scribbling away at something. With the way he kept glancing up at us, I had a feeling he was only pretending to work, just so Cavanaugh wouldn't have something to yell at him about.

"Yes, Detective." Unsure what the proper protocol might be, I reached out a hand. Cavanaugh shook it with a bemused expression. "I've learned a few things about Joseph Danvers's murder. Or the investigation, anyway."

I fully expected Cavanaugh to chide me for poking my nose into police business, but he merely nodded at me to go on.

I quickly told him about my conversation with Chester Chudzinski, and how he believed Christine Danvers might still be alive. As I spoke, Cavanaugh's expression didn't change an iota. He listened attentively, almost passively, though I knew he was cataloging my every word.

"There's a chance Christine killed her husband," I said. "That is, if Chester is right about her."

"I'm aware of Mr. Chudzinski's beliefs," Cavanaugh said. "His name appeared more than once in the case files."

"So, do you think it's possible?"

He shrugged. "Anything is possible, I suppose. But"—he raised a finger before I could speak—"don't read too much into it. His findings were dismissed because he was unable to present the officers on the case with any workable evidence. I don't believe that has changed, has it?"

"Well, no. But what if he is right?"

"I understand why you're interested," Cavanaugh said. "But you need to be careful here. There are people who have worked this thing since it started. Just because they haven't been able to close the case, doesn't mean they have given up on finding out what really happened."

"Like Chester." It came out almost defiant.

Cavanaugh gave me a single nod, conceding the point. "Trust me, we have this covered. Now, was there anything else?"

I felt kind of silly since he'd so easily dismissed Chester's findings, but I wasn't about to hold anything back from him.

"That car I told you about followed me again."

Cavanaugh's entire demeanor changed. He stood up straighter, his eyes going razor sharp. "Did you catch a plate this time?"

"No." I mentally cursed myself for not doing so. I'd been so intent on the driver, it had completely slipped my mind. I, obviously, would never make a good detective. "But I did get a look at the driver's face."

"Did you recognize them?"

I shook my head. "All I can say is that it was a black man, maybe in his thirties. It happened so fast, I'm not totally sure." I gave him a quick description, making sure to note how well-groomed he seemed.

Cavanaugh pulled out a notebook while I talked and took notes. "Was there anything else about him that stood out?" he asked. "Did he look angry? Threatening?"

"He looked kind of scared, actually." Whether it was because he realized I'd gotten a look at him, or for some other reason, I didn't know. "He took off as soon as he had the chance. Now that I've seen his face, I wonder if I'll ever see him again."

Cavanaugh frowned at that and reread his notes before tucking the notebook away. "I want you to be careful, Mrs. Denton. You don't know what this man wants, or what his connection to the deceased might be."

"If there's one at all."

He gave me a flat look that had me blushing in embarrassment. Of course, there was a connection. "If you see him again, don't try to interact with him, don't try to get another look. Find somewhere safe and call me."

"I will."

"I'll send someone right away." He paused, and then, "In fact, I'll have someone periodically drive by your place to make sure your sedan driver doesn't try to make a move against you."

"That won't be necessary," I said.

"But I'll do it anyway. Please, Mrs. Denton, this is a delicate situation. I don't want you to get hurt. If you or your family hear or see anything that sets you on edge, don't hesitate to call. I don't want to scare you, but with a murder on our hands, whatever happens next, could be a matter of life or death."

6

I spent the drive home staring into my rearview mirror, paranoid that every car that pulled out behind me was going to chase me home. None of them were, of course. The brown sedan was long gone, and I hoped that now that I'd seen the driver's face, he wouldn't risk coming after me again.

The house was still empty by the time I pulled up into the driveway. I began unloading Manny's car, making sure to get the ice cream and other freezer items out first. It took multiple trips, which were complicated by the cats, who kept shoving their noses through the gap every time I tried to open the door. I managed to get most everything inside without one of them escaping.

I was just grabbing the last bag out of the car when Joanne appeared behind me.

Twice in one day?

"Liz, a moment, please."

Something in her tone had me turning to face

her, rather than racing for the front door. "Hi, Joanne. What do you need?"

She glanced down the street both ways before her gaze settled on me. She looked worried, which in turn, made my paranoia leap to new heights.

"Did something happen?" I asked.

"I'm not sure." Another glance down the street. "I was out watering my plants earlier and this car drove by all slow like. I didn't think anything of it at first, but then it happened again."

A chill climbed my spine. "A sedan?" I asked. "A brown one?"

"You know it?" Joanne sagged. "I was actually worried they were up to no good. I didn't get a good look at the driver, but I could tell they were watching your house. I suppose it's a friend of yours?"

"No, not a friend," I said. "Did they stop?"

Joanne shook her head. "Drove by three or four times, and then took off. Haven't seen them since."

"When was this?"

"I don't know. Twenty minutes ago?"

While I was talking to Detective Cavanaugh. I didn't doubt it was the same car that had been following me. Did he drive straight here after he sped away from me? If so, why?

Dreadful thoughts popped into my head then, none of them good. If he killed Joseph Danvers and now knew I'd seen his face, could I be next? Cavanaugh's ominous last words drifted through my mind and caused my stomach to churn.

"I'm not sure what you're doing, Liz, but I don't like strangers lurking around my house. I don't want to have to call the police."

"If you see the car again, you should," I said. "That

man is dangerous." I didn't feel safe standing outside talking about it, so I hoisted up my bag of groceries and carried it to the front door without a backward glance.

As I stepped inside, I heard Joanne make a distressed sound and hurry back across the street to her house. I hoped I'd scared a little sense into her. She might be annoying, but I didn't want anything to happen to her. If the killer was after me because he thought I'd seen something, I didn't want him coming after Joanne because she couldn't keep her nose out of other people's business.

Sheamus was pawing through the bags of groceries as I set the last bag down. I returned to the front door, locked it, and then headed to the back door to make sure it was locked as well. I was anxious for the rest of the family to get home. I needed to make sure they were okay.

Stop being so paranoid, I reprimanded myself. Just because someone was following me didn't mean anyone else was in danger.

Keep telling yourself that.

I put away the groceries with both Sheamus's and Wheels's help. The cats had to stick their noses in every bag, bat at every item to see if it would roll away. A job that should have taken ten minutes took nearly twenty because I kept having to step over the cats, and once, retrieve a bag of Babybels that Wheels tried to roll off with.

As I finished putting everything away, there was a knock on the door.

I hadn't heard a car pull up, but then again, I'd been focused on putting the groceries away. My mind had been miles away, thinking about Joe and Cavanaugh and Chester, and wondering how in the world I managed to get myself mixed up in yet another murder. If I hadn't locked the door, I doubted I would have noticed it opening if someone were to have pushed their way inside.

I stood in the kitchen, not quite sure what to do. I could see the door from where I stood, but I couldn't see outside to make sure it wasn't the man from the brown sedan who had come looking to end me once and for all.

The knock came again, this time more insistent.

It was followed by a series of rapid barks.

I just about sagged through the floor. My imagination was starting to run wild, and before long I was going to start jumping at every sound. *Get a grip on yourself, Liz.*

I marched to the front door, and without bothering to peek out the window, I opened it.

I wish I hadn't.

"Liz." My nemesis, Courtney Shaw, was on my stoop, a small dog carrier in hand. Her blond hair was styled in what I imagined was the latest hip trend. It swept around her face in waves and, for as much as I hated to admit it, made her look like a movie star. Her pink van was parked so close beside Manny's car, I wouldn't have been able to open the driver's door. The words *Pets Luv Us* was painted on the side of her van, amid cute baby animals.

"Courtney." It was as close as she was going to get to a hello. "What are you doing here?"

She flashed me the briefest of smiles before she used the dog carrier to force me back into my house so she could come inside. "It's hot out there, isn't it?" She checked her nails like she thought the polish might have run in the heat. "I don't see how you of all people can stand it." She looked me up and down. I could almost see her mentally weighing me.

And, yes, I do mean in pounds.

"I manage," I said, closing the door before one of the cats could get out. "You didn't answer my question." My gaze moved to the carrier. The dog inside was barking, a high-pitched, snarling yap that sounded like the pooch might be half rabid.

Courtney set the carrier down. Wheels had her face pressed up against the door almost immediately. All it earned her was a series of barks and growls. At least there were no teeth.

"It's this dog!" Courtney threw her hands into the air. She sounded as if her entire world had come crashing down. "I tried to find it a good home, I really did, but no one wants it. He nips at everything." She held out her left hand, which had two small bandages on it. "And the barking! Listen to him."

She was right; the dog did bark a lot. It was a nonstop barrage that had Wheels slinking away—and Wheels liked everyone.

I crouched down so I could peer into the cage. Inside, a Chihuahua lunged at the carrier door, barking and snapping. He looked healthy enough at first glance, but he was most definitely agitated. I wondered what Courtney had done to set it off, then scrubbed the thought from my mind.

"And why did you bring him here?" I asked, rising.

"You deal with troublesome pets," she said. "I thought that if anyone could find a home for the little demon, it'd be you."

Alarm bells starting clanging in my head. There was absolutely no way Courtney would bring an animal to me for any reason. She'd believed we were rivals from the moment I started up Furever Pets. No matter how much I insisted we could coexist, she steadfastly refused to view me as anything more than competition.

"I can't take him in right now," I said with some mild regret. "I'm currently housing a cat with health issues, and his latest adoption fell through." *Understatement of the century.* "I wish I could help, but I can't."

"But you have to!" Courtney all but stomped a foot and jutted out her lower lip. "I can't do it. I've tried. If you don't help the poor thing, well, I don't know what will happen."

My heart went out to the Chihuahua, but there was little I could do. I've housed more than one animal at a time, but Sheamus was a special case. Not to mention the fact that the Chihuahua made high-strung seem cool and collected. And with the murder and my stalker on top of that . . .

"I'm sorry," I said. "I really do wish I could do something."

There was a flicker in Courtney's eye, a defiance I'd come to know. It was there for a mere heartbeat, and then was gone again an instant later.

"I know we've had our differences," she said, rivaling my own understatement with one of her own. "But I can't believe you'd let Piranha go homeless because you can't be bothered."

"Piranha?" I asked, shooting a skeptical eye to the carrier.

"It suits him; you'll see."

"No, I won't, Courtney. I can't take him." Despite my words, I could feel myself softening. Every animal deserved to have a happy home, even an ultra-temperamental Chihuahua. "You'll have to home him yourself."

The front door opened, and for a heart-stopping second, my brain registered the face of the man driving the brown sedan, before sense returned and I saw it was Manny.

He stopped just inside the door, a worried look on his face. "Liz. Courtney."

"Hi, Manny." Courtney's voice turned sickening sweet. "I was just dropping off a dog for Liz. I'm thrilled she'll be taking him in and helping the poor thing out."

A series of barks and snarls emitted from the carrier, causing Manny's eyebrows to rise in concern. Wheels poked her head into the room, and then sped away again, apparently having had enough of the noise.

"I never said—"

"Thanks again, Liz. I know you'll do a good job. I've got to go." Courtney spun on her heel and hurried out the door. A few seconds later, her van shot down the street like she was making a run for the border.

"Do I want to know?" Manny asked, closing the door behind him.

I picked up the carrier and held it at eye level. Piranha barked and hopped back and forth in tiny little lunges.

"I'm not sure I know what just happened." I sighed. "But I guess I've got to figure out what to do with this guy."

Manny followed me into the laundry room, which had become the de facto room for pets I've housed over the years. I set the carrier down in the middle of the floor and motioned for Manny to close the door.

"The van's clean," he said, watching me from across the room. He looked ready to bolt. With the way the dog was barking, I didn't blame him. "Inside and out. I also bought you a new battery-powered vacuum to keep inside the van. It has a charger that you can plug into the nine-volt outlet."

"Thank you," I said, and I meant it. Animal hair got everywhere and was impossible to be completely rid of, but every little bit helped.

I left the carrier door closed and checked a shelf we'd recently installed that held all the spare food for my temporary visitors. I chose a dog food I thought would be good for the Chihuahua, and filled a bowl.

"I'll take him into work with me tomorrow," Manny said. "I have an opening in the morning and can run him through his tests then. I can have Ben come with me and he can bring the dog back here once I'm certain everything is clear."

"That'll be great," I said. Already, I was mentally running down my list of people who'd had an interest in a dog recently. Surely one of them would be interested in a Chihuahua I knew nothing about. Normally, I liked to know an animal's history, whether or not it came from an abusive home, or was someone's prized pet. It helped in finding them the perfect furever home.

Unfortunately, I doubted Courtney would be willing to give me anything else to go on about little Piranha. I was on my own.

I turned the carrier so it faced the food—and was facing away from me, Manny, and the closed door—and then carefully popped open the cage.

Piranha shot out of it as if I'd lit a fuse. He barked rapidly, spun in a hopping circle, as if looking for something to destroy, before he settled on attacking the food. Manny and I crept out of the room as quietly as we could to let the dog eat.

"He seems tense," Manny said.

"Very."

"Maybe I'll give him a look tonight, just to make sure there's nothing that needs my immediate attention."

I nodded with a frown. How in the world had a dog like Piranha ended up with Courtney Shaw of all people? She was all about kittens and puppies and cuddly animals. And while a Chihuahua could be cute, Piranha didn't appear to be young. At first glance, I'd put him at seven to ten years old.

"I saw Ben while I was out."

"Hmm?" I turned my attention to Manny.

"Ben. I saw him."

"Is he on his way home?" I asked, confused by the abrupt change in subject.

"I doubt it. He was with a young woman who looked to be five years his junior."

Which would put her at around eighteen, which seemed awfully young. I still wasn't sure how that merited Manny's tone, which had turned somewhat odd.

"Okay?" I crossed my arms, expecting the worst.

"I saw them going into a house."

I blinked at him. What was he getting at?

"There was a 'For Sale' sign in the front yard."

My brain struggled to connect the dots. I *knew* what he was trying to say, yet I didn't want to believe it. "Was he helping her look for a place?"

"That's not what it looked like to me," Manny said. "They went in arm in arm, and with a Realtor. I think he's looking to move out. Honestly, I think it's about time."

Ben's moving out? "Who is this woman?" I asked. "Have you met her?"

"No, I haven't." Manny shrugged as if meeting the

woman our son might be moving in with didn't matter. "But she had that look about her. Pretty, maybe a little self-involved. You know the type?"

"Yeah, like a lot of Ben's girlfriends. How long have they been dating? Is she even out of high school?"

Manny shrugged. "Not long, I don't think. And do you really think Ben would date a high schooler?"

No, I didn't, but he also didn't always make the best choices when it came to women.

I wandered into the dining room and plopped down into a chair. "They've likely just met and they're moving in together already?"

Manny sat down across from me. "It's Ben." As if that explained everything.

"How's he going to pay for a house? Was it a nice place?" I couldn't imagine his bedroom upstairs being empty. I knew the time was coming that he would eventually need to go, but even now, twenty-three years after he was born, I wasn't ready for it.

"He asked for more time at the office," Manny said, referencing his veterinarian practice. "I'm looking for some way to plug him in, but since he's not fully licensed yet, I can't just make him a partner."

Everything was happening so fast, my head was spinning. "He's growing up," I said.

"He did that a long time ago, Liz." Manny stood and kissed the top of my head. "I'm going to go check on our latest resident. You going to be okay?"

I nodded, too stunned to speak. Ben was thinking of moving out. Amelia was looking at a career as a private investigator. A lot had happened over the last year. I wasn't so sure I could handle it, especially not now, after Joe's murder. I needed a mental break.

Manny headed for the laundry room where Piranha waited, leaving me to sort it all out on my own.

It's just one more thing to deal with, I told myself. Besides, how much more could happen?

It was as if the fates decided to pile on.

The house phone rang. I rose to answer it.

"Hello?"

The line was silent.

"Denton household, Liz speaking." I paused. "Is anyone there?"

I could hear breathing, but nothing else.

"If this is a joke—" The line went dead.

I held the phone to my ear. The chill in my spine returned and slithered throughout my body, causing me to tremble.

The caller might not have said anything, but I *knew* who was on the other line, just like I'd known that Courtney was up to no good when she'd brought me Piranha.

The man in the brown sedan. He knew where I lived, knew my face.

And, apparently, he knew my phone number.

7

Sleep that night came in spurts. I kept hearing sounds outside, but when I'd look, nothing would be there. When my eyes finally did close, I'd see a brown sedan and would be awake again almost immediately.

And then there was Piranha.

I'm not one to dislike any animal, but the Chihuahua was working on my last nerve. He was locked safely away in the laundry room, where he couldn't hurt one of the cats or break anything, but his bark carried up the stairs and pierced my ears like a needle.

It took some time, but eventually, the sounds and paranoia couldn't keep exhaustion at bay. When I did finally drift off for good, the sky was already lightening. Two meager hours later, I was dragging myself out of bed, and into the shower.

By the time I was done with my morning routine, everyone was gone, and the house was silent, other than a handful of sneezes from Sheamus. Manny, true to his word, had taken Piranha with him to the vet. Ben must have gone with them because he wasn't in his room. I hoped Manny would get a chance to ask him about his house hunting, because Ben had come home too late last night for me to do so.

"Amelia?" I called. It was punctuated with a yawn that forced me to lean against the wall lest I fall down. Once it passed, I knocked on her bedroom door.

There was no answer.

Like Ben, Amelia had come in late, just before I'd gone to bed. She'd gone straight to her room, barely paying the barking Chihuahua a glance on her way up the stairs. I'd tried to ask her about the investigation, but she'd merely shrugged, and closed her door.

I knocked again, raised my voice. "Amelia? You up?"

When she didn't answer, I opened the door a crack.

Her bed was empty. Not only that, but it didn't look as if she'd slept in it at all. The comforter was rumpled like Amelia had sat cross-legged on it as she was wont to do, but it wasn't bunched at the foot of the bed as it usually was when she slept.

I closed her bedroom door with a frown. Amelia was never up this early. And since she never made her bed, I was positive she hadn't actually slept in it.

But if that was the case, where had she gone? And when?

All those sounds that kept waking me up last night came back to mind. Could it have been Amelia sneaking out? Or did she fall asleep at her desk in her room, and I was worrying myself over nothing?

The brown sedan. If Amelia had left in the dead of night, and if my stalker was lurking around somewhere out there, could he have taken her?

Panic tried to flare, but I swallowed it back. Amelia was a grown woman. If someone were to try to abduct her, she'd have more than a few words to say about it. She also had a set of lungs on her that would wake the dead. I seriously doubted anyone could shove her into a car she didn't want to get into without her blowing out their eardrums and waking the neighborhood.

I forced myself to go downstairs and eat breakfast and scan the news on my phone like it was any other day. Manny had already fed Wheels and Sheamus. Both cats were napping in the living room, next to one another, content as could be.

I was only mildly jealous.

I finished up my cereal, rinsed out the bowl, and was heading to my laptop to see what I could do about Piranha when there was a knock at the door.

I shot a quick glance at the clock. I rarely had visitors, and when I did, they usually called ahead of time. *Unless it's Courtney*, I thought as I veered off toward the door. I opened it with a yawn that turned into a near scream when I saw who was standing on my stoop.

The man was a head taller than me, and was built like a runner. His limbs were long, and he stood with feet spread apart, as if he was ready to break into a jog at any moment. Dark eyes scanned me as I staggered back, away from the door, my shock overcoming my sense of decency.

In the driveway, a brown sedan sat next to my van.

"Excuse me for intruding," the man said in a cultured, somewhat nervous voice. "I didn't mean to startle you."

"You!" I pointed at him, then realized I was doing it, so I jammed my hand behind my back.

The man lowered his gaze. "I'm sorry."

I stood there, torn between asking him what he wanted and making a break for my phone. This was the man who'd followed me all day yesterday. This was the man I thought might be Joe Danvers's killer.

And now, here he was, standing on my doorstep, apologizing.

"If it wouldn't be too much trouble," he said, "I would like to talk." He held up his hands, showing me they were empty. His fingers were long and looked strong. "I know how all of this must look, but I promise I'm not here to hurt you."

That's what a killer would say! I stomped down on the stray thought and did my best to regain some semblance of composure. "Who are you? And why are you here?"

The man straightened, met my eye. Surprisingly, there was a hint of fear in his gaze, like he was afraid I might slam the door in his face or call the police on him.

And there was something else buried deep in his eyes, something I didn't expect to see.

Immense sadness.

"My name is Erik Deavers," he said. "Joseph Danvers was my father."

My mouth fell open, but no sound came out. Now that he mentioned it, I could see the resemblance. They had the same wide nose, the same square jaw. If I'd spent more time with Joe, then perhaps I would have seen it before now.

After a few moments, I managed to close my mouth and come up with something to say, though looking back, I wish I would have said something far more intelligent.

"Joe didn't have a son."

Erik's smile was sad. "He never knew about me."

He motioned toward the door. "Please, may I come in? I would like to explain. And, well, I have questions of my own."

I nodded and Erik stepped through the doorway, and into my house. He closed the door, and then his entire face lit up. "What an adorable kitty." He crouched down as Wheels rolled right up to him. "I've never had a cat of my own. Always too busy, you know?"

Despite how our paths first crossed, Erik earned a few points in my book for how he treated Wheels. "She seems to like you."

He scratched her behind the ears, and ran a hand down her back, before he rose. "Well, I like her." Some of the pleasure went out of his eyes. "Where should we sit?"

I led him into the living room, making sure not to turn my back on him completely, just in case his kindness was all an act. He took the couch, while I sat down in a chair across from him. He sat upright, with good posture, and folded his hands in his lap.

He has manners. I was sure there were plenty of killers with good manners, but it was hard to see him as such when he wasn't threatening me. Could I have been wrong about him?

There was only one way to find out.

"Why were you following me?"

He looked embarrassed when he answered. "I truly am sorry about that. I wasn't sure what to do, who to go to. I . . ." He shook his head as if dismissing whatever he'd been about to say. "It's probably better if I explain from the beginning."

I sat back and motioned for him to go on.

It took him a minute to gather his thoughts. I waited patiently, not wanting to rush him. Besides, it

gave me a chance to study him, to search for deception in his expression or posture. He appeared to be
in his thirties, and as I noted when I'd caught a
glimpse of him yesterday, he looked well-groomed.

"As I said, Joseph Danvers was my father," he said.
"I didn't know this until recently. Well, that's not
true. I knew his name, but didn't know the man himself. We'd never met, but that wasn't for a lack of trying."

"He didn't want to see you?"

Erik's smile was heartbreakingly sad. "As I said, he
didn't know about me."

It took a moment for what he said to click with
other parts of Joe's story. When it did, I couldn't
help but shout my next words.

"You're Christine Danvers's son!"

Erik nodded. "I didn't know that was her real
name until recently. I've learned a lot over the last
few months, more than I ever expected. I knew Mom
as Chris Deavers. She never married after Dad, but
she'd changed her name. She didn't tell me why, and
honestly, I still don't know. There's so much she
never got to tell me."

"Wait, wait, wait." I held up a hand. "I really do
think you need to start from the beginning." Christine was alive! It appeared as if Chester had been
right all along.

Erik crossed his legs and carefully smoothed out
his pants where they bunched up. "I was born thirty
years ago to a single mother. She'd told me my dad's
name, and never once led me to believe she had anything but love for him."

"But she left him?" It came out as a question.

"It took her years to explain," Erik said. "And even
then, she never told me the whole story. She claimed

it was for my own good, that it would be best if I never knew. But she did say that she was forced to run from her home, to leave her husband behind. She said he never knew about me." He closed his eyes briefly, before going on. "She always hoped that one day she'd find him again and would be able to tell him everything she couldn't when she left."

It took me a moment to realize why she'd had such a hard time finding Joe. "He changed his name."

"It took us years to find him. Mom had searched for him ever since I could remember. She never came here, to Grey Falls, but she did ask around. She was careful, like she was still afraid of something, but she tried the best she could."

"Do you know what she was afraid of?" I asked, thinking that whatever it was, it very well might have been what got Joe killed.

"No," Erik said. "She was careful to keep that part of her life separate. If it wasn't for Dad, I think she would have moved on from her old life completely. She really did love him."

I tried to imagine what it would be like to leave my home, my family, and not be able to come back. To leave Manny behind. Ben. Amelia. I honestly didn't think I could do it.

"Whatever she'd run from must have been pretty bad," I said, more to myself than Erik, but he responded anyway.

"She was terrified. When she heard Dad might be living in Grey Falls again, she tried to reach out to him, but we still didn't have his new name, just rumors. By the time she learned who he'd become, it was already too late."

My heart sank. "His death?"

Erik took a shuddering breath before answering. "Before that. Last week, in fact. Mom became gravely ill. It came on fast, and before either of us knew what was happening, she was gone." He swallowed. I noted his hands were shaking where they were folded in his lap. "She desperately tried to contact him, but she was so sick . . ."

I thought back to the room I'd found Joe in. "He was trying to find her, too," I said. "I don't think he ever stopped."

A tear rolled down Erik's cheek. "That's good to hear. Mom said she'd left to protect him, as well as to protect me. She prayed that we'd all one day become a family, but it never happened. It never will."

I was forced to swallow back a lump that had grown in my own throat lest I blubber all over myself. "You followed me," I said. "Why?"

Erik removed a handkerchief from his pocket and dabbed at his eyes. "That day, I was finally going to meet my dad. The day after Mom died, she received an anonymous letter with what was, apparently, Dad's new name. As soon as I read it, I knew I had to come to Grey Falls. I drove by his driveway, I don't know, twenty times. I was scared he'd reject me, scared he'd tell me he'd never wanted me. I guess I was afraid that he'd somehow blame me for Mom's death."

He laughed, though it was a frustrated sound.

"I should have gone right up to his door. Maybe if I hadn't been such a coward, he'd still be alive."

"You can't think like that," I said as gently as I could.

"I know, but it's hard sometimes." He tucked his handkerchief away. "I went back to my hotel room to calm my nerves, and after a good lecture to myself, I headed back to the house. When I got there, you were leaning against your van, and the cops were everywhere. I didn't know what to think. I didn't know who you were, only that you had some connection to my dad. I . . ." He cleared his throat. "I guess I thought you might have been his girlfriend."

I bit back an immediate rejection of the idea. I barely knew Joe Danvers, hadn't even known his real name, but there was no way Erik could know that. "I was taking him a cat," I said, motioning toward where Sheamus was watching us with one sleepy eye.

Erik seemed to notice the Maine Coon for the first time. He practically melted into the couch. "That one?" he asked.

"Yeah. He was adopting him. I was due to deliver him to Joe that day." I almost told him I'd found Joe's body, but decided that probably wasn't something he wanted to hear right then.

Erik smiled fondly at the cat before turning back to me. "Well, I saw you there, and thought you might know what happened. But with the police crawling all over the place, and me being a stranger, I was scared. I followed you, fully intent on asking you about Dad, about what happened, but when you got here, I chickened out."

"And later?"

Erik looked down at his hands. "I have anxiety. I struggle with meeting people, talking to them. I sometimes struggle with people I know." He glanced up at me. "And you were a stranger, one who knew my dad better than I did. I was afraid you'd reject me outright, or worse, had something to do with his death and would come after me next. I didn't know what to do."

"I thought *you* were after *me*," I admitted.

"I only wanted to talk. And then when you led me on that chase, I thought perhaps you were trying to get a look at me so you could find me and finish me off." He laughed. "I realized later that I was being stupid and forced myself to come to your house and introduce myself. Unfortunately, you weren't home."

"Yesterday," I said. "Joanne . . ." My eyes widened. "Oh no!"

I jumped up and rushed to the front door. Erik followed me.

I yanked the door open and peered across the street. The curtains swished closed, a sure sign that Joanne was watching.

"What's wrong?" Erik asked.

"My neighbor." I closed my eyes, cursing myself for being so stupid. "I told her to call the police if she saw your car again."

"Oh."

"I have a feeling we're going to have company soon."

Sure enough, an unmarked car shot down the road, toward the house. It came to a stop, just behind Erik's sedan, and before I could say another word, Detective Cavanaugh was marching toward us.

"I got a call. Is everything all right, Mrs. Denton?" While he spoke to me, he was staring hard at Erik.

"Everything's fine. We're just talking." I don't know why, but I raised my hands in surrender. Too much TV, I supposed.

Across the street, Joanne stepped outside. She looked excited about the prospects of a real life police drama unfolding on her street.

"Is this the man who was following you?" Cavanaugh looked Erik up and down. From his expression, I think he recognized him as Joe's son or, at least, suspected something.

"He was," I admitted. "He's Joseph Danvers's son. Like I said, we were talking. That's all he wanted to do."

"I think you'd best explain," Cavanaugh said.

Both Erik and I took turns retelling the tale, with Erik handling most of the details dealing with Christine. Cavanaugh listened, growing more and more troubled as we went on. It was no wonder, really, considering he'd been running on the belief that Christine Danvers was murdered by Joe some thirty years past.

When we were done, Cavanaugh blew out his cheeks. "I think it might be best if you come down to the station to give an official statement."

"Now, wait a minute!" I said, stepping between him and Erik. "He didn't do anything."

"It's all right," Erik said. "I understand."

"He's not in trouble, Mrs. Denton," Cavanaugh said. "He might have information that could help us discover who killed Joe." His voice *was* gentle, so I supposed he wasn't just saying that to keep me calm.

But still, the man had gone through enough already. His dad, a man he'd never gotten a chance to meet, was dead. There was no fixing that. Dragging him to the police station would only compound the issue.

Erik took my hand and squeezed it. "Thank you for taking the time to talk to me," he said. "I wish . . ." He shook his head. "I'm sorry if I scared you."

"It's all right," I said. "I'm glad we got it sorted out. Wait one sec." I hurried inside, jerked open my purse, and removed one of my rarely used business cards. I returned to hand it to Erik. "In case you need to call me. It has my cell number."

"Thank you." He smiled, and then turned to the detective. "I'm ready."

Cavanaugh led Erik to his brown sedan. I supposed it was a good sign that he was letting him drive to the station under his own power. I watched as they both backed out of my driveway and headed downtown. The urge to follow them was great, but I held myself in check. There were better things I could do with my time.

8

The front room of Chester's office was empty, so I made for the closed door where I could hear muffled voices. A giggle came from inside, and I was pretty sure it was Amelia's voice. It was most definitely not Chester Chudzinski.

A brief flare of motherly protectiveness tried to worm its way through me, but I mentally pushed it away. It was far more likely that Chester had said something funny, causing Amelia to laugh, rather than something untoward happening behind the door.

Still, I cleared my throat loudly before I knocked on the frosted glass.

There was a thump that reminded me of the sound of a cat jumping off a table. Seconds passed where I could barely hear a hushed whisper, then the door opened, revealing Amelia. Her eyes were a little too wide, her cheeks flushed.

"Mom?" she asked. "What are you doing here?"

"I learned something that I thought Chester might want to hear." I peered around her, but instead of Chester Chudzinski, another woman was standing in the room, hands behind her back. She had hazel eyes that stood out against her milk chocolate skin. Her hair, like Amelia's, was colored at the tips, but rather than Amelia's blue, hers was a fiery red.

"Mrs. Denton?" the woman asked, taking two quick strides forward. I noted she was wearing combat boots along with her shorts and black spaghetti-strap tank top. It reminded me forcibly of Amelia's wardrobe. "I've heard a lot about you."

I glanced at Amelia.

She cleared her throat and adopted a more professional tone. "Mom, this is Maya Boyd. She works with Chester."

"Maya," I said. "It's a pleasure to meet you. I didn't know anyone else worked with Chester. Are you an intern as well?"

"No," Maya said. "I'm not a full partner or anything, but I help Chester out on his cases. I do have my license, so I guess I'm officially an investigator." She glanced at Amelia. "And with how hard this one works, I imagine she'll be joining me soon."

"Flattery will get you nowhere," Amelia said with a roll of her eyes. She turned her attention back to me. "Chester will be back down in a few minutes. Was there something you wanted?"

"I think I'd better wait for him to join us."

Amelia backed away from the door and motioned to a chair. I took it, but neither woman sat next to me. Maya moved to lean against Chester's desk, while Amelia stood in the corner, arms crossed. She acted like I was invading her private space, which, I suppose, I was. I wouldn't have liked it if my mother had shown up to my workplace either.

I decided to break the tension with casual conversation. "Have you worked here long?" I asked Maya.

"Couple years. I interned, like Amelia, thinking I'd strike out on my own after a few months. Chester's a good guy, and I've learned a lot from him, so I've kind of stuck around."

"I didn't even know we had a private investigator in Grey Falls until recently," I said.

"We do keep to ourselves," Maya said. "I'm not sure if that's a good thing or not."

"I'm sure it's fine." I glanced around the office. While none of the furniture was new, it wasn't falling apart either. "It's kind of exciting to think Amelia might be working here in an official capacity someday."

"We'll see," Amelia said. "I've still got a lot to learn."

"And get licensed." Maya said it like it was something that they'd discussed before.

"What does that entail?" I asked, genuinely curious. If there was anything I could do to help Amelia expedite the process, I would do it.

Before either Amelia or Maya could answer me, however, Chester hurried into the room. He was flushed, hair ruffled and sticking straight up in places, as if he'd spent the last ten minutes tugging at it.

"I couldn't find it," he said, seemingly looking right past me as he strode to his desk. "I'm pretty sure I boxed it up, but there's a chance it's tucked into my desk somewhere. Oh!" He came to an abrupt halt midway through sitting. "Mrs. Denton. I didn't see you there."

"It's all right," I said. "And please, call me Liz." I glanced to Maya. "Both of you."

"Sorry, sorry." Chester dropped the rest of the way into his chair. "You'll probably have to tell me every single time we meet. I tend to address people formally out of reflex."

"That's all right," I said. In fact, I imagine it was a good habit to have as a PI. "I wanted to talk to you, if that's all right?"

"Mom might have learned something," Amelia said from her spot in the corner. She sounded like she was anxious for me to be gone, but was intrigued at the same time. "She does that sort of thing."

Chester started to open a drawer in his desk, but closed it without looking inside. "Is that right? Is this about Christine and Joseph Danvers?"

"It is," I said, and then I told them about my encounter with Erik Deavers. The moment I mentioned that Christine hadn't been murdered, but had, in fact, given birth to Joe's son, Chester was on his feet.

"I knew it!" He clapped his hands together loud enough that it echoed. "I didn't know about her being pregnant, but I knew Joe was innocent." Some of his excitement faded. "But now, it's too late."

"It sounded like they loved each other very much," I said, then finished the tale.

Chester's expression grew sad as he sat back down. "You say she died?"

"She did. Apparently, she was ill. It wasn't why she left—Erik doesn't know why she fled Grey Falls. But she did try to find her husband again in the hopes of telling him about their son."

Maya closed her eyes and dropped her head. At the same time, Amelia made a sad, heartbroken sound.

"It's a shame they never found one another again," Chester said. "We can't let things stand as they are. We've got to do whatever we can to clear Joe's name." He aimed the last at Maya and Amelia.

"Erik is telling the police everything he knows as we speak," I said. "I'm not sure what good it's going to do in the long run, but at least now, they'll know Joe never killed Christine. That has to count for something, doesn't it?"

"To some, it will," Chester said. "But the more we can discover about what happened, the better it will be."

"What can we do?" Amelia asked, pushing away from the wall to stand at Chester's side. "Even with proof Joe didn't murder his wife, someone *did* kill him. And Christine did run. Do you think it's connected somehow?"

"It very well might be," Chester said. "In fact, I'd almost count on it. It can't be a coincidence that Joe's son arrives in town the same day Joe gets murdered."

"He didn't do it," I said, though I knew no such thing. As far as I knew, Erik had fed me a string of lies. He'd seemed genuine enough, and I doubted the police would take him at his word, so it would be hard for him to keep up the façade if he was, indeed, lying.

"I'm not saying he did," Chester said. "But I bet someone else knew about him, knew that Christine was still out there. They'd almost have to, wouldn't they?"

"If Mrs. Danvers fled Grey Falls, she did so for a reason," Maya said.

"And that reason might be the same one that got Joe killed," Amelia added.

"Exactly," Chester said. "Something made Christine Danvers run and, as Liz here said, change her name. It wasn't her husband, that much is clear since she was looking for him. There has to be something in her life that points to what that might be."

"An old boyfriend?" I chimed in, feeling like an outsider. I'd only seen all three of them together for a few minutes and I could already see the chemistry between them. Amelia was in good hands here, and I couldn't be prouder.

"There were a few, back before Joe," Chester said. "But none of them still live in Grey Falls, and as far as my research could turn up, the men remained on good terms with Christine, even after they'd broken up."

"Gambling, maybe?" Maya said, before shaking her head. "No, that doesn't fit."

"Could it relate to Joe somehow?" Amelia asked. "Like, maybe he had a mistress or was into something dangerous. Christine found out and took off." Even as she said it, she sounded as if she didn't believe it.

"But if that was the case, why look for him later? Or tell her son about him?" Maya asked.

Chester rubbed at his temples. "There has to be something."

"What about her family?" I asked. "Not everyone has a good family life." And even if Christine was a good person, it didn't mean she got her kind disposition from her parents.

Chester snapped his fingers and spun around on his chair. "Where did I put it?" he asked, though it was obvious he wasn't asking anyone but himself.

It took him only a moment to find what he was looking for. The file he dropped on his desk was battered and stained, as if he'd gone through it hundreds of times over the years. He opened the folder, flipped through a few pages, and then jabbed a finger into it so hard, it had to have hurt.

"That's what I thought!" he said, glancing up at me. "Christine Danvers was adopted by Ida and Boris Priestly."

The names meant nothing to me.

"Ugh, who names their kid Boris these days?" Amelia asked.

Chester ignored her. "It says here Christine was eight years old when she was adopted."

"And her real parents?" I asked, wondering what could have caused someone to give up their eight-year-old daughter. There was no way I'd ever give up my children, for any reason. And especially not after I'd gotten to hold them and care for them for so long.

"I was never able to discover that information," Chester said. "Back when I was looking into Joe's case, it hadn't seemed important, so, admittedly, I didn't look too hard."

"So, you have no idea why she was adopted?"

Chester shook his head. "I wish I did. I'm pretty sure Christine didn't have a relationship with her birth parents, though. Joe would have said something if she had."

I wasn't so sure about that, especially if Christine's

birth parents were bad people. It's a natural instinct to protect the people you love.

"I can see if I can dig up the records," Maya said. "Sometimes that stuff is easy to find online, especially if there was no reason for them to keep it a secret."

"Someone should talk to the Priestlys," Chester said. "Perhaps they know something that might help. I talked to them when I first investigated Christine's disappearance, but things might have changed since then."

"I'll do it." Amelia practically tripped over herself to volunteer.

"I could go with you," I said.

She shot me a suspicious look, as if she didn't believe my motives for going with her were pure.

"I want to solve this just as badly as you do," I said, although I did also want to keep an eye on her. I mean, a killer was still out there somewhere. Perhaps the Priestlys had decided to exact revenge on their daughter's suspected murderer once he'd resurfaced, thirty years after the fact.

Yeah, it was a stretch, but it gave me a good reason to tag along.

We filed out of Chester's cramped office, into the main room. Chester seemed energized by the recent revelations, and I had to admit, I was pretty excited myself. Joe deserved justice, for both his murder *and* for having false accusations thrown his way.

Amelia dropped into the chair behind her desk. "Give me a sec to find an address." She did a quick search and then wrote down what she found. "Got it."

Amelia and I were about to head for the door when it burst open and a short, stocky man who appeared to be in his mid- to late fifties strode in. He wore overalls and a faded red ball cap that once had something stenciled on the front—I think it was a sports team—but it had been torn free, leaving behind only a speckled, circular patch in its place.

He looked right past Amelia and me and pointed at Chester. "Leave it alone, old man," he said. He ran his tongue along the inside of his lower lip, pushing something around that was pressed between his lip and gums. Tobacco, I assumed.

Chester went completely still. "I don't know what you're referring to."

"The hell you don't." The guy had the audacity to spit a dark juice onto the floor, as if he was out on the farm somewhere, not inside a place of business. "He got what he deserved. Both him and that woman of his."

"Are you talking about Joe—"

Maya didn't get to finish.

The man spun on her, eyes going hard and dangerous. "No one spoke to you." He looked her up and down. "Shouldn't you be trying to cash in your food stamps?"

Maya took a step forward, fists clenching. "Say that again."

Chester hurriedly moved between the man and Maya, before shooting Amelia a warning look. Amelia was practically seething, and I couldn't say I was faring much better. The stranger was a real piece of work.

"I think you'd best go, Harry," Chester said. "I wouldn't want to have to call the police."

"Go ahead," the man—Harry—said. "I'll just tell them what I saw yesterday."

"Yeah?" Amelia said. "What's that?"

The look the man gave Amelia had me close to knocking him out. He *leered* at her, eyes most definitely not where they were supposed to be.

"Harry," Chester said. "Did you see something?"

Harry's gaze lingered on Amelia a moment longer before he finally turned his attention back to Chester. "I did. It's why I'm here. You're out there, asking questions that no one should be asking, when I know for a fact what happened."

He jabbed at the wad in his lip with his tongue, looked as if he might spit again, but thought better of it.

"What did you see?" Chester asked. He was somehow remaining calm. If it had been me and my place of business, I would have decked the guy already.

"It was like the last time. People don't always see me, but I sure see them."

My brain snapped into focus. *Harry?* As in Harry Davis, the man who'd claimed he'd seen Joe Danvers dragging a body and carrying a shovel at night. This man was the reason Joseph had to change his name to Joe Hitchcock. Could he also be the reason Christine fled town?

"Go on," Chester said.

"I saw him. One of *those* types."

Chester visibly cringed and Maya's teeth snapped tight. Amelia shifted next to me and I put out a hand to keep her from going after Harry. He might be older, but he was still built like a farmer. I didn't trust that he wouldn't hit a woman.

Harry went on, oblivious to the tension flowing around the room. "He was lurking outside and I de-

cided to watch to see what he did. Guy waited until
Joe"—he practically sneered the name—"got home
and then went in after him."

"You saw who killed Joe?" I asked. I hadn't meant
to speak, but it just sort of popped out.

"I did." Harry grinned like he'd done something
he was especially proud of. "And I plan on letting the
police know it too. Facts are facts. Joseph Danvers
killed his wife, and he, in turn, was murdered, just
like he should have been years ago."

"Did you actually *see* it happen?" Chester asked,
but Harry was done answering questions.

"Stop poking around where you don't belong," he
said. "There's nothing for you to discover out there
that we don't already know. Keep at it, and the next
thing you know, you'll end up like the others."

"Is that a threat?" Somehow, Chester's voice remained calm and cool. His eyes, however, were blazing.

"Take it how you want." Harry spat again. "But
don't come crying to me when something happens
to you." He glanced around the room. "All of you."

And with that, Harry Davis waltzed out.

"That guy's a real jerk," Amelia said.

"And a liar," Maya said. "Did you hear what he said
to me?"

Amelia crossed the short space and wrapped Maya
in a hug. Both of them were trembling, and I wouldn't
doubt that if Harry were to walk through the door
again, neither of them would hold back.

"I've got to make some calls," Chester said. He
turned and walked into his office. Just before he
closed the door, I caught a glimpse of the look on his
face.

He looked terrified.

Amelia broke her hug with Maya and cleared her throat. She glanced at me briefly before heading to the door. "Come on, Mom," she said. "Let's go talk to Mr. and Mrs. Priestly. We need to figure this thing out before that jerk manages to ruin someone else's life."

9

Amelia and I sat in a small, tidy eat-in kitchen. The room smelled of flowers in bloom and was bright and airy, despite its small size.

"Here you are." Ida Priestly poured tea into three mugs before returning the teapot to the stove. "I prefer my tea to be hot, never mind the weather." She crossed the room and sat down gingerly across from us. "Now, you said you wanted to talk to me about Christine?" Her eyes misted briefly before her pleasant smile returned.

"If it wouldn't be too much trouble," I said, sipping my tea. It was piping hot and had an odd flavor, as if I were drinking liquid potpourri. It wasn't entirely unpleasant, but left an aftertaste I could have done without.

"It's never too much trouble talking about her." She blinked rapidly as she brought her own teacup to her lips. Ida was in her eighties, and looked every year of it. Her hand shook ever so slightly, yet she managed to not spill a drop of her tea as she sipped. "She was a beautiful child, grown into a beautiful adult."

"Was it difficult adopting her?" Amelia asked. "Considering . . ." She blushed.

Ida smiled. "Because I'm an old white woman? It was. My husband and I never did care one lick about skin color. It's what's inside that counts."

"I wish everyone thought that way," I said, remembering Harry Davis's comments. I had a hard time believing that people like that still existed.

"Me too, dear, me too." She ran her hand over the tablecloth, smoothing out ripples. "Christine was a good child. And when she lived here with us, I made sure she understood where she came from, who she was. She didn't need to change to be more like Boris or me. It wouldn't have been right to ask her to do so."

"Did you know her parents?" Amelia asked. "Her birth parents, I mean."

"No, I didn't." Ida's face clouded over. "But from what I hear, it wasn't a good situation that brought Christine to us. It never really is, is it?"

"Often, no," I said.

"She was scared when I first met her, terrified, really. I thought for the longest time it was because we were new to her, strangers. I eventually realized it went deeper than that. Something happened in that girl's life that traumatized her. I never did get it out of her, but I suppose I didn't press too hard. She was my baby and I didn't want to hurt her or add to her distress."

Amelia and I shared a look. It was Amelia who spoke. "Do you think whatever happened when she was little was why she left town?"

Ida's face transformed into a blank mask. "What do you mean? She went missing years ago, and the police believe her dead."

"Her husband didn't kill her," I said. "Joe was innocent."

"I always knew that," Ida said. "I went to the police myself to tell them they were wasting their time looking into him, but they refused to listen." She shook her head. "That poor man. Hounded until he left Grey Falls, then murdered when he returned. Someone needs to pay for that."

"That's what we're hoping to accomplish," Amelia said. "We want justice for both Joe *and* Christine."

Ida picked up her tea, but her hand was trembling so badly now, she couldn't bring it to her lips. A little slopped over the side, onto the tablecloth, as she set it back down.

"Oh dear," she said, rising quickly. "I made such a mess."

I watched her as she scurried around the kitchen. Her movements were furtive, almost frightened, and I was pretty sure I knew why.

I waited until she'd cleaned up the mess and sat back down before I spoke.

"You knew Christine was alive, didn't you?"

"I always believed so." She refused to meet my eye. "Not quite a mother's instinct, but something akin to it."

"It's more than that," I said. "You *knew* for a fact she was alive. You knew she left town on her own. Do you know why?"

Ida picked at her nails. Her mask fell away and I could see the fear in her eyes. She didn't want to look up, didn't want anyone else to know.

I reached across the table and rested a hand on her own. "We want to help." And then the kicker. "I met Christine's son."

Ida's eyes snapped closed and her lower lip started to tremble. She turned her hand so that she could grasp mine.

"Is he all right?"

"He is," I said, hoping it was true. I hadn't heard from him or Detective Cavanaugh since they'd left my house. And if Harry followed through on his threat to tell the cops that he'd seen Erik snooping around Joe's place, who knew what was happening. "He came to Grey Falls to meet his father. He arrived too late."

"Did you know Christine had a son?" Amelia asked Ida.

The older woman's nod was jerky. "I did. But I never met him." She took a big breath and when she exhaled, she seemed to deflate. "I knew Christine ran, but I didn't know why she did or where to. She never gave me an address or a number where I could reach her. It was hard, to say the least."

"But she contacted you somehow."

"She did." Ida pulled her hand from mine and rose. She left the room briefly and returned a few minutes later carrying a small fire-resistant chest. She set it on the table between us. "It's unlocked."

I turned the chest to face me and flipped open the lid. Inside were postcards, at least a hundred of them. Careful not to bend or tear anything, I picked up a stack and sifted through them.

There was no return address on any of them, and they were all postmarked from different states. The messages were always brief, and gave away nothing about Christine's location. But they did tell me one thing: She loved her mother.

"I'm not sure if she moved around, or if she had other people send those for her," Ida said. "I tried to look for her; I really did. She asked me not to, of course. A few of them say so."

I sorted through a few more until I found one. I read it out loud. "Don't look for me. I'm happy. If you see Joe, please tell him I love him. We'll be together again, I swear it. Love, C."

A tear rolled down Ida's cheek. I was forced to wipe one of my own from my eye.

"She never did find him, did she?" Ida asked.

"She did," I said. "But she got sick. You do know . . . ?" My chest tightened at the thought that I might have to tell her that her daughter was dead.

Ida nodded, saving me from the unpleasantness. "I received a letter. She sent it just before she died, telling me it was her time. I'd show it to you, but—"

"It's personal," Amelia said.

"I wish there was something in it that told me why this had to happen; I truly do. Boris, when he died . . ." She pressed her palms into her eyes as if she could force back the tears. "He never understood. His heart was broken when she left. I don't think he ever recovered."

I tried to imagine how I'd handle it if one of my kids ran away without telling me why. I couldn't do it. It would have broken my heart, just as it had Boris's. I would have done anything to find them again, even if it was against their wishes.

"Did you ever find any clues about why Christine left?" Amelia asked. "Or come up with any theories?"

"No theories," Ida said. "But there was a man."

Both Amelia and I sat up straighter. "What man?" I asked.

"He came to Boris and me a few weeks after Christine vanished. He didn't buy into the rumors that Joe killed her, and I know I didn't do a very good job concealing that I knew something. Back then, I was so worried, I couldn't keep the concern out of my voice. I'm sure he suspected something, but he never outright said it."

"Did you know the guy?" Amelia asked.

"Never saw him before that day. He was, let's just say, not exactly my type. He was older than Christine, but not by much. I thought maybe they were friends or perhaps they had dated once without my knowledge, but the more he talked, the more I realized she wouldn't have had anything to do with him. He was prejudiced, if you get my meaning."

Amelia and I shared another look. Even though neither of us spoke, I could read the name in her eyes. *Harry Davis.*

"What did he look like?" I asked.

"Like anyone else, I suppose. Tanned arms, like he worked on a farm." She tapped her bicep, as if hinting that the tan stopped there. "He was a bit aggressive when he asked after Christine, as if he was desperate to find her. I was glad when he was gone, and glad that I never saw him again until recently."

"You saw him again?" Amelia asked. "Where?"

"Here." She tapped her table with her index finger. "Came to my door, asking me what I knew about Christine and Joe. I slammed the door in his face. At my age, I don't need to deal with people like that. It's bad for the heart."

"Did you ever catch this man's name?" I asked.

"I wish I had." Ida leaned forward. Her gaze was intense. "Christine was scared of something when she left. I can almost guarantee that this man was part of the reason why."

After our chat with Ida Priestly, Amelia dropped me off at my car outside Chester's office, but declined to come home with me.

"I want to help Maya look for Christine's birth parents," she said. "They might be able to help fill in the gaps on her past."

I left her to it and drove home, thinking about Ida and her relationship with her daughter. I couldn't imagine going thirty years without seeing one of my children, only getting postcards.

And then to find out they were going to die, and never getting a chance to be with them or say goodbye.

It hurt too much to even think about it, let alone live it.

I was so lost in thought, I didn't notice there was another car in my driveway until I was parked beside it. It wasn't Erik's brown sedan, or any other car I knew. I looked from the strange vehicle to my front door.

That's when I saw the woman marching toward my car.

"Thief!" She kicked my bumper with her Crocs-covered foot. "Petnapper!" Another kick, this one to the door of my van.

I almost opened the van door, but thought better

of it. I rolled down the window instead. "I'm sorry, but I don't know what you're talking about."

"You're *sorry?*" The woman kicked my van again.

"Please stop that."

She kicked it again, this time harder, with arms flying up over her head. The woman looked strong, as if she'd worked with her hands all her life, though the years had softened her somewhat. I put her in her fifties, though I didn't doubt she could take me if she wanted to.

"You stole my Chico."

"Your Chico?" I asked. "I don't know what that is."

"Liar!" A kick to the tire. "I can hear him barking."

"Wait," I said, a slow understanding dawning. "Chico is a Chihuahua?"

"You know he is." This time she slapped the car door, just under the window. I jerked back just in case her next blow was aimed at my face. "You can't keep him! I'll call the cops."

"I didn't steal anyone," I said. "Let's just calm down so we can talk about this."

"Calm down?" she shrieked. "I don't think so, lady."

I winced at her piercing tone, and glanced in my rearview mirror. Sure enough, Joanne was standing outside her house, hands on her hips, and a disapproving look on her face.

Great. I was positive I was going to be hearing from her about this too.

"I want my dog," the woman screamed. "And I want him now!" This time, she punched my door with a closed fist.

"I can't do anything if you keep beating on my van," I said.

The woman grudgingly stepped back. I eyed her a moment, not quite sure I trusted her not to leap at me, before I opened the van door and stepped out.

"Get him," she said, jabbing a finger toward my door.

"No." I crossed my arms and stood my ground. I would *not* be bullied by this woman, not after dealing with Harry Davis. "I'm not doing anything for you while you're this angry."

The woman actually snarled at me.

"Why do you think I stole your dog?" I asked. I somehow kept my voice calm and level.

"Because he's inside!"

"But how did you know he was here?" I asked. "Did you give him up to Pets Luv Us?"

"Give him up? I'd never do such a thing."

"Then how did he end up here?"

The woman looked like she might yell some more about how I stole Chico, but thought better of it. "He broke his leash," she said. She wouldn't meet my eye as she spoke. "He ran and I didn't know where he went. Then, I received a call that he was snatched up by Furever Pets." She jabbed her finger at the logo on my van.

"I didn't snatch your dog," I said. "He was brought to me." But, apparently, not in good faith. I was going to kill Courtney the next time I saw her.

"Your van was spotted at the scene," the woman said, her voice slowly rising back to a shout. "You, or one of your people, took him. I want him back."

"I'm sure you do," I said, trying to be diplomatic. "Do you have documentation on you?"

"What?"

"Papers. Something that will tell me that Chico is indeed yours?"

The woman narrowed her eyes at me. "Are you calling me a liar?"

"No," I said. "But I need to make sure I'm doing what's best for Chico."

"He needs me."

"I understand. Just show me something that will prove that he's yours." At that point, I would have accepted a photograph.

The woman grumbled something under her breath. When I didn't respond, she raised her voice. "I don't have any with me."

I took a deep, calming breath. "Okay. We can work this out." I noted then I didn't hear barking, nor was Ben's car in the driveway. "Chico is getting checked out at the vet to make sure he's healthy right now, so I couldn't give him to you now, even if you had proof of ownership. Give me your name and number and let me make some calls, and as soon as I have verification that he's yours, and once he's back here, I'll get him to you."

The woman ground her teeth a moment before she stepped closer. I cringed, thinking she might go for my shins with her Crocs, but she merely muttered her name and phone number.

"Okay, Stacy," I said. "I'll call you as soon as I work this out, all right? If you can get me some sort of documentation, I can speed this up. Otherwise, it might not be until tomorrow before I know for sure. Rest assured, I'm going to take good care of Chico until then." And I planned on getting to the bottom of this, even if I had to corner Courtney to do so.

"You'd better." She started to walk off toward her car, before she stopped. "Everyone is going to hear about this." She narrowed her eyes at me. "Everyone."

And then she got into her car, spun her tires, and flew out of my driveway.

I sagged against the side of my van. This was something I most definitely didn't need.

Courtney. My hands balled into fists and I had to restrain myself from following Stacy's lead and punching my van.

I took a deep, calming breath, and then I marched for the house, still seething. I had a call to make.

10

The phone rang, but no one picked up.

I paced my living room, steaming. I *knew* Courtney had set me up, but how was I supposed to prove it? She'd just deny everything or play it off as a mistake. I wanted to believe this was all one big misunderstanding, but knew from experience that it wasn't. Courtney knew exactly what she was doing when she'd done it.

What I didn't get was why she'd stoop so low. I didn't make money with my rescue. In fact, I spent more money than I ever took in. Courtney, on the other hand, had no problem charging adoption fees that allowed her to tuck a few extra bucks away here and there. This wasn't something you did for profit.

So why bother smearing my name?

I disconnected and tried again. After only a handful of rings, I gave up.

"She's avoiding me," I said to Wheels, who was watching me from the dining room. Sheamus was sitting in the living room window, sneezing up a storm. After a few seconds, when I worried I might have to do something, he calmed and settled in to watch the birds outside.

I plopped down on the couch to think about what to do. Wheels rolled over and stared up at me. I scratched behind her ears, shooting a glance toward the laundry room door, which was open. As I assumed, the Chihuahua was still getting checked out.

I could keep trying to call Courtney and hope we could work it out civilly, but how long before she simply blocked me? She wasn't answering her phone for a reason.

"I could pay her a visit," I muttered. Wheels meowed and rubbed against my leg. I couldn't tell if she agreed with me or not.

I wasn't sure how else to go about verifying Stacy's story other than waiting for her to get back to me with documentation. I believed her when she'd said Chico belonged to her, but I still wanted proof. I wouldn't put it past Courtney to have sent this woman here to cause trouble.

The front door opened and Ben bounded inside, dog carrier in hand. The dog was quiet for a change, and I wondered if Manny had been forced to sedate him for his tests. Ben took Chico to the laundry room, set him free, and then joined me in the living room.

"Hey, Mom." He threw himself down into the recliner, propping one leg on the armrest. "Dad says Piranha is good to go."

"It's Chico." I assumed. *And what if I'm wrong about Stacy?* Lately, I was struggling to trust my own instincts.

Ben cocked his head to the side. "What?"

"Never mind." There was no sense getting into it now, so I changed the subject. "I heard you were looking at a house."

Ben grinned. "Yeah, it was strange. Some of the houses we went to were still occupied. You'd walk in and someone else's life would be right there, laid out in front of you. Some people didn't even pick up after themselves before we got there. We're talking dirty clothes on the floor, sinks full of dishes. I'm not sure I'd want someone popping into my room without me being there to watch them like a hawk."

I barely heard what he'd said after one word: "We?"

His grin widened. "Her name's Katie. I think I'm in love."

As if I hadn't heard that from him before. "Are you planning on moving in with this Katie?" I asked. "How long have you known her?"

He took a moment to think about it. "Three and a half weeks now. Give or take."

"Three weeks?" I very nearly shouted it.

"And a half."

"Do you really think you should be moving in with someone you've known for under a month?"

Ben shrugged and seemed to dismiss my concerns. "She's been looking for a place of her own for a while now. And, honestly, I should have done the same a long time ago. We got to talking about it, and both of us figured, why not? I mean, we're both adults. If it doesn't work out, we've got a plan for that."

"You have a breakup plan?" I asked, incredulous. Leave it to Ben to prepare for an inevitable separation. I don't think he'd ever had a relationship that lasted for more than a couple of months, and that might be stretching it.

"Yeah. As you pointed out, we haven't been together for long. Things happen. People move on from one another, grow apart, what have you."

In Ben's case, that seemed like a weekly event. "What about renting a place instead?" I asked. "If you buy, you're going to be on the hook for it if you two break up. It's not like you can just give the house back if it doesn't work out."

"We thought about it," he said. "But decided against renting. Mom"—he dropped his leg to the floor and sat forward so he could look me in the eye—"I know what I'm doing."

Oh, how I wished I could believe him. I loved my son, I really did, but sometimes, I wished he'd be just a little more responsible.

Isn't that what he's trying to do?

"I'll support you, Ben, no matter what," I said. "But please make sure you're doing the right thing. Think it through. Don't make any rash decisions."

"I won't." He popped to his feet. "I'm going to do a little more research online. If you don't need anything . . . ?"

"No, go ahead."

He grinned, kissed me on the top of the head, and then bounded up the stairs.

I watched him go with a worried sigh. He was happy, I could tell. I only hoped that his happiness would last this time.

While I was worried about Ben's future, talking to him did have one good side effect—I didn't want to wring Courtney's neck as much as I had before. I decided to give it a few more hours before I tried calling her again. Maybe, by then, I'd see things clearer, and Stacy will have gotten back to me. Besides, yelling at her wouldn't do either of us any good.

Since Ben was doing his own research upstairs—likely house research, if I didn't miss my guess—I decided to do some of my own. I grabbed my laptop and did a quick search for Stacy Hildebrand, the woman who claimed Chico belonged to her. Finding photographic evidence that she did indeed own the dog would go a long way in easing my mind about her and her motives.

It didn't take long to find her social media profiles and see that, indeed, Chico and Stacy were an item. Nearly every photograph showed her hugging or grooming him. No wonder the woman was so upset; they appeared inseparable.

Once I talked to Courtney to make sure I wasn't overlooking something, and once Stacy got back to me, I'd get Chico back to his owner. Somehow, I'd make sure everyone came out of this happy.

I started to set my laptop aside to give Courtney another call when I realized there was someone else I could do some digging into.

"Harry Davis." I spoke his name out loud as I typed it in.

Unsurprisingly, I found almost nothing on him. There were way too many people with the same name, and digging through them all would take all day. I had no idea how to narrow my search, since I wasn't looking into him for a pet adoption.

But I know someone who might have some idea.

I did a quick search, snatched up my phone, and made a call.

"Chudzinski Investigations. How may we be of service?"

"Hi, Maya, it's Liz Denton. Amelia's mom."

"Oh, hi, Liz. Do you need to speak to Amelia? She's right here."

"No, I was hoping I could ask Chester a question or two. Is he available?"

"Let me check. I've got to put you on hold. I apologize for the music in advance."

"That's all right."

"I'll be quick."

There was a click, followed by music that made elevator music sound upbeat and exciting. It made me wonder if Chester had chosen it to weed out anyone who wasn't serious about employing his services. I mean, you had to be truly dedicated to a call to wait through the toneless tune playing in my ear.

Thankfully, Maya was true to her word and she was back after only a couple of seconds. "Liz? He can talk to you now."

"Great."

Another click. This one was followed by Chester's voice.

"Hi, Mrs. Denton, what can I do for you?"

"Hey, Chester, I was wondering if you could tell me something about Harry Davis."

There was a pause. "What about him?"

"Actually, I'm not sure. Curiosity, maybe? I was hoping you could tell me something that might, I don't know, give me some context on who he is."

"Context? You won't like anything you find on him," Chester said. "I looked into him back when Christine first went missing, and I hated every second of it. It's like walking into a cesspool of prejudice and hatred. You'll need a shower after reading some of the things he's said."

"That's all right; I could use one anyway."

Even though it was meant as a joke, neither of us laughed.

"Do you have an email address?" Chester asked. "I've kept tabs on Harry, and I can shoot you a link or two I've found where his true colors come out. You can take it from there."

"Yeah." I rattled off my Furever Pets email address, which was the only one I had. I wondered if I should go ahead and create a personal address for situations like this. *Not that I plan on doing this ever again.* "Thanks a lot, Chester. It'll ease my mind knowing who Harry really is."

"I don't know about that. Trust me, you won't like it one bit. What you saw earlier today was only a small taste of Harry Davis."

We clicked off and I immediately checked my email. As promised, the links were there. I hovered my mouse pointer over one, took a deep, bracing breath, and then clicked.

Much to my surprise, the first link took me to Reddit. I guess I didn't think a man of Harry's age and persuasion would even know what Reddit was. I only knew of the site because I found it useful in my work when I had questions Manny couldn't answer.

I don't think I could ever bring myself to repeat what I found in that thread. Summarizing it would be bad enough that I'd feel sick to my stomach for days. He used his full name as his handle, so there was no question as to who made the posts. Their vileness made me want to throw my laptop across the room and take that shower Chester spoke of.

The thread started innocently enough. The poster asked about a deli downtown, if anyone had tried it. The first few answers were helpful, even thoughtful.

Then Harry chimed in.

Let's just say he wasn't too keen on someone not originally from this country touching his food.

I ground my teeth together and forced myself to keep reading. I don't know why I did. I mean, the guy was spewing uninformed hatred, using "facts" he obviously made up on the spot to support his argument. No one agreed with his assessment, but that didn't stop him. In fact, it only seemed to urge him on all the more.

And then I spotted something that made my skin try to crawl right from my bones.

> *If they don't pack it up soon, I'll make sure they get what they deserve.*

I read the line twice to make sure I'd read it right before moving on. The responses weren't kind, which was expected. A few posts down, he chimed in once again.

> *These people need to disappear. If they can't manage it on their own, then I'll assist them. I've done it before, and I'll do it again.*

"Assisted how?" I wondered aloud. I thought back to what Ida had told me about a man paying her a visit. Could it truly have been Harry? If so, what was he after? What was his connection to Christine?

And did it tie in to this post somehow?

There was nothing else in the thread of use, so I moved on to the next link Chester had sent me. It was more of the same, but this time he'd made a comment on an online newspaper article. He once again referenced having done something to someone, but didn't clarify what exactly he'd done.

Was he merely trolling everyone, making wild claims, just to get a rise out of people? Or was there something there that pointed to a man ready and willing to commit murder?

He didn't kill Christine, but he very well could be the reason she'd fled Grey Falls. Both links were quite a few years old, so they didn't reference Joe, but those comments about doing "it" before could most definitely be referencing Joe's wife.

I closed my laptop with a frown. Did the police know about Harry's posts? If they did, would it even matter? Posting about something was completely different than actually *doing* it. And unless he gave details, what was there for anyone to follow up on?

I wished I had a picture to show Ida Priestly so I knew for sure if Harry Davis was the man who'd come to see her. Unfortunately, I didn't, and wasn't interested in finding one. Besides, I had nothing to do with the murder, or the ongoing investigation. As much as I wanted to know what had happened, it wasn't up to me to find out. I had animals to take care of.

I picked up my phone and tried Courtney again. After looking into Harry, Courtney's little deception didn't seem so bad.

Like before, the phone rang without anyone picking up. Either she was monitoring her calls and was avoiding me, or she'd forgotten her phone at home. I'd put money on the former.

A new idea struck me then. If I couldn't get ahold of Courtney directly, I knew someone else who could.

I checked the number and then dialed. After two rings, it was picked up.

"Billings residence, Sasha speaking."

"Hi, Sasha, it's Liz Denton. Is Duke around?"

"Oh, Liz." Duke's wife sounded almost disappointed, as if she'd been expecting another, far more exciting call. "Yeah, he's home."

"May I speak to him? It'll only take a moment."

"One sec." There was a clunk that sounded like Sasha had dropped the phone rather than set it down. I waited patiently, wondering how I was going to ask about Chico without upsetting Duke. He worked with Courtney, but I knew for a fact he didn't always agree with her actions. I hoped this was one of those times.

There was a rustle, followed by, "Liz." He sounded unhappy.

"Hi, Duke. I was wondering if you've talked to Courtney lately."

There was a slight pause before, "I have."

"Do you know anything about a Chihuahua she had in her possession? She called him Piranha, but I have reason to believe his real name is Chico."

Another pause, this one longer, before he said, "I'm going to be here all day. We need to talk." His tone was ominous.

"Okay. When?"

"Anytime."

He hung up.

"That can't be good," I told Wheels, who was now hovering near the window where Sheamus was still lying down. At least he wasn't sneezing now, just snoozing.

I glanced toward the laundry room and wondered if I should take Chico with me, then decided against it. There was nothing Duke could do about it, even if he did know what Courtney was up to.

I moved to the bottom of the stairs and shouted up them. "Ben, I'm leaving. Keep an eye on Pir— Chico for me."

A faint, " 'Kay," was the only response I got.

That taken care of, I filled the kitties' dishes, grabbed my purse, and then headed for my van.

11

Duke's house was a ranch style home that sat on three acres, just outside Grey Falls. It was a quiet, serene location, where the only noises were nature sounds. Trees lined the property, giving it an isolated feel. Everything was done in earth tones.

I pulled into the gravel drive and shut off the engine. A trio of black cats swarmed from the front stoop, and zipped around to the back. The last time I'd seen his kitties, they were mere kittens peering at me from a window. It always surprised me how fast animals grew.

The front door opened as I got out of my van. Duke stood framed in the doorway. His arms were crossed, and he had a dour expression on his face. He was broad-shouldered, and I knew from experience, he was as strong as he looked.

"Hi, Duke," I said. "I'm sorry to bring this to your doorstep."

"It's not your fault," he said with a sigh. "Come on in."

I followed him into the house, all the way into the living room. His home was just as serene inside as it was outside. The furniture was done in soft, earthy tones, with a fireplace dominating one wall of the living room. It wasn't currently lit, but I could imagine spending hours sitting in front of it on cold winter evenings.

"Can I get you something?" Duke asked, motioning for me to take a seat on the couch. "Water? Tea? I could put on a pot of coffee if you'd prefer."

"Water's fine."

"I'll be just a minute." He turned and walked stiffly to the kitchen.

The last time I was inside Duke's house, I'd only stopped by for a brief visit. Now that I was staying for longer than a few minutes, it gave me time to really look around, take in the atmosphere.

While the room felt rustic, that didn't mean it was entirely without modernization. The television attached to the wall above the fireplace was large, and I had no doubts was at least 4K. A laptop sat on the coffee table in front of me, though its lid was closed. Speakers were placed around the room, and at first I thought they might be for the television, but then I noted the stereo panel built into the opposite wall.

That single room probably cost half as much as my entire house. It made me wonder what Sasha and Duke did for a living, because there was no way Courtney was paying him anything more than a pittance on every pet adoption where she earned a profit.

Duke returned and handed me a bottle of water. He sat down in a wooden rocking chair that looked antique, yet sturdy. He cracked the cap on a bottle of his own and took a long drink before setting it aside.

"So, Courtney," he said. I noted a heavy dose of frustration in his voice, and all he'd said was her name.

Admittedly, I probably sounded the same anytime she was mentioned.

"Yes, Courtney," I replied. "She's created quite the mess for me. Do you know anything about it?"

Duke ran his hands over his face before he answered. "I'd like to say up front, I had nothing to do with any of what she did."

"So, you know what happened?"

"To a point." Duke sighed heavily. "Last week, Courtney and I were picking up some kittens. She was doing her nonstop self-promotion bit, when the woman mentioned Furever Pets. She said that she's heard good things about you and wondered if Courtney knew anything about your rescue."

I couldn't help but grin. It seemed as if my reputation was spreading. "That was nice of her."

"It was," Duke said. "Courtney, however, didn't think so. Let's just say she made sure to mention Ben as an accused murderer and made outrageous claims that you stole pets from their owners and then turned around and adopted them out for profit."

"I *what?*" I very nearly came out of my seat. "I'd never do such a thing. And Ben . . ." I sat back and seethed. He might have been accused, but his name was cleared. The real killer was currently sitting in prison, where he belonged.

"I know," Duke said, holding out a placating hand. "I did my best to smooth things over, but you know how it is with Courtney. She talked right over me and tried to pretend she hadn't actually meant it literally, even though it was obvious she had."

"Did the woman believe her?"

"No, I don't think so. I did my best to make sure of it. You've been nothing but kind to me and my family. You've tried to play nice with Courtney. For whatever reason, she doesn't see it. She thinks you're trying to ruin her by running her rescue out of business."

"I've tried to be friends," I said.

"You have. And I've tried to make her see reason, but she insists the two of you can't work together. She'd rather see you fail than to admit it's possible for the two of you to coexist."

"So, she brings me someone else's Chihuahua? Why?"

Duke spread his hands. "To smear your name, I suppose. To add credence to her claims. I honestly hoped that when she picked up the dog, she had good intentions. She didn't take me with her, mind you. But I saw him when she brought him back to her place. When I asked about it, she was cagey. I knew something was up, but she wouldn't come right out and admit it. All I managed to get from her was that she planned on taking the dog to you."

"Where did she get Chico?" When Duke gave me a questioning look, I added, "The Chihuahua."

"I'm not sure," he said. "I'd like to say she obtained him in good faith, but honestly, at this point, I'm not so sure."

Which means, she very well might have stolen him right out of someone's yard. Despite what I knew of Courtney, I couldn't believe she'd stoop so low. I mean, to knowingly steal someone's pet, just to make me look bad? Who does something like that?

"I was suspicious of her motives from the start," Duke went on. "And then, after she got back from your place, I truly did begin to question her. When she refused to talk to me about it, I went home."

"This is . . ." I struggled to come up with a word. I finally settled on, "insane."

"That, it is."

"I take it the woman who showed up, claiming Chico was hers, wasn't just putting me on?" I'd looked her up, but a part of me hoped I was somehow wrong and the dog in the photos wasn't Piranha.

Duke shrugged. "As far as I know, it's possible. With Courtney, it's hard to say for sure."

"Great." I rubbed at my temples. I had no idea how I was going to make this right. I could give the dog back to his rightful owner, but that wouldn't clear my name. If I went around town calling Courtney a liar, only half the people would believe me. And even then, some would look down on me for trying to smear *her* name. Once a rumor got started, it was hard to stomp it out.

"I honestly don't believe I can do this anymore." Duke sounded distraught at the thought. "I like working with the animals, and I like making people happy, but this"—he shook his head—"this I can't abide."

"What else would you do?"

Duke picked up his water and took a long drink before answering. "Work, I suppose." He gestured toward the closed laptop. "I don't need to work with Courtney to get by. And when she's not causing trouble for you, she's not as bad as you think. Besides, I like my office here." This time, his gesture encompassed the room. "Sasha and I work together. If I stopped working with Courtney, I'd get to spend more time at home with my wife. Can't say the thought doesn't have its appeal."

"But?" I could feel the word hanging in the air.

"But I'd miss it," he said. "You know what it's like when you find the perfect pet for someone, or when the perfect pet parent shows up to adopt your latest rescue. That kind of happiness can't be replicated."

No, it couldn't. The way everyone's eyes lit up— including the pet's—was as close to magic as I was ever to come.

I heaved a sigh. "I'll figure it out," I said. "Somehow, I'll make things right."

"Good luck with that." He smiled.

"I've already had a crazy week, or else I might have already worked it out with Courtney. Did you hear about the murder?"

Duke nodded, his smile slipping. "I did."

"I was the one who discovered the body." I suppressed a shudder at the memory. "I was taking a Maine Coon to the victim, Joe, when I found him. It wasn't a pleasant experience."

"I imagine not. I suppose not every job can be special."

"Ain't that the truth."

We sat there in companionable silence for a long moment before I spoke up again.

"I honestly wish Courtney's little stunt was the worst thing to happen to me this week, but after finding the body, hearing that Ben might be moving out with a woman he's just met, and then to run into that jerk, Harry Davis, I'm not sure I can take much more."

"Harry Davis?"

Both Duke and I turned to find Sasha standing just inside the room, big, dark arms crossed over her chest.

"Do you know him?" Duke asked.

"I've had the displeasure," she said with a scowl that could peel paint. Sasha was built like a linebacker, and I had no doubts she could crush someone like Harry Davis with her bare hands if she wanted to.

"He showed up at Chester Chudzinski's office and started throwing insults around," I said. "He seemed . . ."

"Prejudiced?" Sasha asked. "Like he walked straight out of some backward country that thinks everyone should look and sound alike?"

"Yeah." That was putting it nicer than I would have.

"What happened?" Duke asked, rising to his feet. While he tended to be gentle, he wasn't a small man. He might not be Sasha Billings big, but he was stronger than most people I knew. If Harry wasn't such an unredeemable jerk, I might have pitied him.

"Do you remember that run-in I had at Sophie's Coffeehouse a few months ago?" Sasha asked.

Duke nodded. "I do."

"That was him."

I could practically see the steam coming out of Duke's ears.

"What happened?" I asked.

"He raised a ruckus because I was there," Sasha said. "He tried to get me thrown out by claiming I was bringing down the quality of the place by my mere presence. He dumped his coffee out onto the floor, screamed that it was tainted, and that my very breath infected everything in the place."

"Wow," was all I could think of to say.

"That's not the half of it," Sasha said. "When he realized that someone in the kitchen was of Asian descent, he threatened a lawsuit, of all things."

"If I'd been there . . ." Duke's fingers flexed.

"You'd have sat right beside me and continued eating," Sasha said. "I ignored him, figuring a man like that wasn't worth the breath it would take to tell him off. He didn't like that much, either."

No, I didn't imagine he would. A man like Harry Davis needed to be heard. Ignore him, and you would wound his self-worth, which was something he obviously couldn't deal with in a decent, constructive manner.

"He demanded that both me and the cook be thrown out of the place. Instead, he found himself being dragged to the door by the guys I was eating with." She grinned. "We'd stopped by after lifting, so you can imagine how that went."

"I hope they left him in a dumpster," Duke said.

"They just tossed him out the door." Sasha crossed the room and put an arm around Duke's waist. He squeezed her close. "Of course, despite getting thrown out on his ass, he had to get in the last word."

"Oh?" I asked, curious. The more I learned about Harry Davis, the more I disliked him.

"He threatened to come after us and make us regret insulting him or some such." She frowned. "If I recall, he was eating with someone who'd watched the whole thing without stepping in. Guy was well-dressed, and got up and walked out without a word. When Harry saw him coming, he shut up real quick, like he was afraid of the guy."

"Do you know who it was?"

"No idea. I've seen him around now and again, but I've never met him."

There was a long moment of silence before Duke asked, "Why didn't you tell me it was Harry Davis back when it happened?"

"Because you would have insisted on defending my honor or something silly." She grinned at him. "I can take care of myself, Peaches."

I tried not to giggle at the pet name. The look Duke shot me was both embarrassed, and a warning.

"Do you think Harry could have killed Joe Danvers?" I asked, hoping, like Duke, Sasha knew about the murder.

"He might have," she said. "But I got the impression he was all talk. He backed down quick enough when someone stood up to him."

"That doesn't mean he didn't kill someone," Duke said.

"Joseph's wife ran away from Grey Falls thirty years ago," I said. "If Harry came after her, perhaps she got scared."

"Perhaps," Sasha said. "The man is a virus. I only met him that one time, and I already know I could live the rest of my life without ever seeing him again."

I left a short time later, mind whirling. Harry was old enough to have been around when Christine fled town. He could very well have been the same man who'd approached Ida, both back then and recently. It wasn't much of a stretch to think he killed Joe as well.

But how to prove it?

Vague Reddit posts and online newspaper comments proved nothing. Even if he *was* the man who'd showed up at Ida's house, it didn't mean he'd killed anyone. Not even his threats made against Sasha amounted to much more than proof that the guy was a jerk.

I did wonder who the well-dressed man Harry was eating with might be. Could it be someone who knows more about what Harry has done? Or was it just a friend who happened to be there at the wrong time?

I had no way of knowing, but it might be something the police would be interested in hearing.

I climbed into my van, waved to the trio of cats watching me from the side of the house, and then headed to the station to tell Detective Cavanaugh everything I'd learned.

12

The Grey Falls police department lot was packed as I pulled in. People were standing outside their cars, many red in the face as they shouted. Nearly all of them were middle-aged women wearing jeans and T-shirts. I found a parking spot in the far back corner, though I had to honk my horn twice to get a pair of angry women to move.

I got out of my van and tried to make sense of what was happening. A pair of young police officers were barring the doors to the station, where a little under a dozen women were trying to force their way inside. It didn't look like anyone was about to riot, but there was a lot of anger going around.

"What's happening?" I asked the nearest woman. She was wearing a light summery dress and flip-flops—a change from the rest of the throng. It was hardly the attire I'd expect out of someone on the wrong side of the law.

"They arrested him," she said. "Right in front of everyone!"

A zing of excitement shot through me. Had they already caught Joseph's killer? "Who did they arrest?"

She turned wide eyes to me. "You don't know?"

"Sorry," I said. "I just got here."

She blinked at me like she couldn't quite believe her ears before she answered. "Travis McCoy. They arrested Travis McCoy!"

The name didn't ring a bell. "Does he live around here?" I asked.

The woman's mouth fell open. "You don't know who Travis McCoy is?"

"Nope. Should I?"

Her hand fluttered to her chest. "Everyone should know about Travis McCoy. He's one of the best country singers out there today. His song, 'Love Nest, Baby,' hit number one just last week. I'm sure you've heard it?"

"Can't say that I have." The woman opened her mouth as if she might start singing, so I hurriedly added, "What did they arrest him for?"

"Drunk and disorderly or some other trumped-up charge," she said. "It was a concert, so what did they expect? I mean, I suppose it was *before* the show was to start, and he *did* punch that other guy, but I'm sure that man deserved it. Travis wouldn't hurt anyone who didn't ask for it."

So, not Joe Danvers's murderer. Disappointment warred with mild amusement. All of this for a country singer? "I see. Thanks for letting me know. And good luck with this." I waved a hand vaguely toward the rest of the crowd. "I'm heading inside to talk to a detective about something else, but I'll let him know about your displeasure."

"You can try," the woman said. "They aren't letting anyone in."

I was hoping that since I wasn't there about Travis McCoy, they'd let me in to see Cavanaugh. I mean, I was there about a murder, which had to take precedence, right?

I worked my way through the crowd, avoiding flying arms and purses, as the women continued to shout. Now that I knew what I was listening for, I noted many of them were screaming, "Free McCoy!" over and over again. Unfortunately, they weren't yelling in any sort of synchronized way, so it ended up sounding like a muddled mess. I had a feeling that a lot of them had imbibed their favorite beverages well before the show had started.

Since ninety percent of the people here were women, it did make me wonder what kind of songs Travis sang. Based on the song title the woman had given me, I was guessing he specialized in love songs. But even then, I'd have thought more men would be present.

Nearby, a woman hoisted a poster in the air that told me all I needed to know about the country singer.

Travis McCoy couldn't be much older than twenty, twenty-two at the most. His jeans were two sizes too small, and he stood gazing adoringly over his shoulder, so you could get a good look at his backside. His shirt . . . well, let's just say it wasn't so much a shirt than it was netting. If it wasn't for the cowboy hat and boots, and the acoustic guitar in his hands, I might have mistaken him for a stripper.

It took some doing, but I finally made it to the doors. The women who'd been trying to force their way inside had backed off and were shouting from a nearby van decorated with more Travis McCoy images. A quick look at his bare torso plastered on the side of the vehicle told me it was unlikely the guy even knew what a shirt was, let alone ever wore one.

"Hi," I said, approaching the two cops. I didn't know either man. "I'm here to see Detective Cavanaugh." I had to raise my voice to be heard over the shouting behind me.

"Get back with the others," the first cop said. His nametag read GRACE.

"I'm not with them," I said, jerking a thumb toward the other women. "I'm here about a murder."

"Was someone killed?" the other officer—Officer Kang, according to his nametag—asked. His gaze moved to the crowd, like he thought there might be a body amongst them.

"Not at the concert, but earlier. I'm here about Joseph Danvers's murder. He was killed just the other day. Detective Cavanaugh has the case. I have some information to deliver to him."

The two officers shared a look. Officer Grace was the one who spoke. "Is it an emergency?" he asked. "As you can see, it's pretty crazy here at the moment."

"Kinda." I cringed as I said it.

"It's as bad inside as it is out here," Kang said, glancing over his shoulder. "It might take a bit to find him."

I heaved a sigh. Leave it to a celebrity to shut down an entire police station. *And of all the times.* I wasn't sure how Detective Cavanaugh was going to be able to focus on his investigation with this circus happening just outside his door.

"That's all right," I said. "I can wait."

"All right," Officer Kang said. "Stay here. I'll check

to see if the detective is available, but I can't promise anything. We are a little swamped, as you can see."

"Thank you." If there hadn't been an army behind me, I might have hugged him.

Grace muttered something under his breath that was lost to the cacophony as Kang hurried inside. There was a surge as some of the women started forward, but it subsided as the doors closed and Officer Grace put a hand on the butt of his gun.

"Guess that singer's a pretty big deal, huh?" I asked, hoping to break the ice a little.

Grace glanced at me and scowled. "Wife loves him. She's going to kill me when she finds out I had a hand in this."

"Sorry to hear that," I said. "Did he really punch someone?"

A smile tried to form at the corners of Grace's mouth, but he managed to keep it at bay. "It was that woman's husband." He nodded his head toward one of the irate women standing by the van. "McCoy got a little too cozy with her before his show and Mr. Mock didn't approve. Mock got aggressive and McCoy popped him one square on the nose. If we hadn't been there working security, McCoy would have been in a world of trouble."

"Other guy bigger?" I asked.

This time, Officer Grace did allow himself a smile. "About twice his size and three times as mean."

The door opened, but it wasn't Officer Kang or Detective Cavanaugh who emerged.

"Oh! Mrs. Denton." Officer Reg Perry looked surprised to see me. "I wasn't expecting you here." He had to shout over the increased volume as the women started chanting in earnest.

"I'm waiting for Detective Cavanaugh. I need to talk to him about his case."

Officer Perry's expression turned sympathetic. "You won't be able to talk to him right now," he said. "But I can try to pass word on to him, if you want."

I frowned. "Is it about the country singer?"

Officer Perry shook his head. "No, he's not in. Is it something I can help you with?"

"I'm not sure," I said. I was glad to see Officer Perry, but I wasn't sure how he could help me. From what little I knew about him, I took him for a kind, gentle man. His gray hair stood out in stark contrast to his dark skin. He looked stressed, but his demeanor was still friendly.

Something shattered in the parking lot—it sounded like a glass bottle—and the noise died down as everyone turned to look. A single voice rose in the silence.

"Sorry."

The shouting picked right back up.

"Let's take this to the side," Perry said, guiding me away from the front doors and around the corner of the building where it was quieter. "I can't wait until this gets sorted out and we can get back to normal."

"You and me both," I said. I knew he was referring to Travis McCoy's arrest, but I was thinking of something else entirely.

"So, is there anything I can do for you, Mrs. Denton?"

"Please, call me Liz."

"Then I'm Reg." He smiled. "I'll be retired soon enough anyway."

It felt strange calling a cop by his first name, but I obliged. "Okay, Reg. It's about Joe Danvers," I said.

"I've heard a few things I thought Detective Cavanaugh would want to know."

Reg's expression turned sad. "It's a real shame about Joe. He wasn't a bad man; never thought he was. And come to hear that his wife was alive all this time." He tsked and shook his head.

"Did you meet his son, Erik?" I asked. "He was here earlier."

"I did. He reminded me a lot of his father, to be honest. Well-spoken, kind, even. He left about an hour ago, which is a good thing considering . . ." He motioned toward where the shouting was still going on.

"You knew Joe?" I asked, surprised. It hadn't occurred to me until then that Reg Perry might have been involved in the case back then. He was old enough for it.

"Not too terribly well," he said. "But I took an interest in the investigation when it happened. Never believed Joe responsible, but wasn't much I could do about it since I wasn't officially on the case."

"You didn't believe the witness?" I asked.

Reg's face clouded over. "Harry Davis."

"That's him."

"By your tone, I can tell you've met him. I never liked that man." The way he said it made it sound like that was a rarity for him. "Didn't trust him the moment he showed up out of the blue, claiming to be a witness. He wouldn't talk to me. He dealt solely with the detective in charge."

"And that would be?" I asked, hoping it was someone I knew, though my knowledge of the Grey Falls police department staff was limited to just a couple of men.

"Detective Wayne Hastings. He was fair, don't get me wrong, but he didn't listen to my concerns about Harry and those he ran around with. I even pointed out other incidents involving Harry, but at the time, Joe was the best suspect—the *only* suspect, really. Taking Harry at his word was far easier than trying to dig through what little we had." Reg lowered his head. "I wish I would have tried harder to get him to see what was right in front of all our faces."

"I'm sure you did the best you could."

"I tried." Reg shot me a smile that was a little sad. "If you see the old detective around, tell him hello for me. He retired years ago, and I haven't seen him since. I'm not even sure he'll remember an old codger like me, but I do remember him fondly, despite our differences."

"I'll do that," I said. "And if you see Detective Cavanaugh, would you tell him I stopped by?"

"I will, but I wouldn't count on hearing from him today."

I wondered what meetings Detective Cavanaugh could be in that were important enough to drag him away from a murder investigation, but didn't ask. For one, it was none of my business. And secondly, I wasn't entirely naïve. Cops often dealt with more than one case at a time. Cavanaugh would be no different.

"Thanks, Reg. I really am happy we got to talk."

"Maybe next time it'll be under better circumstances."

"I hope so." I made as if to leave, but Reg laid a calloused hand on my wrist to stop me.

"Now, Liz, I don't know how deep you're going to get into this thing, but I'd be remiss if I didn't warn you to watch yourself. These things have a tendency to get out of hand."

"I'll be careful," I said.

"You do that. Harry Davis isn't a man to be trifled with. I don't know if he had anything to do with Joe Danvers's death, but I wouldn't put it past him to be a part of it. Despite his unappealing nature, he does have friends in this town. If they think you're going to make a nuisance of yourself, they won't hesitate to put a stop to it."

"Do you think he'd hurt me?" I asked.

"If not you, perhaps your family. He tends to be more aggressive to people who aren't just like him. And since your husband and your children . . ." He trailed off with a frown.

I knew exactly what he meant. Manny's mom was born in Mexico before she'd moved to America, where she met her husband, the man who'd eventually become Manny's father. Manny had taken after his mother far more than his father in appearance, and his heritage could still be seen in my children's faces. It had never been an issue before, but now, it made me worried.

"I'll be careful. I'm not planning on poking my nose where it doesn't belong. My daughter, Amelia, *is* working on the case, however. She's working with Chester Chudzinski, the PI."

"I know him. He's good at what he does." Reg's hand moved from my wrist to squeeze my shoulder. "Your daughter is in good hands, but please, make sure to pass my warning along to her anyway. I don't want to see anyone else get hurt."

"I will."

I left Reg to deal with the crowd, which was just as raucous as it was a few minutes ago. I felt better having talked to him, and despite his warning, I felt a near overwhelming urge to talk to some people, just to gain more clarity into what happened all those years ago. Maybe I'd learn something that could help Amelia.

If nothing else, I had another name. If Detective Hastings could tell me something more about Harry Davis and his connection to Christine and her family, then perhaps I'd come up with a motive for not just Christine's disappearance, but Joe's murder as well.

13

I was met by a pair of cats when I walked through the front door of my house.

"Hey, guys," I said, dropping my purse onto the table. "Hungry?"

Wheels meowed and rolled into the kitchen, where her food dish was kept. Sheamus took a moment to put his front feet on my leg to headbutt my hand in welcome before he joined her.

"You need a brushing," I told the big cat, following after them. "But first . . ."

The bowls were empty but for a few stray pieces. I filled each with dry, and then got them fresh water, before I headed for the laundry room. The door was closed, and it was quiet inside. Unless Ben or Manny had taken him out, Chico would be in there.

As soon as my hand touched the knob, the barking started. I cringed, knowing that Joanne was likely sitting by her window, just waiting for the noise to start so she could come over to complain. After the day I'd had, I definitely wasn't in the mood to deal with her.

I slid into the room quickly and shut the door behind me. "Let me get you something to eat, then I'll call your mommy," I told the irritated Chihuahua.

Chico was practically hopping up and down with every bark. He wasn't being aggressive, outside the bark, of course, but I was leery nonetheless. All it would take is one sudden move the wrong way and the little dog might snap at me.

I filled Chico's food dish, and then grabbed his water bowl to refill it. Once that was done, I went ahead and took him out back, just in case no one else had done so while I was out. I'd asked Ben to keep an eye on him, but when I'd pulled up to the house, his car was gone. Amelia's own car was parked in its place, but I didn't know if he'd told her to watch the dog, or if he'd skipped out the moment I was out the door.

"Good boy," I said, returning the dog to the laundry room. At least he'd gone quickly and quietly. Maybe I'd avoid Joanne's wrath after all.

Once the animals were all fed and comfortable, I checked the notepad by the phone, just in case someone had called. Nothing was scribbled on the pad, and I wasn't sure if I should be relieved or worried. I wanted to get Chico back home where he belonged, but I didn't want to be berated by his owner again.

Knowing Amelia often didn't write down my messages, I headed upstairs to check with her. If she had her earbuds in, it was unlikely she'd have heard the phone if it had rung, but miracles sometimes did happen.

"Amelia?" I knocked on the door as I spoke. I gave

it a heartbeat before I pushed the door open. "Amelia are you—oh!"

Maya was standing on one side of the room, one of Amelia's books in her hands. Amelia was sitting cross-legged on her bed, staring hard at the screen of her laptop, which was open in front of her.

"Hi, Mrs. Denton, er, Liz." Maya cleared her throat and set the book aside.

Amelia shot Maya a look I couldn't interpret before she lowered her laptop lid, though she didn't close it completely. "Mom? What are you doing here?"

A snarky *I live here* was on the tip of my tongue, but I decided not to embarrass her in front of her friend. "I came home to check on the animals. Ben was supposed to be watching Chico."

"The Chihuahua?" Amelia asked. "He told me his name was Piranha."

"That's him. It's a long story." One I didn't want to get into right then. "I take it he left the job to you?"

"He called me a while ago, asking when I might be home. He said he had something super important to take care of, but wouldn't tell me what it was." She glanced at Maya. "He's probably snogging his new girlfriend."

Maya snickered, but didn't otherwise comment.

"Snogging?" I wasn't sure I'd ever heard Amelia use the term before. "Did he say when he'll be home?"

"No, sorry. He wasn't here when we got here."

My gaze traveled around the room. It was messy, as always, but the bed was a disaster. The comforter was on the floor, as was one of the pillows. You'd think that if she had company, Amelia would at least have picked up a little.

Then again, old habits did die hard. She'd never been a tidy person, and I imagined that when she finally did get a place of her own, she'd either have to hire a cleaner, or marry someone who didn't mind a little mess.

"Still working?" I asked, nodding to the laptop.

Amelia nodded. "Yeah. We figured it would do us good to get out of the office for a little while, get a new perspective on things, you know? Ben's call made the decision easier."

"Chester was really stressed," Maya said. "I've never seen him so rattled. That Harry guy really got to him."

"I think that goes for all of us," I said.

Maya nodded. "He's a total creep. I kept thinking about what he said, the threats and whatnot." She clenched her fists as if she might punch something. "Every time I looked up from my desk, I swore I could see him standing there. I needed to get out of the office so I could focus."

"I take it you haven't found anything on Christine's birth parents?"

"Not yet," Amelia said. "But we're working on it."

"I have a few leads that are being followed up on as we speak," Maya added, tapping her phone, which was stuffed into her back pocket. "I'm hoping I'll hear back from someone soon."

"It would be nice to figure this out before someone else gets hurt," Amelia said.

That, I could most definitely agree with. "Do either of you know anything about a Detective Wayne Hastings? His name came up in conversation today."

Amelia shook her head. Maya was the one who answered. "I've seen his name in some of Chester's files. He's the detective who worked Christine's disappearance, right?"

"He was," I said. "I was hoping you could tell me

whether or not he was trustworthy." While Reg had seemed fond of the retired detective, I wasn't so sure I could trust his assessment of his former colleague. The two of them had worked together, probably for years. Just because Hastings might have been good to Reg didn't mean he was that way with everyone.

Or that he wasn't dirty.

"As far as I could tell, he was," Maya said. "I honestly don't know that much about him. It was before my time. Chester would know more since he talked to nearly everyone involved in the case back when he was first working it."

I figured as much. "What about Travis McCoy?"

"What? The singer?" Amelia asked, nose scrunched up as if she smelled something bad.

"Yeah, him. Do either of you listen to him?"

"Ew, no." Amelia glanced at Maya, who shook her head.

"Not my type of music."

It wasn't mine either. Honestly, I wasn't sure why I'd asked. It wasn't like it had anything to do with the investigation.

"I didn't think so, but thought I'd double-check to be sure."

"Did he do something?" Amelia asked. "Like, is he a suspect or something?"

"No. He was arrested earlier today for punching someone. It turned the police station into a madhouse."

"I'm not surprised," Amelia said. "He's always trending on Twitter for doing something he shouldn't."

"It's often someone's wife," Maya added.

That definitely sounded like the man Officer Grace described. "All right," I said. "I'll leave you two alone." I started to close the door, but then remembered my original reason for coming upstairs. "Has anyone called for me while I was out?"

Amelia glanced at Maya before she gave an apologetic shrug. "I wasn't paying attention to the phone. Sorry."

"I didn't hear anything," Maya said.

"All right. I'll be downstairs in case you hear something back." I aimed the last at Maya, who gave me a thumbs-up.

I hesitated at the door a moment. Amelia had opened her laptop again and was focused on whatever was on the screen, and Maya was checking her phone. With a sigh, I closed the door and headed back downstairs.

The cats were already done eating and were snoozing in the living room by the time I returned. I found a cat brush in the dining room hutch, and carried it with me as I headed for the phone. Sheamus needed a brushing, but something else needed to be done first.

I hated having to do it, but I picked up the phone and called Stacy Hildebrand.

"Hi, Stacy," I said when she answered. "It's Liz Denton with Furever Pets. I—"

"Do you have my dog? Where is he?"

Even though she couldn't see me, I plastered a smile onto my face in the hopes that it would come through when I spoke. "He's here. While I have yet to receive documentation from you, I've come to the conclusion that the Chihuahua in my possession is indeed your Chico. I was wond—"

"I told you as much!" she shouted, cutting me off. "I was right there in your driveway, and *told* you that you had my dog. Thief. I've already reported you to everyone I could think of. I hope your business collapses."

The smile was becoming harder and harder to hold in place. "I had nothing to do with your dog ending up here," I said. "He was delivered to my house by someone else." I desperately wanted to point the finger at Courtney, but I refused to stoop to her level. "I took him in on good faith. I promise you, I didn't take your dog from you."

There was a long stretch of silence where I hoped Stacy was actually thinking about what I'd said, but when she spoke, I realized she'd merely been seething.

"You have a lot of nerve trying to blame someone else for your transgressions," she said. "I can't believe you'd stand there and lie to me. You were caught red-handed. You are going to have to deal with the consequences of your actions."

It was my turn to remain silent while I composed myself. I couldn't believe this woman. Sure, I'd be angry if someone had taken my beloved Wheels from me, but to outright refuse to listen to what they had to say?

"I'm sorry you feel that way, Ms. Hildebrand." Somehow, I kept my cool. "I only want what's best for Chico. He's back from the vet with a clean bill of health, and you, of course, won't be charged for his checkup. If you would like to pick him up, or if you'd prefer to have me deliver him to you, we can set something up for today."

"That doesn't work for me."

I blinked. "What doesn't?"

"I can't get him today. You're just going to have to take care of him for another day or so."

After the fit she'd thrown in my driveway, and now

on the phone, she was going to pull *this*? "I'm sorry, I don't understand."

"I can't drop everything to help you fix your mistakes." I could *feel* the venom dripping off her words. "I have a life, and I refuse to bow to your whims just because it would be convenient for you."

"I see." I didn't know what else to say.

"Bring him to me tomorrow morning. I expect him to be in perfect health. If so much as one hair is displaced on his head, I'm going to sue you for all you're worth."

I was stunned into silence. This woman had thrown a huge hissy fit about getting her dog back and now she was going to make me wait until tomorrow to return him? What was wrong with her?

A thought trickled into my head. What if Courtney had set this whole thing up? Could Stacy and Courtney have worked together, all in an effort to smear my name?

Don't be paranoid, Liz. Not even Courtney would stoop *that* low.

Would she?

"Nine sharp," Stacy snapped. "Any later and I'll call the cops."

I had to shake my head to clear it. This wasn't how I'd expected the conversation to go. "I'll need your address."

Stacy rattled off an address so quickly, I knew she was trying to trip me up on purpose. I made her repeat it twice, then recited it right back to her before I was satisfied.

"I'll see you tomorr—" This time, I was cut off by the sound of the phone clicking off.

My mouth worked, forming words best not said aloud. I managed not to utter them, but it was a near thing. I didn't know if this was a setup or not, but I did know I was going to have serious words with Courtney when I saw her next.

I was clutching the brush so hard, my fingers ached. I forced myself to loosen my grip before I headed into the living room where Sheamus was napping on the couch. I sat down next to him and ran the brush down his back once.

He was on his feet immediately, purring so loud, I swear Amelia had to hear it all the way upstairs.

"You like that?" I asked him, some of the tension bleeding away as I brushed him. "I bet you do, don't you?"

Sheamus leapt off the couch so he could rub against my legs as I continued to brush the tangles out of his fur. He didn't mind me working at them, even when I got to his underside. The cat truly did love his brushing, and I couldn't say that I minded it either. It was almost as relaxing for me as it was for him.

It took ten minutes to work all the tangles free. By the time I was done, Sheamus's coat was sleek and shiny. He rubbed up against my leg once more, wrapped his long tail around me, and then walked over to Wheels to wash her.

Apparently, he liked giving as much as he did receiving.

That done, I brought out my phone—which I'd remembered to take out of the van's cupholder for once in my life—and added a reminder to deliver Chico tomorrow.

I was about to tuck the phone away when I changed my mind and did a quick search. I found Wayne Hastings's number, and added it to the note. Once I was done dealing with Stacy—and very likely Courtney—I thought I might just go ahead and give him a call. I wasn't officially working on the investigation, but if I could help Amelia get in good with her boss, why not?

A door slammed open upstairs, causing me to startle to my feet. Footsteps pounded down the stairs, and both Amelia and Maya burst into the room, eyes wide and excited.

"Mom!" Amelia said, spotting me immediately. "You're not going to believe this."

"What's happened?" I asked, not sure if I should be excited or scared. After a quick look at the two of them, I settled on worriedly excited.

"Someone got back to me," Maya said, holding up her phone as if in proof. "I know who Christine's birth parents were." Her grin was triumphant. "And I think it might be the reason Joe Danvers was killed."

14

"Christine Danvers was originally Christine Hemingway," Maya said. "Her parents, Joan and Hue Hemingway, were killed just after her eighth birthday."

"Geez," Amelia said with a sad shake of her head. "That's awful."

Maya checked her phone before going on. "I don't have a ton of information on what happened as of yet, but it does say that her parents were murdered, so it wasn't an accident." She met my eye. "Christine was there when it happened."

"She saw the killer?" I asked.

"That's what it says, but she couldn't ID the guy. I guess when you're eight, you don't notice stuff like that."

"It wouldn't surprise me if she blocked it out," Amelia said. "Trauma can do that."

"It says here that the Hemingways were upstanding people. No arrest records, nothing. A motive was never discovered for their murder. No suspects, either. The cops in charge at the time determined it a random killing and, apparently, moved on."

We all fell silent as we thought about it. It appeared as if Christine's life was rife with misery. Her parents were murdered, and then she was forced to flee her husband and home, all while pregnant with his child.

And then, just after she died, her husband was murdered.

"Do you think she ran into her parents' killer fifteen years later?" Amelia asked.

"I was thinking the same thing," Maya said, tucking her phone away. "If she saw the murder happen as a kid, and then came across the killer later, it wouldn't surprise me if she recognized him, even if she'd blocked him, and the memory, out."

"Which, in turn, caused her to run," I said, thinking it through.

"Yeah, she sees him, and maybe he recognizes her too. Threats are made, and she decides that to protect her husband and unborn son, she needs to escape Grey Falls before something can happen to them too." Amelia tapped her chin. "Or she's told to go, or else they *would* be next."

"But why not call the police?" Maya asked. "I know if I saw a murder and I found the killer years later, I wouldn't hesitate."

"Maybe he's a cop," Amelia said. "It could explain why she couldn't ID the killer the first time. She was only eight back then. If the cop was there, asking the questions, he could have messed with her head somehow, made her doubt what she remembered."

"Or intimidated her," I added.

"Do you think the same person killed Joe, then?" Maya asked.

I did some mental math. "That would put the killer at what? At least fifty? Sixty?" I couldn't see a teenager as a murderer, though I supposed it was possible.

"There's not many cops left on the force at that age," Maya said.

"No, but that doesn't mean they don't still live in Grey Falls." My mind went instantly to the detective who'd worked Christine's disappearance, Wayne Hastings. Could he have killed her parents and then chased her out of town later?

Quite suddenly, I wasn't so keen on paying Detective Hastings a visit by myself.

"All of this assumes the killer is the same man," Amelia said. "Or even if it is a man. We can't be sure the two crimes are connected without some sort of unifying proof."

"But it's awfully convenient if it's not," Maya said. "I mean, who has that bad of luck?"

"We should call Chester," Amelia said. "Let him know what we found. Maybe he'll know something we don't."

"That's a good idea," Maya said. "This could be big."

"If he does, let me know, all right?" I said as they started for the stairs.

"Will do, Mom."

And then the both of them were gone, leaving me to digest what they'd discovered on my own. Could Joe's death have been almost fifty years in the making? That's a long time to hold a grudge.

But if Amelia was right and a cop was involved in the Hemingway murders, then it stood to reason the man had a lot to lose if Joe started poking around in his wife's disappearance again.

But if that was the case, why was Harry Davis so interested in the case? He didn't strike me as a man who'd have friends on the police force, but what did I know? I didn't know *that* many cops.

A part of me wanted to call Detective Hastings and try to weasel some information out of him, but I was mentally and physically exhausted. I'd been going pretty hard the last couple of days, and thanks to Courtney, I had more than just a cat and a murder to deal with.

I spent the next hour doing what I could for Sheamus and Chico. I still had to find a new home for Sheamus, and while I liked the cat, I couldn't keep him. Wheels was all the cat I needed, especially since I always had animals in and out of the house. I didn't know how Sheamus would react if I ever had an influx of hyperactive puppies.

Manny came home not long after, looking as if he'd had a rough day. He kissed me on the cheek before he collapsed onto the couch.

"Want to talk about it?" I asked him.

"Not yet." His chest heaved and I realized it must have been one of *those* days. He tried not to let it show how much it bothered him when he couldn't help someone's pet, but I saw it in his posture, and in his eyes. He was torn up inside and wouldn't want to drag me down with him.

"All right." I squeezed his shoulder and let him work through it on his own. He'd let me know what happened in his own time.

I threw on a quick dinner of spaghetti since it was easy and I had no idea what Maya might like. Neither she nor Amelia had left Amelia's room since they'd vanished upstairs to call Chester, and I wondered if they were making progress on Joe's murder. It would be nice if it all came together nice and tidy, and we could put it all behind us.

Just as I finished dumping the spaghetti into the pan, Ben waltzed through the door, grinning ear to ear.

"Hey, Mom, what's cooking?"

"Your favorite." I held up a bottle of spaghetti sauce.

"Blech." He stuck out his tongue. "Are you sure we can't just dump some tomato sauce on strips of cardboard? It'd amount to the same thing."

"Feel free," I said. "But the rest of us will stick with pasta."

Ben got out the saucepan for me and set it on the stove. "Just think, if I finally move out of here, you won't have to cook for me anymore."

"You mean, you won't have to suffer my cooking anymore."

He laughed. "That too."

While I poured the sauce into the pan, Ben retrieved the parmesan from the fridge. He took it, along with a stack of plates, to the table.

I watched him work without making it obvious as to what I was doing. My heart ached thinking about him moving out, but I'd come to terms with it. There's a point where a grown man living with his parents to help out with a business goes from sweet to pathetic.

As much as I hated to admit it, we were definitely nearing the pathetic end of the spectrum.

"You'll need to grab one more plate," I said as he returned to the kitchen. "Amelia has a friend over."

"A boyfriend?" he asked.

"More like a work friend."

"Uh-huh." But he grabbed the plate anyway.

Dinner was a surprisingly calm affair. I fully expected Ben to hit on Maya, which would, in turn, cause Amelia to get on him for being such a playboy. He must truly be in love with his latest girlfriend, because he was nothing but respectful to Maya. Even Manny seemed surprised.

Somehow, we made it through dinner without talking about Joe's murder. I could tell it was on both Maya's and Amelia's minds. Every so often they'd glance at one another, and I could almost read the questions behind those gazes. It was torture for me to sit there and not ask them if Chester had anything to add to what they'd learned, but I managed.

Manny helped me clean up the table once we were done eating.

"You doing okay?" I asked him as I scrubbed at a dish. He was quieter at dinner than usual, telling me that this was a bad one.

"I'll be fine." He flashed me a smile that didn't reach his eyes. He left it at that.

I wanted to press since I knew keeping it in wasn't going to do him any favors, but everyone processed grief in their own way. Manny always kept everything inside and tried to go on with life as if nothing had changed. When I last asked him why, he'd simply told me that there was no point in upsetting everyone when it was his pain to bear.

I didn't always agree with his assessment, but I wouldn't push him. Sometimes, sharing pain was the only way to get through a tough time. It was what I was there for.

As I handed Manny the last dish to dry, Amelia and Maya entered the kitchen. They were each carrying a laptop bag, and Amelia had her backpack tossed over one shoulder.

"Going somewhere?" I asked.

"I'm going to stay with Maya tonight," Amelia said. "It's kind of crowded in here and it will be easier to work without all the distractions."

"We plan to pull an all-nighter on this," Maya said.

Once again, I wondered what Chester might have told them, but since neither was offering up the information, I let it slide. For now.

"Will you be home for breakfast tomorrow?" Manny asked.

"Doubt it." Amelia elbowed Maya. "I'm going to make her cook me breakfast."

"You might not survive it," Maya said.

"Well, let me know if you learn anything. I might be talking to Detective Cavanaugh soon, so if there's anything he should know . . ."

Amelia rolled her eyes. "Don't worry, Mom, I'll let you know if anything pops."

"Don't work too hard," Manny said.

Amelia and Maya turned and headed for the door. Just as they stepped outside, I heard Maya say, "I like your parents," and then they were gone.

"They didn't invite me," Ben said, coming into the room.

"Looking for another girlfriend already?" It was meant as a joke, but he ignored it.

"Nah, I'm good." He spun on his tiptoes, before he vanished back up the stairs.

"It appears our children are doing well," Manny said, watching him go.

"We've done good."

He put an arm around me. "That, we have."

The rest of the evening was spent cleaning up and working with the animals. Chico was having one of his barking fits and nothing I did made him stop. I wondered if there was something wrong with the dog that caused it. If so, it wasn't something that showed up on Manny's tests, so I chalked it up to a personality quirk, and dealt with it the best I could.

Manny crashed early, and I was soon to follow. I had a to-do list a mile long, and as much as I wanted to get everything done now, it was best left until tomorrow.

Sheamus came upstairs and jumped up onto the bed with me as I slid my legs beneath the covers. He curled up between Manny and me and started purring as he drifted off, which only served to lull me to sleep that much faster.

I dreamt I was sitting in my van. A dog—sometimes Chico, sometimes not—was sitting in the back, barking. And barking. And barking.

My eyes snapped open as I realized the barking wasn't coming from my dream.

Sheamus was gone, and Manny was snoring next to me. I sat up in bed and listened. There was a thump from downstairs, which caused the barking to cease for a heartbeat, before it resumed. Glancing out into the hall, I noted the downstairs light was on.

"Manny." I shook his shoulder, but he only groaned. A quick glance at his nightstand told me he'd taken something to help him sleep.

Another thump came from downstairs. It sounded like the hutch drawer closing.

Amelia? I wondered. She could have forgotten something and had come home to retrieve it. But at this hour?

I decided to let Manny sleep and slid out of bed. I padded barefoot to the door and peeked out into the hall, just as Ben's door opened.

"What was that?" he asked, voice low.

Amelia's door was closed. I moved quickly across the hall and cracked it open. The bed was empty.

"She's not here," I said.

"She's with her friend," Ben said. He started down the hall.

"Ben!" It came out as a harsh whisper. "Wait. Shouldn't we call the cops?"

"What if it *is* Amelia?" he asked, and then started slowly toward the stairs. This time, when I whispered his name, he didn't stop.

The sounds moved from the dining room to the kitchen. The silverware drawer rattled as it was jerked open.

Refusing to let Ben check on his own, I slipped into the hallway bathroom and quietly opened the nearest drawer. Amelia always kept a pair of scissors there. I snatched them up, and clutched them in my hand. When I returned to the hall, Ben was waiting for me.

"Let me," he said, taking the scissors from my hand. "And grab your phone. If it's not Amelia . . ."

"Don't move," I told him, before hurrying back to the bedroom. Manny was still snoring away as I unplugged my phone from the charger. I carried it back to Ben, who then led the way down the stairs.

Chico was still barking up a storm in the laundry room. The noises continued in the kitchen as we reached the bottom of the stairs. The light I'd noted was coming from the dining room, and the kitchen light was on as well. I glanced at the clock on the wall and saw it was just after three in the morning.

Ben and I glanced at one another. Before I could tell him that we should go back upstairs and call the cops to let them deal with it, even if it was indeed Amelia scrounging for a snack, he spoke.

"Hello?" he called. "Amelia?"

All sounds from the kitchen ceased. My breath caught in my throat, and my hand tightened on my phone. If it had been Amelia in there, she would have said something.

"Come on out," Ben said. "I know you're in there. I've got a weapon, and the police are on their way." A lie, but if it kept the intruder from coming at us with a kitchen knife, it was a forgivable one.

"That you, Bennie?"

That voice . . . I knew that voice.

"Jack?" Ben lowered the scissors. "Is that you?"

A man entered the dining room from the kitchen. He was razor thin, cheekbones jutting from a sunken-in face. His hair, which I knew to have once been a shiny brown, was dull and thinning. His clothes didn't look to have been washed in months.

And seeing him, I recognized him. Jack Castle. Ben's best friend from high school.

"Hey, Bennie." Jack smiled, revealing a mouth full of yellowed teeth.

"Jack." Ben sounded as stunned as I felt. "How . . . Why?"

"Yeah, uh." Jack ran a hand over the back of his neck. He was Ben's age, yet he looked twenty years older. "I stopped by to see if you were up, and every-one was asleep, so I . . ."

"Thought you'd poke around and see what you could steal?" I asked, motioning toward the bag sitting on the floor next to him.

"It's not like that." Jack nudged the bag away with his foot before his shoulders sagged. "Maybe it is. Man." He rubbed at his face. "I didn't know what else to do. I have nowhere to go, no money. I knew you lived here, and just couldn't get up the courage to knock."

So, you resort to stealing. It was on the tip of my tongue, but I bit it back.

"Please, man, don't call the cops. I'm having a rough patch is all. I made a mistake." His eyes widened as he noticed the phone in my hand. "You didn't call them already, did you?"

My gaze moved to the back door. I'd had to have the window next to it replaced once before, back when someone had tried to break in. A dog I'd taken in at the time had prevented it. I wondered if Jack was responsible for that break-in too. If he was, at least he didn't break a window this time.

"I'll go," Jack said, raising both his hands. "You won't have to hear from me again."

Ben handed me the scissors. "I'll take care of this," he told me. "Go on back to bed."

"We should call the police," I said at a whisper.

"Please, Mom. He was my friend." He glanced at Jack. "Let me deal with him. Maybe . . . I don't know. Maybe I can get him back on the right path."

Looking at Jack, I doubted it was possible. I wasn't sure what happened to him after high school. He and Ben had drifted apart, as friends are wont to do at that age. I'd assumed he'd gone off to college somewhere, but it appeared as if that wasn't the case.

"Please," Ben said. "I won't let him take anything and I'm not going to give him money."

I hesitated a moment before nodding. "All right," I said. It was hard, but I had to trust my son. He wasn't a kid anymore. *Why is it so hard to remember that?* "But, Ben, be careful."

"I will."

I turned to head up the stairs. Jack spoke up as I started to leave.

"Thanks, Mrs. Denton. It was . . . it was good to see you."

I paused briefly on the stairs, unable to come up with a response to that. I left the two to work things out on their own.

I returned the scissors to the bathroom drawer, and then slid back into bed next to a still snoozing Manny. I strained to hear any sounds from downstairs, but Ben and Jack were quiet as they spoke.

I should have called the cops. My phone was right here. I could still call them and apologize to Ben later. It was reckless of us to go downstairs without knowing what to expect, and while it turned out okay this time, I wasn't going to make that mistake again.

But Ben wanted me to trust him. And, honestly, I used to like Jack. Could I really call the cops on him?

I lay back and waited, hands bunched in my blankets. Twenty minutes later, a door downstairs opened and closed. Five minutes after that, Ben headed to his room. I noted he was alone, and the lights were off. I was hoping that meant Jack was gone for good.

I closed my eyes, but sleep didn't want to come. A trio of questions kept playing over and over in my mind.

Was this break-in an isolated incident? Or had Jack Castle made a habit out of breaking into other people's houses?

And if so, did he break into Joe Danvers's house before the other man was murdered?

15

Everyone was up and out of the house before I'd finished with my morning shower. I'd hoped to talk to Ben about Jack, but honestly, I trusted him to know how to handle his former best friend. If all went according to plan, there'd be no more break-ins at Casa Denton.

And anyway, I had my own troubles to deal with.

After breakfast, and with some trepidation, I loaded Chico into a dog carrier, slid him into the back of my van, and I was off to meet with Stacy Hildebrand.

It hadn't registered when she'd given me her address, but as I pulled onto Stacy's street, I realized she lived only a couple of blocks from Courtney. Coincidence? I seriously doubted it. I just wasn't sure whether Chico's dognapping happened because he got loose and Courtney saw an opportunity, or if there was some amount of conspiring going on between the near neighbors.

The house looked clean and quiet from the outside, which was a good sign. I pulled into the driveway and went to the back to retrieve the dog. Chico was barking up a storm, and while I loved all animals, I was glad he was moving back home where he belonged. I could use some peace and quiet.

"You'll see mommy soon," I told him. He barked and bared his teeth at me before he spun in a rapid circle inside the carrier.

I was surprised when Stacy didn't come storming outside to rant at me the moment I'd pulled up. It was even more of a jolt when I knocked on the door and someone else answered.

"Hi, I'm looking for Stacy Hildebrand," I said in my cheeriest voice. "I have Chico here for her."

The man at the door heaved a sigh and seemed to shrink three sizes. "Oh," he said. "You brought him back."

I blinked, my forced smile cracking. "I did. I'm sorry for the misunderstanding, but Chico is in great health and I'm sure he's looking forward to getting back into his usual routine."

The man—Stacy's husband, I assumed—sighed again. "Do you know how quiet it was without him?" He crouched to peer into the carrier. "No barking. Just . . ." He glanced up at me. "Nagging."

Uh-oh. I wanted no part of any sort of marital strife. "Is Stacy here? She told me to arrive this morning at nine sharp." I glanced at my watch-less wrist. "I'm here just in time." I flashed Mr. Hildebrand a smile in the hopes he would reciprocate, even a little.

He didn't.

Instead, he straightened with a grimace. "I guess that explains why she was so hot to get out of here this morning."

"She left?"

He nodded. "Barely bothered to berate me before she was out the door. Poof." He snapped his fingers before running a hand over his bald pate. "And now, this. I get it now. Let poor old Terrance deal with everything."

We stared at each other. Chico yapped in the carrier. He was growing heavier by the second. I had no idea what to do or say.

Terrance heaved yet another sigh, this one so dramatic, he might have won an award if someone had been filming it. "Fine. Give him here."

I held out the carrier and he took it. "Thank you, Terrance. Please tell Stacy I'm sorry about the mix-up. If there's anything I could do to make things better, tell her to not hesitate to call." Though I hoped never to receive that call.

"Yeah, yeah." He waved me off before setting the carrier down just inside the door. "It's always about Stacy and what she wants. It's me you should be apologizing to." And then he slammed the door in my face.

An urge to knock on the door and tell Terrance I'd take Chico back was so strong, I very nearly did just that. It was obvious he had no use for the dog, and I didn't want the Chihuahua to suffer from neglect, especially since Stacy couldn't be bothered to be here to retrieve her supposedly beloved pet.

But Terrance didn't seem like someone who'd actually hurt an animal, even if he disliked it. And perhaps it was all a show, another part of Courtney's plan to make me look bad. How Terrance's dour performance could affect me, I didn't know. Maybe she thought I'd snatch the dog away for real this time and they could make some real waves.

I returned to my van. After a quick mental debate,

I decided that since I was in the neighborhood, I might as well see if I could put this entire mess behind me for good.

I put the van in gear, shot a worried look toward the Hildebrand house, and then I drove a couple of blocks for what would inevitably turn into a confrontation I'd regret.

Courtney Shaw's house looked like a dollhouse. The outside was lime green and pink. It made my stomach churn just to look at it. Inside, everything was themed, right down to the coasters on the coffee table. The decor fit Courtney's personality perfectly.

I pulled into the driveway, relieved to see Courtney's own van there. The pink was too loud for this early in the morning, so I tried not to look at it as I got out of the driver's seat and strode up to the front door. I pressed the doorbell, gritting my teeth against the princess-themed sound it made.

The door opened and Courtney's voice floated out to greet me. "I'll be sure to let him know, thanks." She clicked off her cell and turned to face me, startled as if she hadn't heard me ring. "Oh! Liz. What are you doing here?"

"Why do you think?" I asked. My anger tried to rise, but I held it in check. Mostly. This was Courtney I was dealing with. This sort of behavior should be expected.

The smile on her face was so fake, it looked painted on. "I honestly couldn't say." Little meows came from behind her. I leaned to the side enough so I could see a pair of carriers filled to the brim with fluffy kittens. They were climbing over one another in a vain attempt to reach Courtney's white Siamese cat, Princess, who was sitting off to the side, looking put out.

As cute as the kittens were, I refused to let them distract me from what I'd gone there to do. "I thought I'd let you know I returned *Chico* to his proper home."

"Chico? Who's Chico?"

"Don't play dumb with me, Courtney. I talked to Duke."

Her eyes widened briefly. "I'm sure I don't—"

I raised a hand, cutting her off. "I'm not here to argue with you or accuse you of anything," I said, which was only partly true. "I know what happened. I know why it happened. I wanted to let you know it's over. Your little scheme didn't work. Chico is back home where he belongs and everyone is happy." Or so I hoped. I was afraid to check to see if Stacy had posted anything about me online, though I figured I would eventually have to do some damage control.

Courtney looked like she really wanted to keep playing innocent, but thought better of it. "I see," she said. "Well, if that's all, I suppose you'd better get going then. I have some little ones to deliver and can't be late."

"Without Duke?" I asked. I didn't know her to do much of anything on her own.

Courtney's face clouded over. "Yes, without Duke. Apparently, he's busy."

Or has he had it with your antics? The question popped into my head, but thankfully didn't pass my lips. I refused to stoop to that level.

"I hope he's okay," I said instead. "Duke's a good man. We could all learn a lot from him."

Okay, so maybe I had to get one little shot in. I'm not above being petty when the situation calls for it. Courtney tended to bring that out in everyone.

Unfortunately, Courtney didn't seem to catch the jab. "I'm sure we could." She bent down and picked up the carriers. "If you'd get the door for me, I really do need to go."

She walked past me, kittens meowing from their carrier. I had half a mind to leave the door hanging open and walk away, but as much as Courtney was getting on my nerves, I refused to risk letting Princess escape. I'd never forgive myself if something were to happen to her.

"Be good," I told the Siamese, as I closed the door. I turned in time to see Courtney pop into the driver's seat of her van, start it up, and back away without a second look my way.

One day . . . I didn't know what I'd do, but darn it, sometimes all I wanted from some people was a little respect.

I climbed back into my van and drummed my fingers on the steering wheel. There was one more thing I wanted to do before the day truly got started, but I wasn't sure I wanted to do it alone. After a few moments of debate, I snatched up my phone and dialed. It rang twice before an aged, trembling voice came over the line.

"Hastings residence. Who's calling?"

"Hi, Mr. Hastings, my name is Liz Denton. I was hoping we could speak."

"Regarding?"

I considered how I wanted to phrase my response before answering. "There's an old case that's drawn my interest and I wanted to talk to someone about it. Your name was given to me by a police officer named Reg Perry."

"I remember Reg." There was a fondness in Wayne's voice that gave me hope that he might be willing to talk. "How is he doing?"

"He's good," I said, hoping it was true. I liked Officer

Perry, but he *was* getting up there in years. "He's considering retiring soon."

"Good for him. He deserves a break." Some of the energy in his voice died away when he continued. "What was it you wanted to speak to me about? You mentioned an old case?"

A car drifted down the road. Irrationally, I waited for it to pass before I answered.

"I did. Do you remember a case you worked some thirty years ago?" I asked. "A missing-persons case? The woman's name was Christine—"

Before I could finish, he did it for me. "Danvers. I remember."

"I'm not sure if you've heard yet, but she's been found."

There was a long stretch of silence on the other end of the line. I couldn't even hear him breathe.

"Alive?" was the response when it finally came.

"She was, up until recently. Her son . . ." I struggled with how to say it, and settled on, "He came to see me. He told me that Christine fled Grey Falls when she vanished, but she wasn't afraid of her husband, Joe. It was someone else who frightened her. I was hoping you might be able to tell me who that might be."

This time, the silence went on long enough that I grew worried. Like Reg, Wayne Hastings wasn't a young man anymore. Too much of a shock might send his heart over the edge.

"Mr. Hastings?"

"I'm here," he said. His voice was choked with emotion, so I gave him a few more moments. "After all this time. She was alive."

"She was pregnant when she ran."

"Joseph's?"

"Yeah. His name is Erik. He came to Grey Falls to meet his dad, but when he arrived, it was already too late."

"Too late?" Wayne said. "What do you mean by that?"

I closed my eyes. Great, he didn't know. "Joe was murdered. I found his body. It's why Erik sought me out."

"Murdered?" He muttered a couple of expletives under this breath. His next word came out stronger, as if hearing about a crime brought some of the old detective back. "How?"

I didn't know if I was breaking some sort of rule by telling him, but since Detective Cavanaugh hadn't told me to be quiet, I assumed it was okay. "He was shot in his home. I think it was because he figured out his wife might still be alive, and why she'd run."

"I . . . I don't know what I can say to you," Wayne said. "Christine's disappearance happened a long time ago, and we'd run on the assumption she was dead. It means most everything we'd thought we'd known about the case was wrong."

"I just have a few questions I hope you can answer," I said. "I'm not a reporter or a detective or anything, but I do have an interest in the case. I was hoping that maybe we could meet and talk about some of the suspects. I know the detective in charge of the murder investigation. Maybe something will come out of our conversation that I can pass on to him."

"I don't see how," he said. I was about to resort to begging when he went on. "But I suppose it can't hurt."

"Thank you!" I almost jumped up and down in my seat. "Where should we meet?"

Wayne rattled off his address and we made plans to meet there in an hour, which gave me time to ready myself for our meeting.

I hung up feeling giddy, and a little frightened. Wayne Hastings seemed nice enough over the phone, but he was still a stranger. As far as I knew, he was the reason Christine fled town in the first place.

And he might have killed Joe.

Good thing I didn't plan on visiting him alone.

This time, when I dialed, I knew the man on the other end of the line.

"Duke. It's Liz."

"Liz? What did Courtney do now?" He sounded almost resigned.

"Nothing, as far as I know. I wanted to talk to you about something else."

"That murder you mentioned."

He knew me so well. "Yeah." I took a deep breath. "This is a big ask, but I have a meeting set up with the detective who was in charge of the case thirty years ago. I was hoping you might be willing to come with me?"

There was a beat where I could almost imagine his confusion before he asked, "Why?"

"It'd make me feel better," I said. "I really want to talk to him, but I don't want to do it on my own. If you can't, that's okay. I could always find someone else." Though I had no idea who.

"No, I'll come."

I was so shocked by how easily he'd accepted the invitation, it took me a few heartbeats to answer. "Thank you, Duke."

"Where do you want me to meet you?"

I almost rattled off Wayne's address, before I changed my mind. "I'll pick you up, if that's okay?"

"All right. That's fine. I'll be here." And then, sounding almost amused, he added, "You'd better not get me killed."

"I'll try not to." I disconnected, hoping that if it came down to it, and we were about to confront a killer, Duke would be the one keeping *me* from a murderer's hand, not the other way around.

16

Duke slid into the van next to me, turned sideways, and said, "Are you really going to do this?"

"Do what?" I asked. "Put on your seat belt."

He did as requested. "Get involved with something better left to the cops."

I backed out of his driveway and drove for a few minutes before answering. "Amelia is working the case with her mentor, who just so happens to be the private investigator who looked into Christine Danvers's disappearance thirty years ago. So, yes, I'm going to do what I can to help."

Duke surprised me by resting a hand on my wrist. "All right. Then let's do this."

It felt like a huge weight was lifted from my shoulders. Or, at least, the little devil that had been whispering into my ear had been swept aside. If Duke approved, then what I was doing couldn't be all bad, could it?

"How are things with Courtney?" Duke asked.

"I'm not sure. I returned Chico to his owner and

let Courtney know I don't approve of her actions. She acted like she didn't know what I was talking about, but I think she got the point." I glanced at him out of the corner of my eye. "She was making a delivery. Alone."

"Yeah." He grimaced. "I couldn't bring myself to go over there when she called. I just don't think I can do it anymore, not with her acting like a child when she doesn't get her way. I hate to walk away from the animals, but what else can I do?"

Something popped out of my mouth then that I didn't plan on saying.

"You could always work with me at Furever Pets."

Duke looked out the side window, and for a moment I feared I'd offended him somehow. When he turned back to me, I saw he was smiling. "You know, that might not be such a bad idea. I might have to think about it for a little while."

There was the faintest twinge of guilt, but it faded away pretty quickly. I hadn't intended to poach Duke from Pets Luv Us, but if he was already planning on walking away from Courtney's rescue, there was no reason why he couldn't come work with me. She'd hate it, and a part of me was glad for it. I guess there was a little childlike spite in me as well.

"So, give me the rundown on what to expect here," Duke said. "All I know is what you told me yesterday, and to be honest, I'm not sure I've got all the facts straight."

The rest of the trip consisted of me trying to explain the tangled web of Christine Danvers's life. I told him about her parents' murder, her later adoption, and marriage to Joe Danvers. I told him of her flight from Grey Falls, of Erik, and then of Joe's murder. I tried not to leave out a single detail, but there was so much to go over in such a short drive, I'm sure I missed something.

"Wow," he said when I finished talking. "I mean, a murder is bad enough, but with everything else tied to it, I . . ." He shook his head. "Wow."

"Tell me about it," I said. "Right now, I'm thinking Harry Davis, the guy that verbally assaulted Sasha, might be involved. He showed up at Chester's and acted awfully invested in what was going on. I mean, why demand Chester stop looking into it if he doesn't have a stake in the outcome of the investigation?"

"He could just be a jerk who thinks that the victim got what was coming to him."

"That's what I'm hoping to find out."

I pulled into Wayne Hastings's driveway a few minutes later. The garage door was open, and hung so crooked, I wasn't sure it could actually close. Inside, an old Dodge Charger sat, polished to a shine. It had one of those strange license plates that indicated it was special in some way. Historic maybe? I'm not into cars, so I could be wrong and the plate was meaningless.

Duke whistled appreciatively as he stepped out of my van. "You need to get one of those."

"Right," I said with a laugh. "I'd probably drive it straight through a wall."

"Car like that might come out of it okay."

I could tell Duke wanted to walk over and investigate the vehicle, but that wasn't why we were there. I led him to the front door, though I walked slowly so he could stare for a little while longer. The front door was open, allowing a faint breeze to air out the house. I could see in through the storm door, and noted the house looked clean and tidy. I didn't see anyone, and didn't want to yell into the house, so I knocked.

The door rattled loudly in its frame, causing me to wince. Wayne's house wasn't as isolated as Duke's, but the metallic banging made me feel like I'd disturbed the peace of the neighborhood.

A man with a stooped back and sharp eyes appeared and made his slow way to the door. Each step shuffled, as if lifting his feet pained him.

"Liz Denton?" he asked through the door. When I nodded, he unlatched it. "Come on in." He turned and shuffled his way back into his living room.

Duke and I shared a look before we entered.

Wayne kept his house well-lit. The floor was clean of debris, and everything seemed to have its place. The house itself was old, and was starting to decay as older houses often did. Water spots speckled the ceiling in places, and the floor sagged in a few well-walked spots. It wasn't that Wayne wasn't keeping up with the upkeep, but rather, the house itself was finally giving in to age.

"Take a seat." Wayne settled into a glider rocker with a groan. "If you want something to drink, the kitchen's that way." He waved a hand toward a small galley kitchen before his gaze settled on Duke. "And you are?"

"Duke Billings." He extended a hand, which Wayne shook. "It's a pleasure to meet you."

"We'll see about that." Wayne winked, and then turned to me. "So, Joe Danvers didn't kill Christine. Christine fled town, had a kid, who is now back in town. And now Joe is dead. Did I miss anything?"

"That's the gist," I said. "There are a few details I'd like to run past you, if you wouldn't mind."

"That's why we're here."

"What can you tell me about the original investigation?" I asked. "I have some of the smaller details, but there's a lot I don't know."

Wayne shifted in his seat with a faint grimace. "Like I said on the phone, I'm not sure how I can help you. I was lead on the case, but there wasn't much to go on at the time. Joe was our best suspect—our *only* suspect—and yet I never did like him for it."

"But you pursued it as if he was guilty anyway?"

"It was the only thing we *could* do," Wayne said. "We didn't have a murder weapon. We didn't have a motive. Hell, we didn't even have a body, which made it all the harder to figure out what happened. It was as if she simply up and disappeared." He paused, expression going thoughtful. "I suppose that's exactly what happened, wasn't it?"

"Did you have any reason to suspect that she'd fled town?" I asked. "Like, did you hear about someone strange hanging around her or anything like that?"

"Not a thing," Wayne said. "As far as we could tell, the Danverses were fine people. Then Christine comes up missing and we had a witness claiming they saw Joe carrying her off into the woods. We couldn't find a grave, shallow or otherwise, but it was all we had."

"Your source was Harry Davis, wasn't it?"

Wayne's face did something I couldn't describe. There was loathing there, and maybe a little bit of guilt. "It was."

"I've met him."

"I'm sorry you had to go through that."

I glanced at Duke and noted his jaw was clenched.

He was likely thinking about what Harry had said to his wife, and quite frankly, I didn't blame him.

I kept as much distaste out of my voice as I could when I said, "He showed up at Chester Chudzinski's place. Do you know who he is?"

"A PI," Wayne said. "Worked the disappearance on Joe's behalf. Can't say we paid him much mind back then, but from what I remember, it sounds like some of what he was saying might have been true."

"He always believed Joe innocent, and Christine alive." I didn't mean it as a shot at Wayne's investigation, but from his involuntary wince, he'd taken it that way. "He's been keeping an eye on the case over the years. Then, just the other day, Harry showed up and warned him off it."

Wayne started rocking in his chair. "Like he had something to hide?"

"I'm not sure," I said. "But he was pretty threatening. When that didn't work, he started up again and claimed that Joe and Christine's son, Erik, killed his own father."

"Claims he saw it?" Wayne asked.

"Pretty much," I said. "Erik *was* hanging around outside Joe's place before the murder, but it wasn't because he was planning on killing him. He was working up the guts to go in and talk to him."

Wayne sighed and rubbed at his wrist like it was hurting him. "I guess I shouldn't be surprised. Looking back, I fear we made a mistake listening to Harry. He tends to stretch the truth when it comes to dealing with people who are, shall we say, different."

"I noticed," I said.

"Back then, no one thought much of it. Harry was Harry. He hung around a couple other people of similar persuasion, though the one he spent the most time with was a man named Martin Castor."

"I haven't heard the name."

"He hasn't been in much trouble lately, so I'm not surprised. But when he was younger." Wayne whistled and shook his head. "He caused quite the ruckus. We chalked it up to wild youth, but there was always more to it. He targeted certain people, and had no qualms about hurting others if he thought they deserved it."

"Do you think Martin or Harry could have had anything to do with Christine's disappearance?" I asked. "Or Joe's murder?"

Wayne shrugged. "Hard to say. It wasn't until, I don't know, two years after we gave up looking for Christine that I realized what kind of man Harry was. When he first came to us with his story, I had no reason to doubt him, but the more we looked into it, the more his story didn't add up. And since his claims seemed to change with the wind . . ."

"And Martin?"

Wayne rocked for a few moments before answering. "He was never a suspect, if that's what you're asking. I don't believe he had anything to do with either of the Danverses. They weren't the kind of people he associated with, and they made sure to steer clear of him."

Of course, that didn't mean they succeeded in that regard. "Could one of them have chased Christine away? Hounded her until she feared for her life?"

"Could have, I suppose. I've had quite a long time to think about it," Wayne said. "My body has started to fail me, but my mind is as strong as it ever was." He shifted in his chair so that he was practically sitting on a hip. When he spoke again, his voice was strained. "If it wasn't for Harry's claim, we might have looked harder at what truly happened to Christine. And if . . ." He frowned.

"If what?"

"You have to understand that while Christine was missing, there was no body. People thought Joe killed her, but it wasn't an official murder investigation. I was buried in bureaucratic nonsense at the time, and I'll be the first to admit it interfered with my investigation." Wayne looked miserable because of it. "I will say, Harry didn't strike me as a killer. He got involved, sure, but to kill someone?" He shook his head.

"He might have been covering for someone else," Duke said, drawing both Wayne's and my eyes. "If his friend went after this Christine woman, then perhaps he claimed he saw her husband disposing of the body to protect this friend of his."

"You know, I've considered a similar angle over the years," Wayne said. "But was never able to prove anything."

"What do you mean?" I asked.

"I never believed Christine was alive." He closed his eyes briefly as if he regretted it immensely. "And after a while, I stopped believing Joe Danvers had anything to do with her death. That meant I needed to ask myself who might have, and Harry's name kept popping into my head."

"You think he went after her?"

"As I said, I don't think Harry has it in him to kill anyone. He's big on threats and making a hell of a scene, but as far as I'm aware, he's never actually hurt anyone physically."

"That's not how he likes to tell it," Duke muttered.

"He would embellish, that's for sure," Wayne said. "But every time Harry's name came up on a scanner, he was always just an accessory. Back then, Martin Castor would be the one to slash a tire, bust a window, and in some cases, a few noses. Harry would egg him on, and would talk just as loudly as Martin, and then afterward would boast that he had a bigger hand in it than he did. The man's all talk."

"So, then, Martin could have done it." I tried to imagine someone akin to Harry, but more violent, and decided I didn't like the image my brain provided.

"Perhaps," Wayne said, but he didn't sound convinced. "There's a lot to dislike about those two men, but Martin's cleaned up last I heard. I can't even say he still associates with Harry anymore. I've been out of the loop these last few years." His smile was almost sad.

Wayne sat up in his chair, planting both his feet firmly on the floor. When he met my eye, there was something behind his gaze, an intensity that had me leaning forward to hear what he had to say.

"I will say, Harry and Martin aren't good people. That's a given. I can't dismiss the idea that either of them might have had a hand in Christine's disappearance or Joe's death, just because I don't *think* they did it. But the more I consider what happened back then, the more I think there's something more going on."

"What do you mean?" I asked.

"Honestly? I'm not sure. There were irregularities with the investigation from the start. As I mentioned, I've had a long time to think about Christine's disappearance. And this last hour, between when you called and when you showed up on my front step,

I've thought even harder about it. I don't think we're dealing with a simple disappearance and murder here. I think we're dealing with something far, far bigger."

I opened my mouth to ask him what he meant by that when my phone went off, startling me so badly, I leapt to my feet.

"Sorry," I said, yanking out my phone. Already, I was regretting carrying it with me instead of leaving it in the cupholder of my van like I used to. I was about to swipe CANCEL when I noted it was a local number I didn't recognize. "One sec." I turned away and accepted the call.

"Liz? Thank heavens you answered."

"Erik?" I walked to the front door and lowered my voice. "Did something happen?" I couldn't think of any other reason he'd call me.

"Someone broke in here." I could hear an edge of panic in his voice. "Someone broke into my hotel room while I was gone. The place . . . It's a mess. What if they were looking for me?"

"Stay calm," I said. "Did you call the police?"

"I . . ." He took a shuddering breath. "No. After what happened to Dad, I didn't know what else to do. I think someone is after me, and I'm not sure if I can trust the police. And since you gave me your number, and you've dealt with the cops here, I thought . . . I don't know what I thought."

"All right," I said. I didn't blame him for not trusting the police, not after hearing his mother's story. Erik had probably asked himself the same sort of questions about them that I had. "Stay there. I'll be right over."

"Thank you, Liz. I know I have no right to ask you for anything, but I didn't know who else to call."

"No, I'm glad to help. Where are you staying?"

He gave me an address. "I'll wait in the lobby. I can't stay in here. What if they're watching the place?"

"Stay calm," I said again. "The lobby is good. Wait there and see if anyone appears out of place, like they're waiting for something. Note anyone who looks at you funny, or threatens you. We can go from there once I arrive, okay?"

"Okay."

I clicked off and returned to the living room.

"Everything all right?" Duke asked, rising.

"I'm not sure." I turned to Wayne. "I'm sorry, but something has come up and I have to go. Thank you for your time, Detective Hastings. You've been a big help."

"I wish I would have been of more help sooner," he said, regret marring his voice. "Maybe then, poor Joe Danvers would still be alive."

17

Erik was pacing outside the hotel doors when we arrived. His cell phone was in his hand and he kept looking at it like he was anxious to make a call, but couldn't decide who to contact. As soon as he saw my van, he jogged across the lot, arms waving.

"I haven't seen anyone," he said as I opened the door and stepped out. "At least, no one that looked at me funny. Well, a few people did, but that might be because I jumped at every loud noise." He ran a hand over his face. "I'm sorry; I'm a wreck."

"It's all right," I said, resting a hand on his shoulder. "Anyone would be."

Erik started to speak, but when Duke came around the side of the van, he stiffened and took a step back. "Who are you?" He looked to me. "Who is he?"

"He's a friend," I said. "Erik Deavers, this is Duke Billings. Think of him as our protection against anyone who would do us harm."

Some of the tension bled from Erik then. Duke

wasn't a small guy; he towered over the both of us, and could probably wrap us both in rib-crushing hugs if he wanted. I hoped his presence would keep whoever broke into Erik's hotel room at bay.

Duke held out a hand and Erik shook it. "I'm sorry for your loss. Liz has told me a little about you and what you've gone through."

"Thanks. It's been rough." Erik's hand tightened on his phone before he shoved the device into his pocket. "I sometimes feel like I'm going crazy. I mean, who does this sort of thing to someone in mourning?"

"Take us to your room," I said, as calmly as I could. Erik sounded ready to flee the state. "You can explain what happened on the way."

Erik tapped his pocket, as if making sure his phone hadn't gotten up and walked away before he motioned toward the hotel. "It's this way." He began walking.

Duke and I shared a worried look before we followed after him.

Erik didn't speak until we were through the hotel doors. "There's not much to say." He led us to the elevator and pressed the button. "I was next door eating a late breakfast when it happened. There's a diner I thought looked pretty good, so I went there instead of staying in my room like I usually would."

"Was it good?" Duke asked.

Erik smiled briefly. "It was. I had the eggs Benedict. You should try it if you get a chance."

The elevator doors opened and we stepped inside. Erik hit 4. The doors closed and we started up.

"I took my time eating," he went on. "I didn't like the idea of spending the day in my room, even though that's sort of my thing. There's really no reason for me to stick around town, but I can't seem to bring myself to leave. What if they find Dad's killer? I think I need to be there for that, just in case the police need a statement from me or something."

"I understand," I said. "I don't think I could leave either, if it was my family." And since Harry Davis claimed Erik was hanging around Joe's place before Joe's death, I doubted the police wanted him to go very far either.

"So, I fiddled around with my phone, drank my coffee, and watched the world pass me by. It was relaxing, I guess. I didn't realize how tense I'd become over the last few days."

The elevator stopped, the doors slid open, and we stepped out into an empty hallway. Erik turned to the right, so Duke and I followed.

"I didn't realize anything was wrong until I stepped into my room," he said. "Everyone here has been nothing but nice to me, so why would I worry? The door was closed, and as far as I could tell from out here, no one had been here." We stopped in front of room 412. He swiped his keycard and pushed open the door. "Then . . . this." We stepped inside.

The room was a mess. The television, the lamps, and anything breakable was still where it should be. But everything else, including Erik's personal belongings, was tossed to the floor. Drawers were hanging open, Erik's suitcase was overturned, and his clothes were strewn across the room. The bed had been stripped, and the mattress was standing on its side against the wall.

I jumped as the door swung closed behind us.

"I haven't touched anything," Erik said. "This is exactly how I found it."

Duke stepped over a pillow to peer into the bathroom. "It's the same in here. Room's been trashed."

I eased through the main room, taking it all in. It appeared whoever broke in was careful not to make too much noise. The clock was still plugged in and was sitting atop the nightstand. An old iPod was charging on the dock pushed to the back of the desk. While the drawers and suitcase had been emptied, Erik's things looked to have been piled up and then shoved over, rather than tossed.

"Can you tell if anything is missing?" I asked, though I doubted it. A thief would have snagged the iPod.

"I'm not sure," Erik said. I noted he had yet to move from in front of the door. "I'm too afraid to look."

Duke moved to the window and glanced outside. "It overlooks the parking lot. And look." He pointed.

I glanced outside. The Sunny Side Diner could be seen from the window. I assumed it was the diner Erik had mentioned. I turned to him. "When you left, did you leave the curtains open?"

"No." Erik frowned. "I always keep them closed when I'm in a hotel. I don't like the idea of anyone being able to look in at me."

Duke checked the window, but it was made of solid glass built into the frame. It couldn't be opened, not that anyone would try to sneak out of it. There was no balcony, and we were four stories up. That'd be a long drop for anyone.

"Whoever broke in here knew you weren't going to be in the room," I said. "They were looking for something, but what?" I looked to him, hoping for an answer.

Erik merely shrugged. "I have no idea. I only

brought a couple things with me, and very little of it is of value."

"Did you ever go into Joe's house?" I asked, thinking that maybe the intruder thought he'd taken something that might tie him to the murder.

"No. I never worked up the nerve, and by the time I did . . ."

His dad was dead.

I walked slowly through the room, but I had no idea what I was looking for. It was obvious the intruder didn't want to be caught. He or she opened the curtains so they could keep an eye on Erik. If they took too long, they could make their escape the moment they saw him leave the diner. Did that mean there was more than one person involved? The bathroom didn't have a window, so if they trashed it too, it would have left them vulnerable without someone else watching for Erik.

"Did you walk to the diner?" I asked.

"Yeah. It's not far."

Which meant the intruder had more than enough time to get out of the room, and very likely out of the hotel, once they saw Erik was returning.

"Think carefully," I said. "When you left, did you see anyone at all hanging around in the lobby? Or maybe the parking lot? What about when you got back? Was anyone leaving the hotel? Or did you see someone both when you left and then again when you returned? Whoever did this might not have been familiar with you, or acted like they were interested in you in any way, but they knew when you left, and were watching for your return."

"I . . ." Erik scowled. "I can't remember." He made a frustrated sound. "There were people, but I wasn't paying attention to anyone."

"You should call the police," Duke said. "This might not have anything to do with you or your father."

"You think it might have been a random break-in?" I asked, trying hard not to think about Jack Castle.

"It fits just as much as anything else," Duke said. "Erik is new to town, so no one really knows him. No threats were made. Nothing is broken. The door didn't appear to be jimmied, and there's no other way in."

"But nothing was taken," I said, indicating the iPod. "Why break in if not to steal something?"

"I don't know," Duke said. "This could be about something else entirely. Think about it. Place is destroyed with no note, no indication as to how anyone got in. I bet they had a key."

"You think a hotel employee did this?" Erik asked.

Duke spread his hands. "Right now, with what we know, I'd say it's likely that if they didn't do it themselves, they assisted whoever did. And if not, then someone might have cloned the key somehow and has been trashing rooms for fun for months. You should call the cops and let them sort it out."

"Yeah. All right." Erik blew out his lip in a huff. "I'm sorry I dragged you all the way down here for this. I didn't know who else to call."

"I'm happy you thought of me," I said. "If anything else happens, don't hesitate to call."

Erik nodded and pulled out his phone. Duke and I left him to make the call.

"How well do you know him?" Duke asked as we rode the elevator back down to the lobby.

"Not too well," I said. "He seems like a good person, though." Though he *had* followed me around town and had called my house only to breathe heavily into the phone. That didn't make someone a bad guy, did it?

"Just . . ." He frowned, looked away. "Just be careful."

"Why?"

Duke didn't respond right away. We stepped off the elevator when it stopped, crossed the lobby, and were halfway to the van before he answered.

"Sometimes, people look for attention and manufacture ways to get it when they can't come by it naturally. I'd make sure he is who he says he is before you take him at his word." He glanced at me. "He might be a good person, might be the man he claims to be, but if he's not, you should be prepared."

I climbed into my van and then looked toward Erik's room. The curtains were still hanging open, and I thought I saw him moving around inside, but couldn't be sure. Unless the intruder was standing directly in front of the window, Erik wouldn't have been able to see them on his way back from the diner.

If there even was an intruder.

"I'll be careful," I said with a slight shudder. Could Erik Deavers be lying to me? Was it only about the room? Or could Duke be right, and he wasn't who he said he was?

I was quiet all the way to Duke's house. He let me think, though he did shoot worried glances at me every now and again. I desperately wished I could reassure him, but I couldn't. What did I really know about everyone involved in the murder? I mean, both Joe and Christine had used multiple aliases. What made me think Erik was any different?

"Call me if you need me again," Duke said when I pulled up in front of his house. "It looks like I have some free time coming up."

I nodded absently, barely hearing him. I kept thinking about how Erik and I had met, how he'd followed
me home, how he'd called me without speaking. That
was stalker behavior, wasn't it? And while he had a perfectly rational explanation for it, I couldn't simply
take him at his word.

Of course, there was one person I knew who knew
how to do proper background checks. I could no
longer trust myself, not after Joe.

I left Duke at his house, and then headed downtown. I found a parking spot across the street from
Chester's office. It took some work to maneuver my
van into the space, since the cars in front of and behind me were nearly sitting on the lines, but I managed. I'd just put the van into park when someone
darted in between the tiny space between my front
bumper and the bumper of the Cadillac in front of me.

It was Harry Davis.

I scrambled out of my van, intent on catching him
before he reached Chester's office, but I was cut off
by a flood of traffic. I watched, unable to stop him, as
Harry burst into the office, already shouting.

Amelia!

I scanned the street, but didn't see her car. I hoped
she and Maya had decided to work from Maya's place
this morning.

I waited until there was a break in the traffic, and
then I ran across the street as fast as my legs would
take me. I took the handful of stairs that led to
Chester's office door by twos, and then burst in about
thirty seconds after Harry.

"I will kill you!" Harry had Chester backed into a
corner. His fists were bunched, but I was thankful to
note he didn't appear to have a weapon on him.

"Calm down," Chester said, hands outstretched in

a warding-off gesture. "Please, Harry, I don't know what you're talking about."

"You have someone following me! I saw them." He raised a fist as if he might throw a punch, but thought better of it. "They thought they were being careful, but I'm not stupid. I *saw* them. I know they're working for you."

"I don't have anyone following you, Harry," Chester said. "If I need someone followed, I do it myself."

"You lie." He snarled the word and pressed closer to Chester. "No one else would have me followed. You and your vendetta against all that's good in this town has gone too far."

Vendetta? I wondered, but I couldn't just stand there and let Harry intimidate the PI, no matter the reason. I planted my feet, just in case Harry decided to charge me like a bull, and shouted, "Stop it right now or I'm going to call the cops."

Harry wheeled around, eyes blazing. "This is none of your business, you—" He gnashed his teeth, wisely keeping whatever he'd been about to say to himself.

"You're threatening my friend," I said, taking a step closer to Harry, even though a voice in the back of my mind was screaming at me to run. "I don't like it when people threaten my friends."

Harry laughed. "And you're going to stop me?"

"If I have to."

Chester eased out of the corner and moved to one of the desks in the room. He didn't reach for a drawer, but his eyes flickered to one. It made me wonder if he had a gun tucked away in there.

"So, it's okay for you people to interfere in my life?" he asked. "I'm not allowed to stand up for my-self?"

"You are," I said. "But threats aren't the way to do

it." And then I took a shot in the dark. "Breaking into people's hotel rooms isn't either."

Harry's brow furrowed. "What?"

"Erik Deavers, the man you fingered for Joe's murder. His hotel room was ransacked this morning. Where were you when it happened?"

Harry looked from me, to Chester, and then back again. "What?"

"The room was trashed. Was it a threat?"

"I didn't break into a hotel room, woman. Are you off your meds?"

"Did you know that Christine Danvers was still alive?" I asked, abruptly switching topics. "Why did you blame Joe for killing her? Do you find lying fun?"

"I . . ." Harry took a step back. For the first time, I saw cracks in his anger. "I saw what I saw."

"Did you?" I asked. "Because, quite frankly, I don't believe you saw a thing. Did he do something to you and you figured accusing him of murdering his wife was a good way to get back at him?"

"I saw what I saw," Harry said again, jaw firming. "Facts are facts."

"You like to say that, don't you?" I said. "But your facts don't seem to align with other people's concept of the idea."

He narrowed his eyes at me, and I had a feeling he didn't quite understand my statement.

"Maybe you're just trying to protect someone." I took another step closer to him, which did nothing to ease the tension zipping through me. Even my *skin* felt tighter. "Maybe Martin Castor had something to do with Christine fleeing, and with Joe's death. What do you think?"

Harry paled at mention of Martin's name. A second passed. Then two.

"You'd better leave me be," he said, wheeling on Chester. "Keep out of my life." He pushed past me and ran out the door. I wondered if he was running to Martin to tell him what had just happened.

"Thank you," Chester said, stepping away from the desk. "But you shouldn't have done that."

I sagged against the other desk in the room as my legs started to tremble. "I couldn't let him threaten you like that," I said. "It's not right."

"Don't get me wrong, I appreciate you stopping him." Chester moved to the door and peered outside, as if to make sure Harry was truly gone, before he turned back to face me. "But if what you said is true and Harry is protecting Martin Castor, I fear that you stepping in might have put a target on your back."

18

Needless to say, Chester's warning had me looking over my shoulder for the next few hours. After Harry left, I mentioned to Chester my concerns about Erik and the possibility that he might be lying about who he really is, and then left him to work on it—if he found the time between looking into why Christine fled Grey Falls and who killed Joe.

At home, I spent the next two hours cleaning the house in an attempt to settle my mind. Wheels and Sheamus followed me around, which meant, of course, a good forty minutes of those two hours were spent cuddling the kitties, rather than actually cleaning. I didn't mind; I needed their comfort as much as they needed mine.

Still, despite my feline companions, I felt alone. No one was home when I'd arrived, and as the minutes turned into hours, and still no one showed, I started to get worried. What if Chester was right and Harry and Martin were going to come after me?

What if their preferred method was to hurt those I loved instead?

It didn't seem like Harry's way, but what did I know about Martin Castor? From what Wayne Hastings told me, Martin didn't sound like anyone I wanted to meet.

I finished sweeping the floor and shoved the broom into the closet before I reached for my phone. I knew my kids hated it when I called them just to check up on them—especially since they were adults—but I needed to hear their voices, just to be sure everything was okay.

As soon as I brought out my phone, a car pulled into the driveway. My heart jumped into my throat when I didn't recognize it, thinking that Harry had decided to seek me out. I was just about to call the cops when the doors opened and three of my friends stepped out.

I hurried to the door. "What are you doing here?" I asked them. "Game night isn't until next week."

"We heard about what happened," Holly Trudeau said, hoisting a bottle of red wine for my inspection. She was married to Ray, a veterinarian who worked with Manny, and she was rarely seen without a glass of wine in her hand. "We thought we'd come by to cheer you up."

Behind her, Evelyn Passwater snickered. Well into her sixties, Evelyn had one of the sharpest minds of anyone I knew. "She's probably enjoying all the attention."

"That's not true, is it, Liz?" Deidra Kissinger stepped up and gave me a kiss on the cheek. She was a high school teacher who looked as if she could be a fitness model. She was also one of my best friends, though I didn't get to see her—or the rest of the ladies—as much as I'd like.

"I'm fine," I said. "And no, murder isn't exactly my idea of fun."

I led the women into the dining room, and then stopped, unsure what to do next. Normally, they showed every first Wednesday of the month so we could play board games and gossip. But, as I'd noted before, we were a week away from that. What were we supposed to do now?

Deidra went straight into the kitchen and returned with four wineglasses. The women settled around the table in their customary spots, so I joined them.

"You say you're fine, but is that really true?" Holly asked. "You look pale."

"It's been stressful." I gave them a quick rundown of Christine's disappearance and Joe's murder, throwing in my troubles with Courtney to boot. "It seems like every time I turn around, some new disaster strikes. I feel like I'm being pulled in a hundred directions at once."

"You should stay in more," Evelyn said. "Can't find dead people if you never go out."

"I guess that explains why you only leave when we drag you out of your house, kicking and screaming," Deidra said.

"I'll have you know, I had a date just last week. I won't tell you how *that* went." Evelyn winked.

Holly filled the wineglasses and I gulped down half of mine in one go. They all stared at me like I'd grown a second head.

"What? I said I was stressed."

"Hey, I'm not one to judge," Holly said. "I've just never seen you drink so much at once."

"It's good for you," Evelyn added. "It's how I've kept up my youthful appearance." She drained her entire glass, though I noted her eyes watered from it.

"I'll be fine," I said. "You don't know how much I needed this."

"Oh, we figured you would," Deidra said. "We're here for you."

"Here, here." Holly raised her glass and then took a drink.

"I remember when Christine Danvers disappeared," Evelyn said with a shake of her head. "The police said her husband killed her, but I for one never believed it."

"You knew them?" I asked.

"Only casually." Evelyn seemed to know everyone, and I was okay with that. It gave me someone to go to whenever I had a question about someone around town. "We'd bump into each other at the store and say hi, but it never really went past that."

Both Holly and Deidra were likely too young to remember much of what happened back then, but Evelyn would have been right around the same age as the Danverses, if not a little older.

"They seemed like nice people," Evelyn went on. "Never could understand why Christine would vanish like she did. Always assumed it was something beyond her control."

"Like an abduction?" Holly asked.

Evelyn shrugged one bony shoulder. "Or someone threatened her. She was always fiercely protective of her family, so whatever it was, it had to be pretty darn bad for her to leave them."

My ears perked up at that. "Did you ever hear anything that hinted that someone might have threatened her?" I asked. "Did Joe or Christine have problems with anyone in town?"

"Not that I'm aware," Evelyn said, before frowning. "I suppose that's not entirely true. I do recall one evening, I'm guessing it was around the Fourth of July because I distinctly remember the fireworks, when I saw the two of them together. I was about to go over to say hello when Christine looked as if she'd seen a ghost. She said something to Joe, who looked confused, before she hurried off. I happened to be standing where I could see that she left Joe for some other guy."

"Did you see who it was?" I asked, growing excited. If this other man was the reason Christine fled town, it might go a long way in figuring out who killed Joe. *That is, if the two are connected,* I reminded myself.

"No, I didn't," Evelyn said. "He was wearing a suit, though. Looked all prim and proper where he stood off to the side. He wasn't facing my way, so all I saw was his backside, before the two of them vanished down an alley. Since it was none of my business what Christine was doing, I left them to it, so I never saw if or when they returned."

"Did you ever tell the police what you saw?" Holly asked.

"Why would I?" Evelyn looked annoyed by the question. "This happened weeks before she vanished. I didn't even think about it until now, and I'm not even sure it had anything to do with her disappearance."

"It might have given the police something to go on, if they'd known," Deidra said. "Even if this guy wasn't why she left, he might have known something that would have helped."

"He may have," Evelyn admitted, "but it's too late

now, isn't it? Besides, back then, they were pretty sure Christine cheated on Joe and he found out about it and killed her for it. I never believed it, but who knows? She *did* hurry off with that other man. As far as I knew, they were lovers, and I witnessed the beginning of the end of both Christine and Joe Danvers."

There was a long stretch of silence before Holly grinned over her wineglass. "Speaking of cheating, are we going to play Scrabble again this month? Or are we going to change it up a bit so Evelyn can't palm any more tiles?"

Evelyn's eyes widened. "I never cheat! I can't help it that none of you have vocabularies that extend past the second grade."

"Maybe we need to pat her down before our next game," Deidra said. "There's only so many places you can hide spare tiles."

"Just you try it," Evelyn said, pointing a finger at Deidra.

My attention was pulled from the lighthearted argument at the table as another car pulled into the driveway. I rose from my seat with a distracted, "Excuse me," and checked the window. Ben got out of the driver's seat of his car.

He wasn't alone.

The woman looked younger than Ben, so much so, she appeared to be fresh out of high school. She wore shorts far too short for her long legs, and a navel-baring shirt that left little to the imagination. I fully expected her to snap her gum as she made her way to the front door. She was hanging from Ben's arm so casually, she almost looked bored.

"Liz? Is everything okay?"

I glanced back to see Holly had risen from her seat

and the other two women were looking at me with a healthy amount of concern in their eyes.

"Yeah. Quickly! Sit down." I hurried back to my seat. "Act natural."

"Why?" Evelyn craned her neck in a vain attempt to see out the window. "What's going on?"

The door opened then and Ben walked in. "Mom?" He paused in the dining room. "Oh! Hi, Evelyn. Holly. Deidra." He nodded to each of the women in turn. "I was wondering who was here since I didn't recognize the car in the driveway."

"It's new," Holly said, eyes raking over the woman on Ben's arm. At first glance, she didn't look approving. I couldn't say I disagreed. "Are you going to introduce us?"

Ben blushed, even as he grinned. "Mom, ladies, this is Katie Sprig."

Katie's eyes passed over us as if we were beneath her notice.

I rose and planted myself in front of her so she couldn't ignore me. "Hi, Katie. I'm Ben's mom, Liz." I stuck out a hand.

She eyed it a moment as if it was covered in filth before slipping her fingertips into my hand. I noted her nails were painted bubblegum pink. The "handshake" lasted all of half a second before she jerked her fingers free.

"I thought we'd stop by and say hi before we hit the movie later," Ben said.

"You're watching a movie tonight? Which one?"

"We haven't figured that out yet," Ben said. "I was hoping for the new Rock movie, but Katie isn't into action flicks."

Katie glanced at him, rolled her eyes, and then turned back toward the door.

"Guess we'd better go," Ben said. He looked a little peeved, considering they'd just gotten there. "See you later tonight."

"Be careful," I said, trying hard not to frown. While Ben had dated a lot of women, I couldn't say I had actively disliked any of them until now.

"She's not going to last long," Deidra said as soon as they were gone. "Ben's got better taste than that."

"They're moving in together," I said, collapsing into my chair. I polished off my glass of wine and held it out for a refill.

"No." Holly sounded shocked as she poured. "There's no way."

"It'll fall through before they make it that far," Deidra said. "Trust me."

"People are judged by the friends they keep," Evelyn said. "Ben will realize that soon enough."

"I hope so," I said, but my mind had shifted gears. *Did Christine have any friends in Grey Falls?* It had been years since she'd lived in town, but someone might still be around. If anyone would know more about Christine and Joe's relationship, it would be a close friend.

The conversation after that turned to frivolous things. It was good to talk—and think—about something other than murder or my family. By the time the wine was corked and everyone was standing, I felt better. I was still worried, mind you, but at least I wasn't jumping at every loud sound and thinking about buying a new series of locks for the door.

As soon as my friends had piled into Holly's car and had backed out, however, my brain jumped right back onto the murder. Within seconds of them leaving, I was on the phone, calling the one person I knew who might know if Christine still had friends in town.

"Hi, Chester, it's Liz. I have a question for you. Do you know if Christine Danvers had a best friend who still might live in Grey Falls?"

"I believe so. One moment." The phone clunked to the desk and I could hear a drawer opening and papers being sifted through. It took two minutes before he returned. "Penelope Pringle. She was Christine's closest friend at the time. Knew each other since high school. She lives at"—more rifling of papers—"1221 West Clairmont Street."

While popping in unannounced might allow me to meet Penelope, I doubted it would earn me any favor with her. "Do you have a phone number for her?" I asked.

"I do." Chester rattled off her number. "Is there anything else I can do for you?"

"No, I think that's it. Thanks, Chester."

"No problem, Liz. Let me know if it amounts to anything. I first talked to Penelope back when Christine vanished, and we've kept in contact ever since. She's a good woman, but her life has been hard. Go easy on her, all right?"

"I will."

I was about to hang up when a new voice came from the background. "Is that my mom?"

There was a rustling sound and Amelia came onto the line. "Mom, Maya and I discovered something new."

A muffled voice I took to be Maya's followed. I couldn't make out what she was saying, but she sounded excited.

"What is it?" I asked.

"You know how we were looking into Christine's birth parents?" Amelia asked.

"Yeah? You found out they were murdered. Did you discover something else?"

"We did. Maya and I decided to look into it some more, see if we could find anything that might link to the current investigation." She paused, obviously waiting for me to respond.

"Uh-huh."

"At first, there wasn't much to find. They were killed, and Christine saw the killer, but could never place him, right?"

"Right." I shifted from foot to foot, anxious for her to get to the point.

"Well, I thought that was odd. I mean, if someone were to come in and murder my family, I'd have everything seared into my brain. There's no way I wouldn't be able to recognize the killer if I saw them again, or at least, wouldn't be able to give the police a proper description."

"You think she knew the killer?" I asked, following her train of logic. "And then protected them?"

"I don't know," Amelia said. "Maya has floated the idea, and honestly, it doesn't sound too far-fetched, not after what we discovered."

There was more muffled conversation from the other end of the line. This time, Chester's voice joined Maya's, before Amelia returned.

"The question became," she said, "why would she protect a killer? And if she did, why would she then run from her parents' killer and leave her husband behind?"

"If that is what happened," I said, unwilling to jump to conclusions just yet.

"I think it is," Amelia said. "Some guy kills her parents; she sees it, but keeps quiet for years. Then something happens. What, I don't know. But he comes after her for one reason or another. Maybe he threatens to hurt her family if she doesn't leave, so she does. Then, Joe realizes Christine might still be alive, starts looking into her disappearance again, and this time, what if he comes across new information? What if he discovered who killed her parents?"

"All right," I said. It sounded plausible enough, but there were a whole lot of maybes and what-ifs. "So, the killer kills him to keep him quiet. But who would do such a thing?"

I could almost *feel* Amelia's grin across the line. "How about Christine's real dad?"

"Her real dad?" I asked. "Do you mean Hue Hemingway?"

"No, not Hue." There was another pause before she hit me with it. "We don't have the records to prove it, but Maya and I have come across information that hints that Hue Hemingway might not be Christine's father after all."

19

Amelia didn't have much else to add, but that little tidbit she had discovered was exciting enough. She didn't have a name for Christine's real father, nor did she have any solid evidence to support her theory that we could take to the police; yet, if what she said was true, we might now have a motive for both Christine's disappearance and Joe's death. Amelia promised to keep me informed if she or Maya came up with anything new, and then disconnected.

The house felt painfully empty now that everyone was gone and I wasn't talking to anyone. I tried to turn my attention to Sheamus's needs, yet every time I considered calling someone about him, I found I couldn't bring myself to do it.

What if they had deep, dark secrets that could cause them to end up like Joe? What if they were like Terrance Hildebrand and were lukewarm to animals at best? I knew I shouldn't be worried—I hadn't had an issue finding the right home for an animal before

Joe—but it was hard. I didn't trust myself to make rational decisions.

So, I decided I might as well be irrational.

I picked up my phone, checked the number Chester had given me, and dialed.

"Hello?"

"Hi, my name is Liz Denton. I'm looking to speak to Penelope Pringle, if she's in."

There was a pause. "I'm Penelope. What is this about?"

It was my turn to hesitate. I had no official authority to be asking her questions about Christine. There was nothing wrong with a couple of women chatting about the past, but would she want to talk to me about someone she'd likely thought dead for the past thirty years? Penelope had already told the police everything she knew, and our conversation would bring back all the painful memories she might wish buried.

Could I do that to her?

"Are you still there?" Penelope asked. She had a kind, gentle voice.

Go easy on her. Chester's words drifted through my mind.

"I would like to talk to you about Christine Danvers," I said. "I have some news you might like to hear. I've met her son."

Her gasp was audible through the phone. "Her son?"

"Please, if I could have a few minutes of your time, I'll happily explain everything."

"Yes. All right." She took a shuddering breath. "Do you know a place called Sophie's Coffeehouse?"

"I do."

"Would you mind meeting me there? I think I

need the comforts of a good cup of coffee if we're going to talk about this."

We agreed to meet within the hour. I made sure the cats had water, gave each a good scratch behind the ears, and then I was on the way.

Sophie's was once an old Victorian house that was converted into a business, much like every other building on the street, including Chester's office. Many of the buildings were once mansions, but Sophie's was smaller, more personal. Honestly, I preferred it that way.

I parked in the small lot out back and then made my way in through the front door. Penelope promised she'd meet me just inside, and she didn't disappoint.

"Liz?" she asked, clutching a handbag like she feared I might try to snatch it from her. She was wearing a floor-length dress, and had her hair pulled up tight to her head in a bun. When she spoke, she didn't look directly at me. "Liz Denton?"

"I am. How'd you know?" I asked her.

She nodded to my shirt, which had the name of my rescue on it. "I checked you out after your call. You do good work."

"Thank you." Hopefully, that meant Courtney's plan to ruin Furever Pets's name had failed. "Shall we?"

Penelope led the way to a table in the corner. I could see the statue of Grey Falls's founder, Sebastian Grey, down the street. Penelope made sure to sit so she was facing the windows and took the time to check them carefully before sitting.

Paranoid? I wondered. Or was she socially awkward. I had my answer immediately.

"I like coming here, but I'm not much of a people person," she said. "Never have been. Christine and I were good friends, mind you. She kind of took me under her wing when we were young because I couldn't make any other friends. You know how kids can be." Her eyes flickered to me briefly, before returning to the window.

"I have two kids of my own," I said. "They both had their moments when they were younger."

Penelope flashed me a quick smile and nodded. "I was surprised you called, honestly. I think of Christine every day, yet I feared everyone else had forgotten her. She was such a good person. I miss her."

I started to speak when a waiter named Roman appeared to take our orders. He was young and good-looking. From the way he smiled, and the confident tone he used to address us, he knew it too.

As soon as he was gone, I spoke. "I didn't know Christine while she was . . ." I paused, wondering what Penelope knew of the investigation, and what she'd merely speculated at. "While she was living in Grey Falls."

"She was truly a fantastic person." She glanced at me before looking down at the table. "She never would have hurt anyone, which makes me wonder how anyone could have ever thought to harm her. You said she had a son?"

"I believe so." I hated not knowing for sure. I mean, I felt Erik was honest with me, but as Duke said, you can't always take someone at their word. "It's complicated."

"Oh?" The hopeful look on Penelope's face gave me no choice but to tell her everything I knew.

I did the best I could to explain in the gentlest way possible. I told her about Erik first, how he was the one who told me about Christine's flight from town, how she changed her name, but still cared for Joe. I told her about Christine's illness, how she'd hoped to find her husband again, but failed. And I told her about my conversation with Ida Priestly, but I did keep mention of Harry Davis to a minimum.

During my monologue, Roman returned with our coffees. I didn't stop talking, and he briefly stopped to listen before wandering off to wait on another table. Once I finished speaking, Penelope and I both sipped our coffees quietly. There were tears in Penelope's eyes and I was afraid that if I said the wrong thing, she'd completely lose it.

It took a good five minutes before she was able to speak. "I never knew." It came out as a whisper. "She was my friend and she never said a thing to me about any of this."

"She was trying to protect those she loved," I said. "I don't know what happened, but I do know it was hard on her." I leaned forward. "Do you have any idea why she would run away like she did?"

Penelope shook her head. "Christine never even hinted that something was going on. She loved her family, her friends. None of this makes sense to me."

Speaking of her family . . . "Did she ever talk about her birth parents to you?" I asked.

"A little." A man strode in our direction, causing Penelope to tense. He didn't so much as glance at us as he turned and headed back to the bathrooms. Penelope's eyes never left him until he vanished through the men's-room door. "She never liked talking about that time in her life. It was hard, you know?"

I nodded. "Was it a good relationship?"

"I got the impression that it was. She never said anything bad about them to me, anyway. I know she wished they hadn't died. She told me once that she had so many questions to ask them, and that she hated the fact she'd never get a chance to do it, but I never really put it all together. They were murdered?"

"Yeah. And it's believed she saw who did it, but she was never able to ID them."

Penelope closed her eyes briefly. "That's terrible. She told me they'd passed, but never said how."

"What about Joe? Did Christine have a good relationship with her husband?"

A smile lit the corners of Penelope's mouth. "Joe and Christine were a perfect couple. I envied them for the longest time. She adored him and talked incessantly about how they were going to raise a family together." The smile slipped away. "They never did get that chance, did they?"

"She had Erik," I reminded her. "Joe might not have known about him, but Christine did tell her son about his father."

"It hurts my heart to know they didn't get to spend time together as a family," she said. "After everything the both of them went through, they should have been given that kindness."

I couldn't say I disagreed. "I take it there's no chance Christine would have stepped out on Joe, then?"

Penelope's eyes took on a heat that I didn't expect out of her. "Never! Christine was faithful, as was Joe. If you'd known the two of them, you wouldn't even consider it a possibility." She frowned. "Although . . ."

I waited her out. Roman started our way, but I covertly waved him off. I didn't want Penelope to lose her train of thought.

She sipped her coffee, the frown growing ever deeper. When she met my eyes again, there was a concern there that hadn't been there before.

"There was one man," she said. "Christine never spoke of him, and I don't believe she wanted anyone to know about him at all. I know I didn't ask; it wasn't my place."

"A man her age?"

Penelope started to shake her head, then nod, then ended up shrugging. "I can't say for sure. I only saw him a couple of times, and it was always from a distance. Christine would see him first and would excuse herself and hurry off to talk to him."

"What did he look like?" I asked.

"It was a long time ago," Penelope said with an apologetic tone. "He's just a blur in my mind. I'd guess he was of average height, average build. Nothing that stood out." She brightened. "When I did see him, he was always wearing a suit. It was a nice one." She pointed out the window. "Just like that."

I turned in my seat to look.

Across the street, wearing a suit that looked brand-new, was Chester Chudzinski.

I didn't know what to think as I drove home a little while later. Chester became Joe's PI *after* Christine had come up missing. Could he have known Christine *before* she vanished? Was that why he agreed to work for Joe?

And was Chester's involvement the reason why what truly happened to Christine never came to light?

I hated to think it, especially with Amelia working with the private investigator, but it was hard not to. I'd heard from more than one person that a man in a suit had been hanging around Christine, and Chester always wore a suit, though not always a nice one. He was involved in the case from the start. And he knew Joe was getting closer to finding out what had happened to his wife.

Could Chester Chudzinski have killed him for it?

I just couldn't see it, not with what I knew of the man.

But I couldn't dismiss the idea out of hand either.

Fortunately for Chester, I doubted he was the only man who ran around in a suit all the time. Detective Hastings could have worn one back when he was on the job, as many detectives did. Could Christine have been meeting with him? Had she gotten involved with something and was working with the detective to take down a criminal of some sort? If so, why wouldn't he have told me when I talked to him about her disappearance?

I supposed the case could have been—and still might be—sensitive, but he could have told me *something*. If nothing nefarious was going on between them, why would he cover it up?

The answer was obvious, though I didn't much care for it. I hated to think that anyone in law enforcement could be a bad person. It was their job to protect the innocent, not chase them out of town and then kill anyone who looked into their disappearance.

The last thought didn't sit well with me as I pulled up in front of my house. Maybe it wasn't Martin Castor I should be worried about, but rather Wayne Hastings. Of course, I knew nothing about Martin either. That was something I needed to remedy.

I went straight to my laptop and brought up the browser. I debated on how to go about it, and then chose just to type in his name to see if there were any hits. It didn't take long to find a Martin Castor who currently lived in Grey Falls. It was the website that surprised me.

I clicked the link and went to the staff listing. Sure enough, Martin Castor stared back at me with a wide smile.

He was old enough to have been around when Christine vanished, but he didn't appear to be old enough to have been her mysterious real father. He had to be close to retirement age, but from the look in his eye in his photo, I had a feeling he planned on working until he was in his eighties.

I clicked another link, still not quite sure I had the right man. I mean, the Martin Castor Detective Hastings described was a horrible, vicious person. I was having a hard time seeing a man in this Martin's career being a killer.

I skimmed the next page, unease growing. Below a brief bio that spoke glowingly of Martin's academic career was another photograph. This time he was holding a small plaque bearing his name.

"He's a doctor," I said out loud, causing both Wheels and Sheamus to look up at me. The cats had been playing pretty hard while I'd searched, and looked ready for a break.

I couldn't fathom how a doctor could be tied to a man like Harry Davis. Wayne *did* say that Martin hadn't been in much trouble lately, and I supposed his profession was the reason why.

But still . . . Could a *doctor* of all people have killed Joe Danvers? Like police officers, I thought of doctors as people who helped others, not hurt them.

It took me a good couple of minutes of staring, of trying to rationalize how a man like Martin could be involved with a murder, when I realized one important feature about all the photographs that stood out. Normally, it wouldn't have mattered, but after my conversation with Penelope, it was seared into my mind.

In every single photo, Martin Castor was wearing a suit.

20

Sheamus purred on my lap as I ran my hand down him. He'd gone through a rough couple of minutes, sneezing like he might never stop, but the fit seemed to have passed. Now, all he wanted was someone to love him.

"I'm trying," I said to him. So far, my attempts had been in vain, but I knew that there was someone out there for him. I just had to trust that they'd find me.

Trust. It was a hard thing to come by these days. I wasn't trusting my judgment, or my research when it came to prospective adopters. I wasn't sure I could trust Chester Chudzinski or retired detective Wayne Hastings. Could I trust that Erik Deavers was who he said he was?

The only thing I was sure of was that I couldn't trust Martin Castor or Harry Davis.

And don't even get me started on Courtney Shaw.

I leaned my head back as it started to spin. I missed the days when the most I had to worry about was how I was going to get an old Saint Bernard with bad hips packed into my van for transport.

Before I could drift off into a well-deserved nap, the phone rang. I considered ignoring it since Sheamus was comforting and warm, but decided it would be irresponsible of me. Despite everything that was happening, I still had a business to run.

I laid the Maine Coon carefully onto the couch, where he promptly curled back up for his nap, and then I headed for the phone, mentally threatening any telemarketer that might be on the other end of the line.

"Denton residence, Liz speaking."

"Hi, Liz, did I interrupt you?" It was Manny. "You sound distracted."

"No, I was about to take a nap. It's been a long day. What's up?"

There was a series of loud voices, mixed with even louder barks on the other end of the line. Manny must have pressed the phone to his chest, because the sound became muffled for a few moments before it finally faded.

"As you probably can hear, we have an emergency here at the office. It's looking like I might not make it home in time for dinner. I just wanted to let you know so you didn't wait up for me."

"Is it serious?" I asked. While any emergency is, well, an emergency, not all of them are life threatening.

"It might be." He sounded worried, which in turn made me worried. I might not know the animal in question, but any time someone's pet gets sick, it upsets me. "I might stay late to monitor them if everything goes well."

I noted the use of the word "them" and my concern grew tenfold, but I knew not to push Manny too hard with questions. He was already stressed enough.

"I'll put leftovers in the fridge if you are hungry when you get home," I said. "I might just get takeout anyway, so I'll be sure to pick you up something that's good warmed up."

"Thanks, Liz." His sigh was both weary and, to my ears, frightened. "I'll hopefully see you tonight."

"Good luck."

I hung up with my stomach churning. I don't care whether someone is a good person or not; their pets aren't guilty by association.

I gave everything I had to finding homes for seemingly unwanted pets. I'd even gone so far as to turn bad pet owners in to the authorities when they mistreated the animal who looked to them for love and protection. Every animal deserves a loving home. Every. Single. One.

And I was going to make sure every one of them did.

I was about to head to my laptop to get to work on finding Sheamus his furever home once and for all, when the door banged open and Ben came barreling in. I was about to ask him how his movie was when I noted the expression on his face.

"What happened?"

Ben threw himself into a dining room chair. "Katie dumped me."

"What? Why?"

He glanced up at me. "She didn't like your friends."

It took a moment for me to register what he'd said. "She what?"

"She badmouthed Evelyn, Holly, and Deidra after we left. I defended them. She didn't like it." He scrubbed at his face. "We didn't fight or anything. I told her that she needed to get to know them better, that they're pretty cool people. Katie didn't buy it. She said they were too old and stuffy for her."

I eased down across from him, torn between feeling sorry for him, and being thankful. Katie Sprig hadn't left me with a good impression, and hearing what she'd said didn't change my mind in the slightest; it merely confirmed my suspicions about her character. Ben deserved better.

And besides, Deidra and Holly weren't *that* old. Good grief, what did she think of *me*?

"So, after a while, she told me she was going to go back to her old boyfriend, some dude name Greg." He rolled his eyes as if there was something wrong with the name. "I guess I should be thankful she left me before we got married or something."

I couldn't suppress the shudder. *Was he actually thinking of marrying her?*

"I'm sure it's for the best," I said as diplomatically as I could manage.

"Yeah, I guess." He didn't look convinced.

It took a moment for me to realize why he was so upset. "The house," I said. "You were hoping to move in with her."

He nodded. "We put an offer down this morning before we left for the movie. It's why I'd come home, but when I saw the others here, I decided to wait to tell you later."

"You what?" My heart did a little hop.

"I know, I know. Looking back on it now, I guess we rushed things a bit, but I was so sure that this would work out." He frowned. "She was adamant I put everything in my name. I guess I know why now."

"What are you going to do?" I asked. I wished Manny was there to help. Like me, he might not know what to say to make things better, but at least he'd be there to show support.

"I'm not sure." Ben sat up straighter and managed a smile. "Maybe you're right and this is all for the best. You know, a blessing in disguise. I'll figure it out."

"You know your dad and I are here for you, right?"

Ben rolled his eyes. "I know." A sly, almost cocky smile spread across his face. "And hey, there's lots of women out there, right? Now that I've proven I can afford a place of my own, maybe they'll come rolling in."

It was my turn to give him a big eyeroll. "Or maybe you'll start to be a little pickier."

He laughed. "Stranger things have happened."

I was going to let him go about his business, when I remembered we had yet to talk about our nighttime visitor. "What happened with Jack last night?"

Ben's smile faded. "We talked. He's had it pretty rough lately, you know? He can't keep a job, which is why he was here, obviously." He actually blushed, as if Jack was somehow his responsibility. "I tried to talk some sense into him, but I'm not sure if it'll do much good. He doesn't have anyone in his life to help him out of his bad situation."

I wasn't surprised. Too many people turned their backs on those who need help. The same went for pets. It made me wonder why kindness was so hard to come by sometimes. "What are you going to do?" I asked.

"I'm not sure." Ben raked his fingers through his hair. "I asked him where he was staying, thinking that I might stop by every now and again to see how he's doing, but he said he doesn't have a place to stay. Not a house, anyway."

"He's homeless?" I asked, my stomach dropping. I knew Jack was bad off, but didn't realize it was so bad.

"Yeah. He's living out of a tent. I guess there's a camp in town where others in similar situations go to sleep and hang out."

It was like a slap to the side of the head. "Is this tent camp on Ash Road?"

Ben nodded. "That's the one. Why? Do you know it?"

I didn't answer him right away. When I'd delivered Sheamus, I'd seen the camp. It was within viewable distance from Joe Danvers's home, but I hadn't put together exactly what it was. I'd mostly forgotten about it, in fact.

"Jack might have seen something," I said. *Or did something*, I added silently. There *had* been evidence of a break-in at Joe's place. Could Jack be involved in this somehow?

"Mom?" Ben looked concerned. "What are you talking about?"

"The murder. It took place right across the street from this camp. I need to talk to Jack." I stood. "He might have seen who killed Joe."

Ben rose with me. "I'm coming with you."

I started to tell him to stay home, but realized it might be a good idea to have Ben with me. Not only would he serve as protection in case someone there did have something to do with the murder, but Jack was also his friend. If anyone could get something out of him, it was Ben.

"All right," I said. "But you're driving."

Ben grinned. "I wouldn't have it any other way."

The camp was mostly empty when we arrived. Tents were still pitched, but many of them were empty. A stray shoe lay a dozen yards from the road, but otherwise the area was clean of debris. Not a discarded plastic bottle or pop can was in sight.

Wary eyes watched us from the few occupied tents as Ben and I made our way into the camp on foot. A fire that had burned down to embers sat off to the side. It was tended by a pair of girls I swore had to be sixteen or under. They watched us with eyes so solemn, it broke my heart.

"Jack said his tent is the red one at the far edge of camp." Ben pointed to the tent in question.

On the drive over, I'd taken a few minutes to look into the campsite. It was owned by a wealthy farmer, C. J. Adams, who'd all but retired. Instead of selling off his fields, however, he'd loaned the space to the homeless of Grey Falls. We didn't have nearly as many homeless in town as a bigger city might, but a quick count of the tents told me we had more than enough.

The flaps to Jack's tent were closed. I allowed Ben to take the lead as we neared. The tent looked old and well-used. I didn't know if it was because Jack had been living out of it for a long time, or if he'd nicked it from someone's trash. Either way, it was an upsetting sight. I'd known him when he was just a kid, had spent hours with him at my house. It was hard to believe someone I knew was having such a hard time of it now.

Ben approached the flaps, and since he couldn't knock to see if Jack was in, he merely called his friend's name in a hushed voice.

The tent opened and a bedraggled Jack Castle crawled out. He looked a little better than when I'd last seen him, but that wasn't saying much. He looked at us with red-rimmed eyes that didn't seem to want to focus. It took a moment for recognition to kick in.

"Ben?" He looked to me, confusion growing. "Liz? What are you doing here?"

Ben glanced back at me. I nodded at him to go on. Along with looking into the camp, I'd briefed him on the way over on what I wanted to know. I figured the less I said, the easier it might be to convince Jack to talk.

"I have a few questions for you, Jack," Ben said. "Do you think you can do a little remembering for me?"

"Yeah, sure." He grinned, exposing teeth in serious need of a dentist. "What do you need?"

Ben patted him on the shoulder and then guided him a few steps away from his tent. From there, he had a clear view of Joe's driveway. Ben pointed. "You see that drive over there?"

Jack squinted, but nodded. "Sure do."

"Couple days back, a guy was killed in the house at the end of the drive. Do you remember that happening?"

Jack's face turned solemn as he nodded again.

"Police showed up. Started asking everyone questions about it."

"Did they talk to you?" Ben asked.

"Nah." Jack grinned. "I saw them coming and decided to take a walk. I wasn't interested in talking to the cops."

"No one came back to talk to you afterward?" Ben asked.

"Some big detective guy showed up a few times, but I made sure to make myself scarce each time. I didn't need no one browbeating me, you know? It wasn't like I did anything." He glanced away at that.

"Jack," Ben said, obviously catching the gesture. "What aren't you telling me?"

Jack shrugged, wouldn't meet anyone's eye. "I've been to the house before. Thought, at first, that was what the cops wanted."

"You broke in?" Ben asked.

Jack stared at his feet. It was answer enough.

Ben glanced at me, so I took over.

"You aren't in trouble for breaking in," I said. "But if you know anything about what happened to Joe, we need to know."

Jack's face screwed up as if it was hard for him to think. It probably was. "Joe?"

"The man who lived at the end of the driveway," Ben said.

"Oh. I never knew his name."

"How long ago did you break in?" Ben asked. "Did you see anything while you were there? Take something?"

Jack scuffed his shoe in a patch of dirt. "I don't want to talk about it. Mr. Adams won't let me stay if he finds out." He finally looked up with pleading eyes. "Please, don't tell him. I have nowhere else to go. I promise I'll stop."

"It's all right, Jack," Ben said. "We won't tell." He looked at me.

"No, we won't."

"I didn't take anything of value. The guy came home and I ran. All I did was get inside and start to look around. Decided against going back after that. Didn't know if he had an alarm system or anything."

I supposed that explained why the break-in hadn't been reported. If nothing was missing, and if Jack had closed the door on his way out, there was a chance Joe hadn't even realized someone had been in his house.

"Look, I was desperate," Jack went on. "Liz. Ben. I'm sorry I broke in to your place. It was a mistake, one I wish I could take back."

"It's all right, Jack," Ben said. "We understand."

Jack wiped a hand across his eyes. He looked as miserable as he sounded. I truly believed he was sorry for his actions.

"Forget about the break-in, and think about the other night instead. Did you see anything strange that day?" Ben asked, shifting the questions back to the murder itself. "Like, before the police showed up."

"No." Jack started to shake his head, but stopped. "Wait."

I took an involuntary step toward him. "Did you see something?" I asked.

"I'm not sure." Jack jammed his fists into his eyes as if he could knock the memory free by sheer force. "I didn't see no people, if that's what you're asking."

"All right," Ben said. "If not a person, then what did you see?"

"A car." Jack pointed toward the road. There was no car there now, but I knew what he meant. "Drove by real slow-like."

My mind immediately shot to Erik and his fear of meeting his dad. Could that have been what Jack had seen? "What did the car look like?" I asked.

"Fancy." Jack crossed his arms. "A rich-guy vehicle. Think it was one of those Mercedes or something."

"Are you sure?" I asked. Erik most definitely didn't drive anything close to a Mercedes.

"Positive," Jack said. "It was black, and since it was at night, it was hard to see details. But I'm positive it was a nice, fancy car that drove by. Never see cars like that around here. It's why I remembered it."

Ben and I shared a look. Pieces were slowly falling into place, but were they the right pieces? There were tons of fancy cars out there, and I was afraid that too many details were coming from unreliable sources. Would the police accept anything Jack had to say? Or would they dismiss it out of hand, just because of his current living situation?

"All right, thanks, Jack," Ben said. "You've been a big help."

Jack smiled, though it was sad. "It's good to be useful for something every now and again. It doesn't happen much these days."

Ben glanced at me to see if I had more questions, but I shook my head.

"Stay warm, all right? I'll see you soon." Ben patted Jack on the shoulder and then started to walk away, but I lingered. After a brief, internal struggle, I fished out a twenty and handed it to Jack.

"Get something hot to eat," I told him.

A genuine tear formed in his eye as he took the money. He nodded once, and was clearly too overcome to speak.

I left him then, hoping that the money ended up in the hands of a waitress somewhere, not at the nearest bar. I was still mad at Jack for breaking in to my house, but I wasn't heartless. He needed help, and if nothing else, I could make sure he didn't starve.

Ben was standing outside the van. He gave me an approving smile, mouthed "thank you," and then, together, we climbed in and headed for home.

21

"Good morning," I said as I filled the dishes on the floor. "Sleep well?"

Both Wheels and Sheamus looked up at me like I was crazy before they both dug in.

"Guess so."

I threw together a quick breakfast and ate it alone. Ben and Amelia were up at first light, which was becoming a trend with both of them these days. I'd hoped to talk to Ben a bit more about what he was going to do about the house—and quite possibly, Jack—but it could wait until he wasn't so busy.

Manny had come in after I'd gone to bed and didn't say a word. I vaguely remember waking up briefly when he'd lain down, but I'd drifted off almost immediately afterward. He was still out, sprawled across the bed like he'd desperately needed sleep, and while I was curious to know how his pet emergency had gone, like Ben's house, it was something that could wait.

The clink of the spoon in my bowl of cereal sounded loud in the nearly quiet house. The only other sounds were coming from the kitchen, where the cats were eating, side by side. Sheamus sniffled as he ate, but his sneezing had calmed down considerably from when I'd first picked him up. It would never go away completely, but that was all right. In some ways, his little sneezes were cute.

I finished eating and deposited my bowl into the sink about the same time the cats finished up their meals. Sheamus sauntered from the room as soon as he was done and plopped down on the couch to wash his face. Wheels made her way over to me and wound around my feet the best she could with her wheels catching my ankles every few seconds.

"Give Daddy lots of love when he gets up," I told her, kneeling so I could run a hand down her back. I checked to make sure her harness wasn't rubbing her skin raw, and then checked her wheels. Everything was fine, as it always was. "I'm going to be gone when he gets up, so I need you to take care of him, okay?"

Wheels purred and rammed her head into my shin. I took that for a yes.

I scribbled Manny a note to let him know where I was going, grabbed my keys and purse, and then was out the door.

The day was overcast, but it didn't feel like it was going to rain. Joanne was sitting on her front steps, watching the neighborhood with a mug of coffee in hand. She started to rise when she saw me, but changed her mind and sat back down. I hoped that meant she didn't have anything to complain about, which would be a change. I raised a hand to her, and she returned the gesture slowly, as if uncertain of my intent.

"Just being neighborly," I said under my breath as I climbed into my van.

I was going to make the best of the day, no matter what. Between the murder, Courtney, Chico, Jack, and finding Sheamus a new home, I'd been near tearing my hair out. I was done overstressing. Courtney and Chico had been dealt with. Jack was, well, Jack. Sheamus would find his furever home soon enough—and it's not like I was anxious to be rid of him, anyway.

And the murder? Admittedly, the investigation wasn't going as smoothly as it could be, but it wasn't like I was a detective or anything. I was merely doing my part as a concerned citizen—and a mom.

I found myself whistling as I drove. There were a few concerns I wanted to alleviate, and then I could go on with the rest of my day. If I could manage to ease my mind about Chester's role in Joe's death, then I thought I could focus solely on Sheamus's well-being, and maybe have a nice, quiet day at home with my husband for once—if I could talk him into taking the day off from work, that was. I think we both needed a little quiet relaxation.

I parked two spaces down from Chester's office, right behind Amelia's car. She'd been putting in a lot of time at work and I was beginning to wonder if she'd ever finish college, or if she planned on transitioning straight to private investigator once she learned the ropes and got her license. I assumed Chester was paying her for her work, but I'd never outright asked her. I wasn't entirely sure it was my place *to* ask.

Amelia was sitting at one of the desks just inside the office. She didn't so much as glance up from her laptop as I entered. She was staring at the screen with an intensity that would melt steel. Her earbuds were in, music turned up so I could hear it by the door, which was why she hadn't heard me enter.

I slipped quietly by her since what I wanted to ask Chester was between the two of us. I didn't want to upset Amelia, not when it could be prevented with a private one-on-one.

I knocked gently on Chester's closed office door.

"Come on in, Amelia," he said. "Did you find anything?"

I opened the door just enough to slip in, keeping an eye on Amelia to make sure she didn't see me, and then closed the door behind me once I was safely inside.

"Oh, Mrs. Denton." Chester rose from his desk. I noted he was wearing a suit that looked an awful lot like the same suit he'd worn the last time I'd seen him. As I'd noted when Penelope had pointed him out, it looked new. "I wasn't expecting you today."

"Call me Liz," I said absently, though at this point, I doubted it would do any good. Some habits did die hard.

"Liz, right." He smiled and then motioned to a chair. "What can I do for you today?"

I sat with deliberate slowness so I could gather my thoughts before speaking. What would I do if my concerns proved justified? There was no way Amelia would listen to me if I warned her off working with Chester. Her stubbornness would get in the way; it was a trait she'd gotten from me.

"I talked to Penelope Pringle," I said. "Christine's friend."

He folded his hands on his desk. "Did she have anything enlightening to say?"

"I'm not sure." There was no good way to go about asking him, so I just said it. "She, like a few others I've talked to, mentioned seeing someone wearing a suit talking to Christine before her disappearance. Ida Priestly also mentioned a man coming to see her, both after Christine vanished and then again recently." Though Ida had described her man as being rough around the edges, not a man wearing a suit. "Penelope pointed you out, saying your suit was similar to what she remembered."

The only reaction I got out of Chester was a slight widening of his eyes. "I see."

I fidgeted, uncomfortable by his stare, though I think it was mostly because of the twinge of guilt I felt for even thinking he could have had anything to do with Christine's disappearance or Joe's death.

Chester seemed to note my discomfort, because he visibly eased as he sat back with a smile. "I understand your concern," he said. "And while I approached all the women you mentioned in the course of my investigation, I only did so in the name of finding the truth."

"You didn't know Christine before she vanished?" I asked.

"No, I did not." He kept his smile in place, but I noted a flash of pain in his eyes. "I never did get the chance to meet her. Joe came to me once he realized she was gone. It was the first time I'd met him as well. I've spent so much time on the case, I do feel like I've known the both of them forever, but no, I had no contact with either of them before Christine left town."

I was taking him at his word, but boy, hearing him say it made me feel a whole lot better. "Do you have any idea who this man in a suit might be?" I asked, my mind going straight to Martin Castor, but I wanted to hear Chester say it.

"I wish I did." His smile slid from his face. "You said someone told you Christine was talking to this suited man before she vanished? No one ever said anything to me."

"I don't think anyone thought it important back then," I said. "From the sounds of it, Joe and Christine had a good relationship, so it wasn't like anyone believed she'd cheat on him." And yeah, I was pretty sure I'd tell the cops if someone I knew and loved vanished and had been sneaking around with some strange guy beforehand, but not everyone thought like me.

Chester frowned and drummed his fingers on his desktop. "What do you know about this guy? Did anyone give you a description?"

"Not really," I said. "No one got a good look at his face. The only thing that keeps coming up is how he was always in a suit." And then, because it kept playing over and over in my mind, I said, "Martin Castor wears a suit."

Chester's face clouded over. "I'm aware of that."

"Do you think he could be the man we're looking for? I was told he is one of Harry Davis's friends, so it would make sense if they were working together."

"It's possible," Chester said before leaning forward. "But, please, stay clear of Martin Castor. I was never able to prove he had anything to do with Christine's disappearance, but that doesn't mean he didn't participate in it. He . . ." He shook his head and sat back, unable—or unwilling—to say whatever had popped into his head.

I had no intention of putting myself in any further danger, though if it came down to it, I might end up having to have a little chat with Martin, especially if Harry kept coming around harassing my daughter.

"Did you ever find out if Erik Deavers is who he says he is?" I asked, deciding to alleviate one more of my fears while I was at it.

Before Chester could answer, there was a knock at the door and an awfully familiar voice called out.

"Mr. Chudzinski? It's Erik."

Chester's face brightened. "Let's ask him ourselves, shall we?"

I opened my mouth to beg him to wait, but it was already too late.

"Come on in," Chester called.

The door opened and Erik entered, a worried expression on his face. When he saw me, his entire demeanor changed. He reached out and gripped my hands in his own.

"Thank you so much for coming when I called yesterday," he said. "I contacted the police after you left and they eased my mind considerably."

"Please," Chester said. "Take a seat."

Erik released my hands and eased down into the chair next to me.

"Erik came to see me after the cops paid him a visit at his hotel room," Chester explained. "We went over details, for verification purposes only." He gave me a telling look. "Erik was able to provide sufficient evidence that he is, indeed, Christine's son."

"That's good to hear," I said, glancing at Erik to see if he was offended. He merely smiled at me. I hated to ask, but I needed to know. "Do you know for certain if Joe was your father?"

Erik shrugged. "I wish I could say yes, but all I have is Mom's word. I have no reason to doubt her."

"Neither do I," Chester said. "And I'm sure Erik

would be willing to take a DNA test if it comes to that."

"Whatever I can do to help."

"Did the police find any evidence of who broke in to your hotel room?" I asked.

"No," Erik said. "But I think they have a few leads. At least, that's the impression they left me with. Mr. Chudzinski is helping me with a few details."

I realized that meant I was delaying their meeting. I rose. "I'm glad to hear everything is working out," I said. "I'd better go."

"If you hear anything else . . ." Chester said.

"I'll call you right away."

"It was good to see you, Liz," Erik said. "If you get a chance in the next couple of days, there's something else I'd like to talk to you about. It's not important now, but I'd like to discuss it before I leave for home."

"Of course," I said, before slipping out the door and letting them get down to business.

Amelia was leaning against her desk, arms crossed, eyebrows raised, as I closed Chester's office door.

"I wasn't going behind your back on anything," I said before she could speak. "I didn't want to disturb your work."

"Uh-huh."

I didn't want to fight, so I motioned to her laptop. "Did you find anything?"

Some of the tension eased from her shoulders. "Not a lot. I've been trying to find a connection to Harry Davis and the Danvers family, but so far, I've come up blank. Same goes for a man named Martin Castor. Heard of him?"

"Yeah. I didn't know you knew about him."

"Chester told me to see what I could dig up." Amelia patted her laptop. "I have this feeling that one of those two men killed Joe Danvers, but I can't figure out which, or why. I've been working here online, rather than doing face-to-face meetings."

Noting the concern in her voice, I asked, "Is that what Maya's doing?"

Amelia glanced toward the door, as if she hoped to see Maya walk in at that very moment. "Yeah. She's talking to a few people, but Chester warned us off of confronting either Harry or Martin directly." She made it sound like her boss was hamstringing the investigation. "Has your police detective friend learned anything new?"

"Detective Cavanaugh isn't my friend," I said. "And, honestly, I haven't spoken to him much about it. He wasn't in the last time I was at the station."

Amelia frowned. "I was hoping he found a print or something that might help."

"Not that I'm aware of." Though, I figured I should pay Cavanaugh a visit before long to see what, if anything, he'd discovered. While none of this was really any of my business, I *had* found Joe's body. Cavanaugh didn't owe me anything, but I could always play the angle of a distressed witness to get a little something out of him.

"I should get back to work." Amelia rounded her desk and sat in her chair with a weary sigh. "I didn't bring enough coffee for this."

I wished her good luck and then made my way to my van. As much as I wanted to get back to Manny to see how he was doing, thoughts of Detective Cavanaugh had me setting my sights on the police station instead. It wasn't too far away, so it wouldn't take me long to make a quick stop and see where the investigation stood. I could always check in with Manny afterward.

Fate, of course, had a different plan for me.

My phone rang just as I started the engine. I answered without glancing at the screen.

That was a mistake.

"You!" Courtney's shrill voice had me jerking the phone from my ear. "I can't believe you'd do this to me!"

I gave it a moment to make sure she was done before I replied. "What am I supposed to have done this time?" I asked.

"You know. Meet me at my place. Now." She hung up without waiting for me to respond.

"Great." I dropped my phone into the cupholder like it was responsible for the call. It would be so easy to just ignore Courtney's wishes and go about my day like she'd never called.

But did I really want to deal with the consequences of ignoring her?

With a weary sigh that mirrored Amelia's own, I put the van into gear, and headed for what was sure to be a headache-inducing meeting with Courtney Shaw.

22

The moment I shut off the engine next to Courtney's pink van, she came storming out the front door of her house. She was dressed as if she was going on a date, with a tight skirt and thin blouse, complete with high heels, yet the expression on her face was anything but date friendly. I debated on simply leaving and avoiding the whole mess, but decided it best if I faced it now so she didn't end up showing up at my front door later.

I got out of my van and waited for her to reach me.

"How could you do this to me?" she shouted. Her voice was so high-pitched, it caused me to wince.

"I didn't do anything to you, Courtney. This is all on you."

"I'm not the one who told Duke to stop helping We Luv Pets! *You* poached him! I know it!" She stomped one high-heeled foot. "Just because your family can't handle their own business, doesn't mean you need to interfere in mine."

I took two calming breaths before I spoke so I didn't end up yelling. "Duke made up his own mind. Maybe you should have thought about the consequences of your actions before you went and dropped off someone else's dog at my place."

Her mouth slammed shut so hard, I was afraid she might break a tooth.

"Look, Courtney, I don't have a problem with you." Mostly. "I'm perfectly content to let each of us run our rescues how we see fit." I held up a finger when she opened her mouth to speak. "*But* . . ." I eyed her, made sure she was listening, before going on. "I will not tolerate you trying to sabotage me. Duke left you because of how you were acting. It had nothing to do with me. It's all on you."

A flurry of emotions washed over Courtney's face as I spoke. Anger. Guilt. Embarrassment. Something akin to pity had me softening my tone.

"I'm sorry about Duke, I really am. He stood by you for a long time, but you finally pushed him too far. Maybe if you find a way to work with me, rather than against me, perhaps he'll come back. Just don't try to lay this at my feet."

Courtney swayed where she stood, as if rocked by my little speech. I hoped that some of my words finally hit home and she'd extend a truce, and that, somehow, despite everything, we'd find a way to co-exist.

My hopes were, of course, in vain.

Disgust splashed across Courtney's face. "I can't believe you'd try to blame this on me," she said. "I can't believe you don't realize what you've done."

"What *I've* done?"

"Call Duke. Tell him to come back to me, where he belongs."

"I'm not going to do that, Courtney."

Her eyes flashed in anger. "You'd better." Another foot stomp. "I won't take this lying down, Liz Denton. I will take everything from you." Her grin was practically a sneer. "Even Manny, if that's what it takes."

Before I could sputter out another word, Courtney spun on her heel and marched back to her house. At the door, she shot me a withering look, before she stormed inside. Her entire house rattled when she slammed the door closed.

"Why did you bother calling me out here if you're just going to walk away?" I shouted after her, but if I expected a response, I didn't get it.

I knew I shouldn't have been surprised by how the conversation had gone, but I was. I expected accusations, sure. I expected some anger too. But to flat out ignore her own role in what happened?

Then again, this *was* Courtney I was dealing with. I'm not sure she's ever taken responsibility for anything in her life.

Since there was nothing else I could do, I climbed back into my van. Maybe after a few days, she'd see reason. There was no reason we couldn't find middle ground.

Putting Courtney out of my mind, I backed out of her driveway and focused on bigger troubles.

Thankfully, the Grey Falls police station was much quieter this time around. There were no women protesting outside, no hint that anyone of any importance might be locked away. I did wonder how that had panned out, but decided that I didn't really care. I parked, got out of my van, and then headed for the station.

When I reached the doors, I did note a Travis McCoy sticker had been stuck to the door and a glossy substance wiped over it. Someone had tried to pick it off, but whatever the glossy stuff was, it prevented easy removal, so only the tiniest corner was missing.

With an amused shake of my head, I entered the police station. Cops were lounging around, some working, others merely gabbing. A few heads rose when I entered, and then lowered again when they realized I wasn't anyone important.

I started for the desk where Officer Mohr was seated, looking miserable, when I heard a voice from down the hall.

"I know." Detective Cavanaugh sounded flustered. "I'm doing everything I can."

There was no response I could hear, so I assumed he was on the phone.

"I get that. I understand. I will." It was followed by a growl that told me he must have hung up.

A few moments later, Detective Cavanaugh himself strode down the hall, into the reception area. He paused when he saw me, then veered over to where I stood.

"Mrs. Denton," he said. "Is there something I can help you with?"

"Is everything okay, Detective?" Cavanaugh was looking pale, and his eyes had dark circles beneath them. From the tone of his voice, I knew for a fact that things were indeed *not* okay.

"It's fine," he said with a sigh. "I'm fine. It's just . . ."

He glanced back to where a few other cops were pretending like they weren't listening in, before he gently took me by the arm and led me to the door. "Meetings."

"Meetings?"

"Every day, almost every damn hour. I can't get anything done."

"What about the investigation into Joe Danvers's murder?"

"I'm doing what I can, but Mr. Wright has claimed most of my attention for the last couple of days."

"*Mr.* Wright?" I asked. "As in Sterling Wright?"

"The one and the same."

"Isn't he a civilian?"

"He is," Cavanaugh said. I noted there was some resentment in his voice. "But he's an important member of our community. He's on the city council. Hell, he *runs* the council. If he decides he wants to involve himself in something, no one is going to stop him."

Something clicked in my head then. "He was at Joe's house, wasn't he?"

Cavanaugh nodded. "He's taken an interest in the case. Says it hurts the image of Grey Falls that this hasn't been wrapped up as of yet. Apparently, he was around when Christine first vanished and is using that to put pressure on us to get things done faster."

"Doesn't he realize how forcing you into meetings is impeding your investigation?" I asked, more annoyed than anything. If Cavanagh wasn't working the case, then who was? Me? Chester Chudzinski? Even if we found something, there wasn't much we could do about it without police support.

"He does." Cavanaugh ran his fingers through his

short-cropped hair. "But city business comes first, apparently. Once I finish with the meetings, I do what I can, but by then, everyone is either asleep, or too far into their drinks to be of any use to me."

I considered adding a visit to Sterling Wright to my list of things to do, but decided against it. I got why he was angry. Wright had been on the council forever—likely was back when Christine first vanished—and now that Joe was dead, the failure to find her, or prove Joe's innocence, had to make the police look bad, which, in turn, made the town look bad.

But why did that matter to him so much?

Higher aspirations. If he involved himself in the case and Joe's murder could be solved, it would make him look good.

"I've got a meeting to attend," Cavanaugh said, cutting into my thoughts. "If you're here to see me, you'd better spit it out now, or else you'll have to wait."

It took me a moment to align my thoughts. "It's about Joe Danvers's murder."

Cavanaugh groaned, but didn't look surprised. "All right. Out with it."

"I ran into someone who might have seen something the night of the murder." I told him what Jack told me about the car he'd seen, without actually using Jack's name. I didn't want him to get into trouble for avoiding the police.

"He didn't get a look at the driver?" Cavanaugh asked, scribbling notes into the notepad he always kept with him.

"He didn't," I said. "But it has to mean something,

doesn't it? A strange car that obviously doesn't belong rolls by right around the time Joe dies. I doubt it's a coincidence."

"It could be," Cavanaugh said. "But I'll look into it." He glanced at his watch. "Later, I suppose. Is there anything else I can do for you?"

I considered telling him about my suspicions about Martin Castor, but decided it could wait. At this point, Cavanaugh looked impatient to go and I didn't want to distract him any more than he already was.

"No, that's it."

Cavanaugh left with a warning to watch my head. I almost followed him out the door, but saw Officer Perry watching me. I waved to him, and then motioned him over. He rose from his seat with a wince I'm not sure anyone else saw, and then he joined me by the doors.

"Mrs. Denton."

"Liz, remember," I said. I was going to have to start wearing a nametag that said CALL ME LIZ so I could stop having to remind everyone.

He smiled. "I do, Liz. How's your son, Ben?"

"Good." Or so I hoped. "I have a quick question for you."

"I aim to serve." He dipped his head in something of a mock bow.

"You mentioned Detective Wayne Hastings the last time we talked."

"I remember."

"You said he didn't listen to you when you raised concerns about Harry Davis's eyewitness account." I paused, uncertain how to phrase my next question without making it sound like an accusation. The two men were colleagues, and while Reg hadn't been happy with being ignored, he had said he had fond memories of the retired detective.

"It's all right," he said. "I won't get offended by whatever you have to say."

I sincerely hoped not. "Do you think it's possible Detective Hastings knew what happened to Christine Danvers?"

Reg's expression darkened. "You believe he covered it up?"

"I'm not sure," I said. "He was the detective in charge, so he likely had more knowledge of the case than anyone. Yet, he believed Harry, even knowing that Harry was prejudiced against Joe and Christine from the start."

"So, you think he was covering for Harry?"

"Or Martin Castor."

Reg shook his head. "I don't believe it. Wayne made mistakes; we all do. But I never once believed him dirty. He did the job, and in most cases, did it well. He would never help a man like Harry Davis get away with a crime. He wouldn't have it in him."

"That's good to know," I said, feeling somewhat better. I didn't want to think the police could have had anything to do with Christine's disappearance, because once you lost faith in those that were supposed to protect you, it was hard to get that faith back.

"I saw you talking to Detective Cavanaugh," Reg said. "Was it about the investigation?"

"It was, but he seems pretty busy."

"He has been." Reg looked worried by the fact. "Too much is getting heaped onto his shoulders and it's starting to show. I remember when Detective Hastings dealt with much the same thing. Nearly caused him to retire on the spot."

I didn't want to see Detective Cavanaugh retire. He and I didn't always see eye to eye, but he was a good man. And as far as I could tell, he was good at his job—when he was allowed to do it.

"I don't get why Mr. Wright is so involved," I said. "He's only getting in the way."

"That's politicians for you," Reg said. "Just you wait and see, by Christmas, he'll be using this to put restrictions on us somehow."

"Or will use it to run for president."

"Perish the thought."

"Has the Travis McCoy situation been taken care of?" I asked, changing the subject to something a little less frustrating.

Reg grinned. "It has. Let's just say some money got passed around and quite suddenly, no one wanted to press charges anymore. If I didn't know better, I'd say the Mocks planned the whole thing from the start."

Why wasn't I surprised? It seemed like anytime a celebrity got into trouble, they threw money at it and it went away. I might not know the Mocks, but it would not shock me to learn that they *had* planned the entire dustup, just to milk Travis McCoy for a few thousand bucks.

"Well, you keep yourself safe, Liz Denton," Reg said. "I've got to get back to work."

"I think I should be the one telling *you* to be careful," I said. "You're the cop."

"Always do," he said with a wry chuckle. "But

you're the one risking her neck for a man she hardly knew."

And with that, he turned and headed back to work, leaving me to wonder if I was doing the right thing, or if I was putting myself at risk for no good reason.

23

"Hi, Mom."

I jerked to a stop, just inside the veterinary office doors. "Ben?"

He stood from where he sat behind the counter. "Last time I looked, yeah."

"I mean, what are you doing here?" I closed my eyes, already anticipating his answer. "No, don't say it. You're working."

"Last time I looked." He grinned at me.

"Where's Trinity?"

Ben shrugged, even as he got a dopey look on his face. He'd had a thing for the pretty veterinary assistant from the moment they'd met, though she'd never reciprocated his affections. I can't say I was too upset about that, considering how Courtney-like she could be.

"Okay, then, where's your father?"

Ben pointed to exam room 3. The door was, of course, closed. "He should be done soon."

I wandered over to the exam room door and peeked

inside. A woman who could be no more than four foot seven stood just inside, a miniature poodle in her arms. Manny handed her something, then, noting me, patted her on the arm, and together they left the room.

"Hi, Liz." He turned to the short woman. "I'll see you next week, Mrs. Tuttle." He bent down so he could look the poodle in the eye. "And you too, Mr. Fluffkins."

As soon as the woman and her dog were gone, I grinned. "Mr. Fluffkins?"

"I didn't name him," Manny said with a chuckle. "I'm not sure if that's the dog's actual name, or if it's a nickname that stuck. You know how that sort of thing happens."

I did. When I was a little girl, I had a cat named Marx, but everyone called him Whiskers because he had these long whiskers that looked two times too big for his body. The nickname suited him far better than his real name, and so, from then on, he'd become Whiskers.

"How's everything going?" I asked with a pointed look. Manny appeared to be in a good mood, which made me hope that everything had worked out last night, but I couldn't be sure since he was so good at hiding his emotions. "I was hoping you'd take the day off to decompress."

Manny leaned against the doorframe. I was happy to note his smile didn't slip. "The emergency turned out the best I could have hoped for. Everyone came out of it okay, though it was pretty sketchy for a little while."

I breathed a sigh of relief. "That's great." Manny wouldn't want to show it, but if something had happened during his emergency last night, he would have been torn up pretty badly. "And Ben?" I glanced back at our son, who was fiddling with his phone, much like Trinity would have been doing if she'd been there.

"I needed him today. Trinity never showed."

"She skipped out on work?" I was shocked. As far as I knew, she had yet to even call in sick in all her time working for Manny.

"Apparently so," Manny said, his face growing troubled. "I tried calling, but she didn't answer."

"I hope she's all right."

"I'm sure it's nothing," he said, but he didn't sound convinced. "Ben's been asking for more time, so it all works out." He crossed his arms and ankles. "So, what did I do to deserve your presence today, my angel?"

I playfully smacked him on the arm for calling me a pet name—which I normally hated—but couldn't stop the smile. "I thought I'd check in to see how you were doing. You seemed pretty upset on the phone last night. I'm glad it all worked out."

"That's all?" Manny pouted. "I thought you were here to whisk me away to my favorite restaurant and feed me grapes while I bask in a sunlit pool."

"Maybe tomorrow," I said as the door opened and a man with six leashed dogs walked through the door. "It looks like you're going to be too busy for pampering today."

Manny straightened and sighed. "I suppose I can wait. I fully expect those grapes by tomorrow."

As I left Manny and Ben to the army of dogs, a weight lifted from my shoulders. I hadn't realized how stressed I'd become over Manny's late-night emergency. I practically skipped to my van, all thoughts of Courtney and murder a distant memory.

That was, at least, until I started up the engine and debated where to go next.

Home was the obvious choice. I was struggling find-ing Sheamus a home on my own, but I could always take him to Pets on Main, the pet store I frequented. The owner, Jamison Crowley, wouldn't mind if I left the cat there to show off for adoption. I'd used him before, but preferred not to if I could help it. I hated putting a cat in a cage, even if it was for his own good.

No, Liz. You can do this.

But is the cat what's most important this very second?

I frowned as I realized that something else was tug-ging at the back of my mind, something I couldn't simply ignore and go on with my day.

I didn't have Martin Castor's personal number, but I *did* know where he worked.

It took only a quick search to find the number on-line. I dialed, heart hammering. This was the man who very well might have chased a pregnant Chris-tine Danvers from town, who might have murdered Joe Danvers because he was getting too close to the truth. And here I was, making a nuisance of myself.

It's not like Detective Cavanaugh is doing much at the moment.

While I couldn't blame him for his slow progress, it was still frustrating. A killer was out there, and the detective who was supposed to be finding him was likely sitting in an office somewhere, being lectured by a politician who cared more about his career than keeping the town safe.

"Doctor Castor's office, this is Uma. How may I be of assistance?"

"Hi, I'd like to speak to Doctor Castor."

"What is this regarding?"

I considered lying. I could say I had a personal problem that I couldn't bring myself to discuss with his nurse. Or I could say I was his girlfriend or wife, not that I knew if he had either.

But would that get me what I wanted? The moment he picked up the phone and realized I wasn't who I said I was, the conversation would be over.

"Tell him it's Liz Denton," I said, settling on honesty. "I'm calling to discuss private matters."

"Mrs. Denton, if you'd care to set up an appointment, I—"

"Just tell him that, please. I bet he'll want to talk to me."

Uma sighed audibly into the phone. "One moment." There was a click, and then soothing music played over the line.

A car pulled up next to me. A woman got out, carrying a fat tabby. She glanced into my van, and then startled back when she saw I was sitting in it. I gave her a finger wave, even as she scurried off.

There was a click in my ear. "What makes you think I'd want to talk to you?"

"Doctor Martin Castor?" I asked to be sure.

"I've heard about you," he said. "Don't think Harry and I haven't done our research. Anyone who works for that poor excuse of a private investigator will know retribution before this whole thing is over."

"Retribution for what?" I asked, anger simmering just under the surface. The guy had no idea what I wanted, yet he was already threatening me. It made me wonder if he was the reason Harry kept showing up.

"I see your watching eyes out there. You think you know something, but there's nothing there. If you haven't figured it out by now, we don't use the cops here when we have a problem. We take care of things on our own."

"I'm not sure what you're so worked up about," I

said, all while thinking that this sure didn't sound like an innocent man. "I was just calling to ask you about your car."

"My what?"

"Your car. If you want to meet, I'd happily do so. We could discuss it then."

"I'm not meeting with you," he snapped. Then his voice lowered to a near whisper. "I know who you are, who your family is. I know where they work, where you live."

"Is that a threat?" I asked. The anger was now a roaring inferno. *How dare he?*

"Take it as you like. I'm not telling you anything, and I'm sure as hell not going to contaminate the air I breathe by meeting with you. The people you associate with . . ." I could almost visualize his disgusted shudder. "You're all a plague."

I sat there, stunned. I thought I knew what he was talking about, and while my encounters with Harry Davis reminded me that these kinds of people still existed in this day and age, a part of me held out hope that Harry was an outlier, a relic.

Martin proved me wrong.

"Don't call me again." A click told me Martin had hung up on me.

It was probably good that he did. I doubted the next words out of my mouth would have been very ladylike.

If I questioned whether or not I thought Martin Castor capable of murder, I had my answer now. Just because he was a doctor, a man sworn to heal the sick, the infirm, didn't mean he was a good person. It made me wonder how many people who'd gone to him for help left in worse shape than when they'd gone in. He wouldn't be the first doctor to overprescribe drugs or misdiagnose someone.

And I wouldn't put it past him to do so on purpose.

Now, Liz, don't prejudge. I took a few calming breaths before I put my van in gear and started driving. Just because Martin was a jerk of the highest order, didn't mean he was bad at his job. It didn't mean he was a killer either, but it sure helped me believe he *could* be.

I pulled up out front of Chester's office for the second time in the span of a couple hours. When I went inside, I found Amelia waiting.

"Is Chester in?" I asked her.

"He's busy right now. New client." She rolled her eyes, as if the new client might not be entirely legit. The tittering laugh from behind the closest door told me that might be right. "Is there something I can do?" She sounded eager.

"I'm not sure." I debated on waiting for Chester to be done with his new client—or whatever she really was—because I wasn't so sure I wanted to involve Amelia in anything that involved Martin.

But then again, this was what she wanted to do, and she was already involved, whether I liked it or not. Besides, I'd vowed to support her in her work, and darn it, holding back on her wasn't supporting her.

"What more can you tell me about Doctor Martin Castor?" I asked her.

"Martin?" She rounded her desk, sat down, and typed briefly on her laptop. "There's not much. I found some complaints about him that were buried beneath glowing reviews. If these complaints are to be believed, Martin tends to treat only a certain portion of Grey Falls's population."

"Meaning?"

"Meaning straight white males. Young, pretty women.

If you're a woman over the age of forty, don't bother trying to get an appointment. Most of the complaints I found are from women who'd been dropped by him after they reached a certain age. Guy's a creep."

Why wasn't I surprised? "What about his car?"

Amelia raised an eyebrow at me.

"Jack—you remember Jack Castle, right?"

She nodded.

"He's had some . . . troubles recently." It was the nicest way I could put it. "He was near Joe's house when Joe was killed, and claims he saw a dark car, possibly a Mercedes, driving slowly down the road around the same time. All he knows for sure is it was a nice, fancy car, and that it looked out of place. I'm wondering if it could have been Martin."

Amelia focused on her laptop for a few minutes before she shook her head. "There's nothing here."

"Nothing?" I asked, surprised. I'd figured it would be easy enough for her to find out what Martin drove, especially since she was working as a PI. It was the sort of thing investigators did.

Her brow furrowed as she continued to type. After a few moments, she sat back. "Nothing at all."

"I take it that's not normal?"

"No, it's not. It might explain why I had trouble finding much else on him too. It's like someone scrubbed his online data as clean as they dared without making it too obvious it was happening."

"But his car? Why remove a record of that?"

She shrugged. "Could be he doesn't own one. Or he'd obtained it in some way that wouldn't pop up here. Or I'm just looking in the wrong spot." She blushed. "I'm still pretty new at this."

"I called Martin to ask him about it, but he wasn't in a talking mood."

"You *called* him?" Amelia sounded incredulous.

"It's better than not knowing," I said. "If he was the one who killed Joe, then maybe his car will be the evidence we need that will put him away."

"It's shaky," Amelia said, but her tone had turned thoughtful. "The police couldn't use the car to arrest him for Joe's murder."

"But it might give them probable cause to investigate him further." That was, if Detective Cavanaugh found time to look into him between meetings.

"One sec." Amelia popped up and hurried across the room. She knocked on Chester's office door, and then slid inside when he answered. She was gone for a good five minutes before she returned with a wide grin on her face.

"I'm not sure I like that look," I said.

She didn't say anything. She went to her desk, shut down her laptop, and grabbed her purse. She fished around until she found her keys and then held them up to me as if victorious.

I watched her, my stomach tightening. *What did I just do?*

"Let's go," she said, marching toward the door.

"Where are we going?" I asked. "What are we going to do?"

She glanced back over her shoulder. The excitement in her eyes was both infectious *and* terrifying.

"Don't worry, Mom. I have a plan."

24

"I don't know what to say."

Amelia grinned at me as she sorted through the various wigs and outfits in the trunk of her car. "I figured it would be a good idea to have a stock of this stuff, just in case. Maya has a trunk-load as well." She plucked out a blond wig, a pair of thin, stylish glasses, and a box of makeup.

"This is my fault, isn't it?" I asked as she continued to sort through the wigs. She found a black one and handed it to me.

"Put that on," she said. "You gave me the idea when Ben was in trouble. Once I started working with Chester regularly, I realized it would be prudent to have a few disguises in case I ever needed to confront an enraged husband or something. I wouldn't want them recognizing me on the street later, you know?"

It *was* a good idea, but I had a hard time believing that anyone would be fooled by a wig and a pair of glasses. Of course, these weren't like the cheap ones

I'd bought her before. The wig she'd handed me felt like real hair, and the glasses looked like glasses you'd get at an optometrist's office.

"How much did all of this cost?" I asked.

Amelia tied her purple-tipped hair up so that it didn't touch her neck, and then pulled on her blond wig. "Enough."

We used the bathroom in Chester's office building to put on our disguises. It took us nearly twenty minutes to get ready. Amelia helped me with my wig, and while I didn't get a pair of glasses, I did get a fake mole at the corner of my eye. She found herself a pretty cotton-candy-pink dress, while I ended up with a pantsuit over a size too small. The makeup took the longest to apply, and I let Amelia handle it. By the time she was done, neither of us looked like ourselves.

"I'm impressed," I said, checking myself out in the mirror. "I didn't think you knew how to put on makeup other than black eyeliner."

"Ha. Ha." Deadpan. Her lips were bubblegum pink. Made up as she was, Amelia kind of reminded me of Courtney, which was terrifying.

"So, what's the plan?" I asked. We were in Amelia's car, with her in the driver's seat. "I don't see how disguises are going to help us discover what kind of car Martin drives."

"The costumes are for our protection," Amelia said. "I have a plan, and figure we won't want Martin realizing who we are. I'm not too keen on a guy like that showing up on our doorstep."

I thought back to my phone conversation with him. "No, neither am I. But he knows who I am, knows your name. I don't see how this is going to help."

Amelia was still grinning. "He won't know it's us. Trust me."

I spent the rest of the ride looking at myself in the sun-visor mirror. I looked younger, despite the pantsuit, which was surprisingly thinning, despite how I'd had to cram myself into it. I most definitely didn't look like Amelia's mom anymore. While she'd gone for a manufactured beautiful, Amelia had turned me into an insurance adjuster.

I tugged at my clothes, wishing she'd had something in my size, but unfortunately, that wasn't to be. I guess I should be thankful she'd had the pantsuit at all. "I intentionally bought one two sizes too large," she'd said. "It's a lot easier to wear padding under that than one of these dresses, if ever I need to look bigger."

Not the most flattering of statements—especially since it felt like I might pop the stitching if I breathed too deeply—but hey, I never said I was a petite flower.

We pulled into the lot of Martin's private practice a few minutes later. The building was small and butted up against a nail salon on one side and a defunct Blockbuster on the other. The lot shared space with the local first-care building, and a small grocery aptly named Downtown Grocer.

My heart sank as I scanned the lot. "There has to be a hundred cars here." There was no way I'd be able to pick Martin's car out of the sea of vehicles. "Do you see a Mercedes?"

"No," Amelia said, getting out of her car. "But that doesn't matter."

"Doesn't matter? How are we—" I hurried to catch up to her. "Amelia, what are you doing?"

She was marching straight for the door to Martin's

practice. She paused outside it, whipped out a compact, and checked her makeup one last time. "You're a witness," she said. "Just verify everything I say, okay?"

"What? Wait!" It was too late; she'd already yanked open the door and was inside.

"Oh dear!" Amelia wailed, her voice an octave higher than normal. "Is the doctor in? Please, tell me I didn't hurt his car."

The nurse behind the window rose—Uma, I supposed. She looked to be in her early twenties, and was made up more like a stripper who was dressed as a nurse for her routine than someone who actually worked at a doctor's office. The top buttons of her blouse were hanging open, leaving very little to the imagination.

"Who are you?"

"Me?" Amelia asked, hand fluttering to her chest. "I'm Amy Tan. I was heading in to get my nails done, and was so worried about not chipping one while driving, I dinged another car. Someone told me it was the doctor's vehicle." She looked at me. "She saw it and I just had to have her here as a witness so he knows I didn't do it on purpose. I really, totally didn't mean it, I swear."

It was hard not to gape at her. Not only did she have a very Courtney-like look about her, she *sounded* like an over-the-top version of her.

The nurse seemed completely flummoxed by Amelia's outburst. She blinked through the window, a near vacant look in her eye. I know it's not nice to judge, but looking at her, I couldn't figure out how she'd made it through medical school, let alone landed a job at an actual doctor's office.

That's not true. I knew *exactly* how she'd gotten the job, and it was through no fault of her own.

"Get Doctor Castor," I said, changing my voice so it was rougher, and a smidge deeper. "He'll want to assess the damage."

Uma blinked a few more times before she scurried off into the back, presumably to get Martin.

"You didn't hit his car," I whispered, despite the fact we were alone in the waiting room.

"I know. But if he *thinks* I did, he'll want to see what kind of damage I've inflicted. I'll pretend I forgot where I parked, and have him take me to his car, which, of course, will be perfectly fine."

"He won't like you wasting his time."

She shrugged. "Who cares? I'll get a look at his car, and then apologize and grovel. He'll be annoyed, but it's not like he'll shoot me for *not* damaging his ride. And while I'm out there with him, maybe you can learn something about him here."

Uma returned then. "The doctor is with a f—err, patient. He'll be out in a moment."

"Thank you," I said.

"Oh, bless you." Amelia rushed forward and reached through the window to take Uma's hand. "You're a lifesaver."

Uma looked both pleased and kind of worried, as Amelia withdrew her hands and joined me by the door.

"Overplaying it a bit, aren't you?" I asked under my breath.

"Maybe a little." A ring of red was creeping up her neck. "It's not like I do this sort of thing often. Besides, she seems to be buying it."

Uma was watching us with a worried expression on her face. I didn't think she suspected anything, which was a plus, but the longer this played out, the more likely I found it to be that we'd be discovered as frauds.

It didn't take long for the door to open and an older man to stride out. He was wearing a nice suit and looked agitated. It took me a moment to realize I'd seen him before, just a few days ago.

"Mr. Wright?" His name popped out of my mouth before I could stop it. "Sterling Wright?"

Mr. Wright paused, halfway out the door, and glanced back at me. "Do I know you?"

"No, I just recognized your face. Are you one of Doctor Castor's patients?"

"That, my lady, is none of your business." He started to push his way out the door, but I stopped him.

"I know Detective Cavanaugh." And then, to add a personal touch, I added, "Emmitt."

"And?"

"He's mentioned he's been in a lot of meetings lately," I said. "He's working on a murder investigation and the meetings have been getting in the way of him doing his job. Weren't you supposed to be with him now?"

"I don't need to attend every meeting." Mr. Wright glanced at his watch. "They are a necessary evil, and I hope that in the coming days we can reach a point where we are all happy. I'm certain the detective is doing the best he can under the circumstances. Now, if you'll excuse me, I have somewhere to be."

Before I could say another word, he pushed out the door and walked away.

I wanted to follow after him and press him into going easy on Detective Cavanaugh, but by then Martin Castor had joined us, and he was steaming mad.

"Who are you?" he demanded. "And what's this about hitting my car?"

Amelia hitched in a breath, but did good by not showing fear. Martin was an intimidating man in person. He was in good shape and had a piercing stare that was almost a physical force. For an older man, he held himself like someone who would happily get into a fistfight if it would solve his problems.

"I'm sorry, Doctor," Amelia said, breathless. "It was an accident. I'm sure my insurance will pay for it if it really is your car."

"What car did you hit?"

"I, well . . ." She fumbled for a moment. "I didn't look to see what make or model or anything. I don't know that sort of stuff. Someone told me it was your car, though, and I just had to rush in and tell you what happened."

Martin closed his eyes briefly and rubbed at the lids. "Fine. Show me."

He didn't so much as pay me a second glance as he walked out the door with Amelia. As the door swung closed, I heard her say, "I sure wish I could remember where I parked."

I was left alone in the office with Nurse Uma, so instead of just standing around like a dope, I approached the window with a friendly smile. "Hi."

"Hello." She looked me up and down, and by the expression on her face, she didn't approve of what she saw.

"What's Doctor Castor like?" I asked. "I was thinking of changing doctors, and his name came up, so I figured I'd ask about him while I was here."

"He won't take you on," Uma said. She lifted a perfectly manicured hand and spread the top of her shirt open a little farther.

Was that a hint?

"Well, can you at least give me an idea of what he's like? Just in case." I winked.

Uma sighed. "He likes things his way." Another head-to-foot glance. "You aren't his type."

"His type?" My smile was faltering, but I somehow kept it in place. "I'm not trying to date him."

"Sorry, he's not going to be interested." And with that, she closed the window.

I bit back a retort, knowing it would do little good. If I needed any more evidence that Martin Castor was a sexist jerk, Uma was proof enough. I wondered if she hated her job, or if she liked the attention.

Then again, it didn't matter either way. It was Martin who made the decision to hire her. *And maybe she's a damn good nurse*, I thought as I returned to my spot by the door. Good-looking people could be just as qualified for their jobs as the rest of us. Martin's prejudices were causing me to make assumptions I wouldn't normally make.

The door banged open just as I reached it. Martin stormed inside and walked right into me, nearly knocking me off my feet. Without so much as an excuse me, he shoved me aside and stormed to the back.

"Jerk," I muttered. When Amelia didn't follow him in, I headed outside to find her. It took me a moment to realize she was sitting in the driver's seat of her car. When I climbed in next to her, I noted her hands were clutching the wheel, and they were shaking.

Amelia took a trembling breath, and then pulled off her wig. "His car is a white Lexus. He was . . . unhappy about being disturbed."

My motherly instincts were in full force seeing Amelia so shaken up. "Did he say something to you?"

"He might have said a few things I won't repeat to my mother." Amelia glanced at me out of the corner of her eye. "I'll be okay. He was pretty pissed, but he'll get over it."

I wanted to march right back into the office and give the doctor a piece of my mind, but I restrained myself. It wouldn't help anything. "What now?" I asked instead.

"Jack said it was a black car he saw that night?"

"Or dark colored; he wasn't sure. And while he said it was a Mercedes, he allowed that it could have been another fancy car."

"Like a Lexus?"

"Yeah, but Martin's is white."

"*This* car is white," Amelia said. "Do you think an arrogant, vain man like Martin Castor only has one vehicle?"

She put the car in gear, and we were moving. I didn't need to ask where we were headed. Amelia had a determined look on her face, one that told me she wouldn't drop this until she found something to pin Martin to the wall with. Whatever he'd said to her, it must have been pretty bad.

We were soon cruising through a residential district where only the rich could afford to live. Nearly every driveway was gated, every house a mansion. I saw more than one nice car that would have fit Jack's description parked in many of the driveways, which worried me. If there were that many nice cars in Grey Falls, how could we use a sighting of one to prove Martin's guilt?

You're not even sure he's guilty, a little voice in the back of my mind said. While I *wanted* both Harry

Davis and Martin Castor to get what was coming to them, I wasn't going to accuse them of murder without proof.

"I found his address while doing my research," Amelia said as we drove. "At least, the address on record."

"Do you think he's somehow hidden that too?"

She shrugged. "I don't know. As far as I know, he has more than one home."

Which made sense. A lot of rich folk had multiple places of residence, but most of the time, the second and third homes were on beaches or off on some mountain somewhere.

"There." Amelia slowed down and pointed. "That's his place."

"That's a big house."

Martin's home had to be the biggest house on the street. Like most of the other properties, the driveway was gated, but the fence was short and spikey, so you could see over it.

"There's got to be what? Twenty rooms in that place?" Amelia asked.

"At least." The front of the house was done in red brick that looked new. The windows were wide and clean. There had to be at least three floors, and that didn't count any basement levels. "Can a doctor who lives in Grey Falls afford something like this?" We didn't exactly live in a big city.

"He *is* pretty old," Amelia said. "He could have been saving up for years."

She slowed to a stop, just outside his driveway. There was a roundabout in front of the house, complete with a fountain at its center. There were no cars in the driveway.

"He has a garage," I said, pointing to the structure. "If he has another car, it'll be in there."

"He could fit five cars in there." Amelia leaned forward, as if she might be able to see through the doors. "We need to get a closer look."

"How?" I asked, noting a neighbor standing outside on his lawn, watching us with a hose in hand. "Someone will see us."

Amelia sped up again, and put Martin's house behind us. The neighbor went back to watering his flowers. "Not now," she said. "But tonight."

My heart did a little hop in my chest. "I'm not going to like this, am I?"

She shot me a look out of the corner of her eye. "Trust me, Mom, I have a plan. And this one is even better than the last."

25

Dinner held no taste as I mechanically chewed and swallowed. Manny and Ben were chatting at one another about their day at the clinic, while Amelia and I kept mostly to ourselves.

The hours following our visit with Martin Castor were torture for me. Amelia wouldn't tell me what she had planned, only that she wanted me there to help her. I supposed I should be glad she'd chosen me to go, and not Maya, because this way I could keep an eye out for her.

I only wished I knew what I was watching for.

"Liz? Are you all right?"

I found a smile buried beneath the worry and flashed it across the table at Manny. "I'm fine. Just tired. After everything that's happened lately, I guess my head is a bit floaty."

He didn't look convinced, but he dropped it. "Ben did a good job today. If Trinity decides to skip out on me some more, I think we have a suitable replacement."

"You could always schedule me alongside her," Ben said with a wink. "I won't mind."

"Uh-huh. I'd like you to keep your mind on your work, if it's all the same to you."

"Just as long as you don't need my eyes." He waggled his eyebrows.

"Pig," Amelia muttered, though I noted she was grinning.

Ben put a hand to his chest. "Hey, I'm not the one who wants to become a cop here."

"I'm working as a PI in training, *not* a cop."

"Maybe I'll have you run a background check on my next girlfriend," Ben said. "It'll help me avoid any nasty surprises."

"Yeah, no." Amelia finished her meal and shoved her plate aside. "You can make your own mistakes."

I glanced down at my mostly full plate. My appetite was sitting at zero, but I was trying to make a show of eating. I took a small bite and chewed it into oblivion.

"What about helping me?" I asked between bites. "I could use some help finding Sheamus a home without any more drama coming out of it. You know, background checks and the like?"

"That should be easy enough," Amelia said. "I'll just need to do a surface check, right? See if they have a history of animal abuse or anything like that?"

"Pretty much. You'll make sure they can handle a pet financially and emotionally, and make sure they don't have violent tendencies or anything."

"I can do that." Amelia's face grew worried briefly. "Just as long as it doesn't take away from my work with Chester."

"It won't," I said. "I promise."

"It appears as if our children are moving on with the rest of their lives," Manny said with a mock sigh. "Soon, we'll have an empty nest." He grinned. "Then we can move to a beach and live out *our* lives in luxury."

"You're not going to a beach without me," Ben said, rising. "So don't even try it." He began gathering the plates and silverware.

The next hour was dedicated to cleaning up. I was glad to note both Ben and Manny were yawning from their long day at the clinic. Whatever Amelia had planned, I didn't want either of them to know about it. Not only would they worry, I was pretty sure Manny would try to put a stop to it.

Once the kitchen was spotless, Manny headed for the living room, while Ben went upstairs to his room.

"Care for a movie?" Manny asked me as he stretched his feet out in front of him. "I'm sure I can find something we'll both enjoy."

My mind raced as I tried to come up with a way to beg off without hurting his feelings. If I claimed I was too tired, he'd expect me to go to bed. If I said I needed to clean up after the cats, he'd merely laugh and pitch in.

"She can't," Amelia said, stepping into the room. "I made her promise to come with me tonight. I'm meeting Chester and Maya for a little pow-pow about our investigation, and since Mom was the one who found Joe . . ." She shrugged.

"I see." Manny yawned. "I suppose it's for the best." He rose and cracked his back with a pop that reverberated throughout the house. "I could use a good night's sleep. Any idea when you'll be home?"

"It shouldn't be too late," I said. "But don't wait up for me. I'll tell you all about it in the morning."

Manny crossed the room and kissed me on the cheek. He did the same to Amelia. "Well, you two have fun."

"We'll try, but you know: murder." Amelia made a face.

As soon as Manny headed to bed, Amelia and I made for the door.

"I don't like lying to him," I said. "What if he finds out?"

"He won't." Amelia glanced back toward the house. The upstairs lights were on, but I had a feeling that wouldn't last long. Manny *had* looked exhausted. "And besides, sometimes you have to lie to protect those you love. Would you really want to know what I was up to if I were to sneak out late at night?"

"Yes. Yes, I would."

Amelia rolled her eyes as she got into her car. "Well, sometimes it's necessary."

"Are we going to need disguises?" I asked. "What are we doing, Amelia?"

She didn't answer until we were well down the road. My heart was in my throat and my stomach was somewhere down around my feet. Sneaking around at night wasn't the kind of thing I'd planned for my life, yet here I was.

"We're going to look to see what kind of cars the good doctor drives," she said.

"How are we going to do that?"

She glanced at me. "You'll see."

I subsided and sat back for the ride. That's not to say I was relaxed or had a good feeling about what we were doing—not that I really knew—but at least I wasn't asking a million questions like a ten-year-old on a road trip.

As we neared Martin's house, Amelia slowed. All the downstairs lights were on, and as we crept by, I noted a shadow moving around inside.

"He's home," I said, needlessly. Amelia had seen the same thing I had, yet she didn't seem perturbed by it.

"That's fine. I planned for that."

She drove us down the block, found a place to turn around, and then she snapped off her lights. She coasted back toward Martin's house until she found a spot where the road widened. She pulled off onto the shoulder and turned off the engine.

"Okay," I said. My skin was crawling. I scratched at my arm absently. "What now?"

Amelia pulled out a flip phone and dialed.

"Martin Castor?" Her voice was lower, deeper, to the point where I had to do a double take to make sure she was actually speaking. "I know about you and Harry Davis. I know what you've done. Meet me at your office in twenty minutes and we can talk a deal." She clicked off.

My mouth was hanging open as she stuffed the phone back into a bag. "What are you doing?"

"We'll want to dump this to be safe," she said, tossing the bag into the back seat, before she settled back.

"Amelia?" My voice had risen a few octaves in my nervousness.

She sighed. "Just wait. Martin will be scrambling to figure out what I know, who I might be, and will likely take a few moments to worry."

"And then?"

She nodded toward the driveway, which was now lit up by headlights.

"And then he'll go see what I want."

The gate opened and Martin's white Lexus pulled out of the driveway. He turned down the road, thankfully facing the opposite direction from us, and then he sped away. The gate began to slowly close.

"Do we need to make a run for it?" I asked, hand on the car door, just in case. I seriously doubted I'd be able to make it in time, but perhaps Amelia could.

"No." Amelia popped open the trunk and then got out of the car. I followed after her. "Carry this." She plopped a thick blanket into my arms before she closed the trunk and started toward Martin's property.

"Amelia!" I scurried after her.

Martin's wrought-iron fence was short enough I could touch the spikes on top without having to stand on tiptoes. It was obviously meant for decoration more than to keep anyone out, yet its effect on me was the same as if it had razor wire strung across it. I wanted no part of it.

Amelia took the blanket out of my arms and draped it over the top of the fence, covering the spikes. "After you." She grinned as she motioned toward the fence.

"I'm not climbing that thing," I said. "This is illegal."

"It's only illegal if we get caught."

"Is that what Chester teaches you?" I asked, before

a new thought hit. "Did he show you how to do this? How many times have you broken into someone's home, Amelia?"

She gave me a patented Amelia eyeroll. "This is my first time," she said. "And no, we aren't breaking into his house. We're going to go to his garage, take a peek inside to see if he has any other cars, and then we're going to go home."

I still wasn't convinced, but I really did want to see if the car Jack saw was in that garage. I'd have to figure out how to tell Detective Cavanaugh about it without telling him how I'd discovered it, but that was a problem for another day.

"Fine," I said. "But only a peek. Then we never do or speak of this again."

"I should have come alone," Amelia muttered.

I considered the fence a moment before wedging my foot between two of the bars. It was a tight fit, which served my purposes just fine. I grabbed the top of the blanket, which wasn't quite thick enough. One of the spikes poked painfully into my palm where I gripped it, but at least it didn't break skin. I counted to three, and then I pulled myself up and over. I landed so hard on my hands and knees, my teeth rattled.

Amelia was up and over in one smooth motion, making me wonder if she'd lied to me and she did this sort of thing on a nightly basis now. She landed on her feet, before dropping into a crouch. She scanned the grounds briefly before she said, "All right, to the garage." She kept low as she made for the building in question.

A light kicked on in the driveway as we neared, startling a scream from me. Under her breath,

Amelia muttered, "Chill out, Mom, it's a motion sensor."

"You chill out," I shot back. "What if he has security cameras? We didn't wear masks."

Amelia hesitated. "I don't see a camera," she said, but I noted she brushed her hair into her face with fingers that trembled ever so slightly.

A walkway connected the garage to the rest of the house. The garage doors themselves were closed, as expected, and when I gave one an experimental tug, it didn't budge.

"How do we get in?" I asked Amelia while I wondered, *Should I have worn gloves?* Now that we were here, past the point of no return, I was regretting letting Amelia talk me into this. There were so many ways this could go wrong, and none of them were within my control.

"Side door," Amelia said, and then she vanished around the corner, presumably to check to see if there even was a side entrance.

I used my shirt to wipe at the door where I'd touched it, and then followed after Amelia. When I rounded the corner, I found her standing in front of an open door.

"It was unlocked."

I really wanted to believe her, but wasn't so sure I did. I kept my concerns to myself, however, as we entered the gloom of the garage.

While Martin could fit five cars in the garage, there were only two vehicles currently sitting inside. One of them was covered with a white tarp. The other was a black SUV.

"Could that be it?" Amelia asked.

"It's not a Mercedes," I said, noting the Lexus logo. "But Jack wasn't very specific, so I suppose it might be." The SUV was dark *and* fancy, so it could very well be the one, though he'd said it was a car, not a bigger vehicle.

Amelia walked over to the covered vehicle. She lifted the tarp enough so she could peer under. "Red. Corvette. Definitely not a black Mercedes."

"Now what?" I asked, frustrated. It looked like we'd hit a dead end.

Amelia glanced toward the door leading to the covered walkway that led to the house.

"No," I said. "We came to check his cars."

"What if there's something inside?" she said. "Rich people like Martin often have home offices. If he had any connection to Christine or Joe, the proof might be in there."

"He wouldn't keep evidence of his crimes lying around where anyone could find it," I said. "I bet he has cleaners come in every couple of days."

"One quick look," Amelia said. "We won't touch anything we don't need to. We won't take anything. If we see something suspicious, I'll have Maya call it in tomorrow as an anonymous tip."

"I don't like this," I said in my latest understatement of the year. "Martin might not have cameras outside, but I can almost guarantee there'll be some inside."

"Maybe." Amelia sounded thoughtful. "But what if he doesn't?"

I closed my eyes. *This is how it ends.* "One quick look," I said, knowing I was going to regret it.

"This is kind of exciting, isn't it?" Before I could

tell her that, no, this wasn't exciting for me in the slightest, Amelia was at the door. She glanced at me once and then turned the knob. "It's unlocked." She opened the door and stepped inside.

I looked skyward and pressed my hands together. "Please forgive us." And then I followed my daughter into Martin Castor's house.

26

Amelia moved from room to room, quickly glancing inside each before moving on to the next. I trailed after her, anticipating the moment when the police would arrive and ship us to a maximum security prison. While Amelia was hurrying, I willed her to go faster. Every room she dismissed was one room closer to getting out of there.

Everything was high-end in Martin's house. The floors were real hardwood, the appliances top-of-the-line. Televisions took up entire walls. Sound systems were displayed in every corner. The only thing missing was a library, though we still had quite a few more rooms to go where one could pop up.

At least an alarm hadn't sounded. As far as I could tell, there were no cameras within plain sight. Maybe we had lucked out and Martin's overconfidence would allow us to escape unnoticed.

"Here we are," Amelia said, slipping into a room on the second floor.

"How do you know this is his office?" I closed the

door part of the way. It wouldn't help us if Martin were to come home, but it gave me a false sense of security anyway.

"The desk. The safe." She rolled her eyes. "Geesh, Mom, it's not hard to figure out."

"Yeah, yeah." My face was hot. I wasn't used to being shown up by my daughter. "What are we looking for?"

"I'm not sure." She moved to the desk and started scanning the things set atop it. There was a monitor, a date book, and a few files, but little else. "We'll know it when we see it."

I moved to the only bookshelf I'd seen in the entire house. It was full of medical texts that looked brand-new. Pulling one free, I noted the pages had that unbroken look to them, as if he'd never once opened the books. *It's all for show.*

It didn't surprise me. After seeing Nurse Uma, I had a feeling that image mattered more to Martin Castor than results. I reshelved the book, careful to make sure I put it back exactly where I'd found it.

As Amelia went through Martin's desk, I moved slowly around the room, looking for anything that jumped out at me as a clue. Not that I knew what that looked like. I was so out of my depth here, I felt like I was drowning.

There were photographs on the wall. All of them were of Martin standing with important-looking people. I recognized a few, but most of them were unfamiliar to me. I was halfway through them when Amelia's excited voice broke the silence.

"Got it!"

I spun to find Amelia holding a memo pad and grinning. "You've got what?"

"The dingbat keeps his safe combination in his

desk." She handed me the pad, and sure enough, it was there, scrawled across the top. He'd even written *safe combination,* at the top of the page.

"Are you sure it goes to *this* safe?" I mean, what's the point of having a safe if you're just going to leave the combination lying around?

"There's only one way to find out." Amelia turned and rested her hand on the dial. "Read off the numbers for me."

Feeling even more like a criminal than I had before, I read off the combination, while Amelia spun the dial. I kind of expected a man like Martin to have a high-tech safe, one that required a numerical code that changed every day and you needed a descrambler to decode it.

Or maybe I just read too many books.

I had to admit, as Amelia spun the dial to the final number, a sense of excitement washed over me. Sure, what we were doing was illegal, but it was for a good cause. There was a chance Martin Castor was a murderer, and finding evidence of his crime was paramount. So what if I got into trouble? If it put him in jail, it would be worth it.

Of course, there was the tiny little problem of explaining how I'd come by the evidence if we did get out of there unnoticed, but I'd cross that bridge when I came to it.

Amelia glanced back at me as the safe made a click. She grabbed the handle, grinned like she was about to open a Christmas present, and then pulled.

The door swung open.

The bottom of the safe held a box of files. Amelia knelt and went straight for them, an eager gleam to her eye.

I, however, noted the single folder on the top

shelf. I wouldn't have seen it if it had been placed farther back, but as it was, it sat crooked on the shelf, as
if it had recently been tossed inside without care, so I
was able to see its corner. I gingerly pulled it free,
fully expecting an alarm to go off as I did.

It didn't, of course.

"These are patient records," Amelia said. "I don't
see anything about Joe or Christine Danvers, and I
don't recognize any of these names."

I opened my file, scanned the page. My heart did a
hiccup and then started racing. "Amelia. Stop."

She glanced up. "Did you find something? I don't
think any of this stuff will help us." She shoved the
file she was holding back into the box.

"I think so." I scanned the page again, my head
started to pound in time with my heart. "I think I
know what happened to Christine."

Amelia rose and snatched the folder out of my
hand as my mind tried to process what I'd just read.

"Wait . . ." Amelia's eyes widened. "These are DNA
results." She scanned the page. "Does this say what I
think it says?"

I nodded. "Hue Hemingway wasn't Christine's father."

Amelia met my eye. "Sterling Wright is."

It made so much sense. I don't know how it happened, but somehow, Sterling Wright and Joan Hemingway ended up together. I wasn't sure if it was
consensual or not, but the results were the same. Joan
became pregnant with Sterling's baby.

It wasn't difficult to draw the line from that moment, all the way to Joe's death. Something happened and Sterling killed Joan and Hue—or at least,
had them killed. Maybe they wouldn't let him see his
daughter. Maybe he found out about the pregnancy

and cover-up later and was angry about being left out.

Either way, they're killed, Christine is sent out for adoption, and then, as an adult, she discovers who her real father is—and that he killed her parents.

It would explain why she ran, rather than turn him in. She might hate him for what he'd done to her parents, but Sterling was still her real father. She leaves town, changes her name so he can't find her, but doesn't take her husband for some reason. Maybe Sterling threatened his life or she simply didn't have time.

Joe is blamed for her murder, he vanishes, changes his name as well. Then, when he comes back to Grey Falls and resumes looking for his wife, he discovers something that leads back to Sterling, who then kills Joe to cover his tracks.

"It explains why Sterling is keeping Detective Cavanaugh locked away in meetings," I said, working it through. "Even Wayne Hastings said something about being distracted at the time of the original investigation."

"We have to get this to the police somehow," Amelia said. "They'll know what to do with it." She shook the file at me. "Martin is implicated in this too. He ran the tests. I bet he's been covering for Wright this entire time."

"What about Harry Davis?" I asked.

Amelia shook her head. "His name doesn't come up, but I think it's pretty obvious he's involved somehow."

"He *did* show up screaming at Chester about him poking around in his life and following him."

"Yeah, but we *weren't* following him," Amelia said. "Someone else must know."

"Or maybe Sterling is getting nervous," I said. "Martin acted like someone was following him too. What if Sterling Wright was getting worried and had Martin and Harry watched to make sure they weren't going to turn him in?"

"It makes sense," Amelia said. "Perhaps Martin kept this file for blackmail purposes." She held the file as if it might catch on fire at any moment.

"I bet you're right." It made me wonder if there was some way we could talk Martin into turning on Sterling. If he turned the file over to the cops himself, then there'd be no reason for Detective Cavanaugh to ever become aware of Amelia's and my transgression.

The windows lit up, cutting our conversation short.

"Is that . . . ?" I asked, unable to finish the question. Some part of me hoped that if I left the question hanging, then it couldn't possibly be true.

"He's back!" Amelia rushed to the window and glanced outside. "There's others with him." She cursed. "I see Harry Davis. And Mr. Wright!"

Panic tried to blank my mind. "What are we going to do?"

Amelia was already moving. She shoved the box of files back into the safe, and then, after a moment's hesitation, placed the file with Sterling and Christine's DNA comparison back onto the top shelf. She closed the safe door, spun the dial, and then dropped the memo pad back into Martin's desk.

Together we made for the door, but it was already far too late to escape. The office was on the second floor, which meant we had to go down the stairs, which spilled out into a large open area that could be seen from any number of rooms. All it would take is one glance and we'd be caught.

Still, Amelia made for the stairs. She'd just reached the top step when voices came from below.

"It had to have been a crank call," Harry said.

"They claimed they knew about us," Martin said. "She mentioned our names!"

"Not mine," Sterling said. "You shouldn't have called me. You risked everything by being so stupid."

"Me?" Martin's laugh was near hysterical. "You're the one who couldn't leave well enough alone. He didn't have anything. But no, you just had to put an end to his pointless investigation, all for *your* sake. You didn't even think of how this might come back on the rest of us."

Amelia and I shared a knowing look.

"No one is in any danger here," Sterling said. "Keep your heads about you and everything will turn out as it always does. I'm keeping the detective in charge of the investigation busy. He won't be able to work the case, which means, we are at no risk."

"People are asking questions," Martin said. "It's getting too dangerous."

The voices moved deeper into the house. Amelia and I gave it a count of ten, then started down the stairs. I couldn't make out what was being said, at least, not until we reached the bottom step.

"I'm not doing this anymore," Harry was saying. "I had nothing to do with any of this, yet people are looking into *me*. I saw them following me."

"It's your imagination." Sterling said it in a way that made me wonder if, indeed, *he* was the one keeping an eye on Harry. "Like I said, no one is in any danger."

Amelia started toward the front door, but I hesitated. While what I'd heard would help me convince Detective Cavanaugh to look into Sterling Wright, along with Martin Castor, I was still missing the smoking gun. If I could just get one of them to confess, to say something that wasn't so darn vague, then maybe I could put an end to the investigation right then and there.

I motioned for Amelia to keep going, mouthing that I'd be along in a minute. I was close to the door. If they started to come my way, I could make a run for it.

Amelia gave me a frightened look, but I waved her off. I would be okay. After a moment, she carefully opened the door and slipped outside.

"I'll get you set up so you can trace any further calls," Sterling said. "We'll find out who did this, and see what they know."

"I bet it's that PI, Chudzinski," Martin said. "He's been working the investigation again. Apparently, he's got a couple girls working for him now."

"They'll find nothing," Sterling said. "That is, if Harry doesn't ruin it for all of us. You never should have brought him in on this."

"I needed help," Martin said, his voice lowered. "He did his part."

"And then turned around and screwed it all up again. I've had to put someone on him to make sure he doesn't do anything stupid. If he keeps it up, he's going to end up like Joe Danvers."

"Now, Sterling, we don't need to go that far."

I leaned forward, straining my ears to hear any hint of Harry's presence. They were talking about him like he wasn't in the room with them.

A cold chill crept up my spine. If he wasn't with them, then where was he?

I decided now would be a good time to get out of there. I peeked around the edge of the staircase to make sure no one was looking my way, and then, seeing the coast was clear, I made a run for it.

And walked right into a very surprised Harry Davis.

There was a moment when neither of us knew what to do. We stared at one another, mouths agape, hands outstretched, but not touching.

In that brief moment, I might have been able to do something. I could have shoved him over, could have rushed the door and gotten away. Even if he recognized me, he wouldn't be able to go to the police without it coming out about his part in Christine's disappearance and Joe's murder.

Instead of running, however, fear had me frozen to the spot.

"Martin!" Harry shouted, regaining his composure faster. "Someone's here!"

I made a belated attempt to make a break for it, but now, Harry was between me and the door, and he looked ready to tackle me if need be.

So, I went the other way.

I bolted around the staircase, both away from Harry and from where I'd last heard Martin's and Sterling's voices. Unfortunately, I was also running opposite the direction in which the garage was located, which meant I was fleeing into the unknown.

Footfalls and voices came from behind me. After only a few moments, the sounds spread out, and I realized they were separating to better trap me. I rushed to the nearest window, tried to open it, but it didn't budge. The window beside it was the same.

All this money and he doesn't have windows that open? I wanted to scream, but that would only give me away.

Footfalls neared. I was in a sprawling living room with only one large exit, which spilled out into the rest of the house. I, of course, was nowhere near a place where I could escape without getting caught, so I did the only thing I could think of.

I ducked down behind the couch.

"I know you are in here." Sterling's voice was hard, uncaring. "There's nowhere for you to go."

I clamped a hand over my mouth and nose and tried not to breathe. Little whimpering sounds tried to burst free, but I somehow managed to swallow them back.

"What part of our conversation did you happen to hear?" Sterling asked. "I'm assuming you're the one who called Martin this evening?"

The light clicked on, blinding me briefly. The jig, so they said, was up. I couldn't hide behind the couch forever. All it would take would be for Sterling to walk around the room and he'd have me. There was always a chance I could make a run for the door once he came around one side of the couch, but it was going to be a close thing.

Martin and Harry came into the room then, and spread out. So much for my escape plan.

"Come out," Sterling demanded. "There's nowhere to run."

I closed my eyes, prayed that Amelia was long gone by now. She'd seen the file, knew who killed Joe. She could go to Cavanaugh and tell him everything. He'd find a way to get a warrant, and then Sterling Wright, Harry Davis, and Martin Castor would be taken where they couldn't hurt anyone ever again.

Unfortunately, it might be too late for me by then.

I rose from where I crouched, determined to meet my fate standing.

There was no recognition in either Martin's or Sterling's eyes, but Harry knew me. He was running his hands through his hair incessantly and looked ready to rabbit out of there. It made me wonder if he'd actually had a part in Joe's murder, or if he was a convenient scapegoat for the other two.

"The police know I'm here," I said.

"I seriously doubt that." Sterling's voice was surprisingly calm for having been overheard discussing his crimes. He glanced at Harry. "Make sure she was alone."

"I am," I said. "I know everything."

"This isn't good." Harry tugged at his hair.

"Go make sure she's alone," Sterling said, never taking his eyes from me. "I'll take care of this."

Harry hesitated only a moment longer before he hurried out of the room.

"What are you going to do to her?" Martin asked. "I'm not covering for you anymore."

"You won't have to. No one will know what happened here tonight." Sterling stepped forward and held out a hand. "If you would, please, come with me."

"I'm not sure I want to do that," I said.

"You really have no choice."

I considered making one last attempt at escape, but ended up allowing Sterling to walk forward and grab me by the arm. As long as Amelia got away, then I'd suffer whatever fate he had planned for me.

Martin produced a ball of twine from a drawer in the room. He handed it to Sterling, as if they'd done this sort of thing before, and Sterling proceeded to tie my wrists behind my back. He moved with a calm calculation that spoke of someone who always got exactly what he wanted. He wasn't afraid, which in turn made me terrified.

"Let's go," he said, guiding me out the door. And then, to Martin, "Keep Harry contained. Explain to him that everything will be fine. Go about your day tomorrow like any other day. If you think he's going to cause us trouble, do whatever you think is necessary to make sure that doesn't happen."

"I understand."

Sterling shoved me in the back, causing me to stagger. He took me to his car—a black Mercedes, no less—and opened the back door for me. "Slide on in, Ms. . . . I didn't catch your name."

"Denton," I said almost mechanically. If I was going to die, I might as well go being called by my name, not Miss or Lady or whatever he'd decide on. It was the only comfort I could give myself.

That, and Amelia got away.

I got into the car, knowing it was probably one of the last things I'd ever do. Sterling reached in and buckled me in securely. "Can't be too careful," he said, before getting into the front of the vehicle. He glanced back at me and smiled. "Let's go for a ride, shall we?"

27

Twine bit into my wrists as I tried to work my hands free of their bindings. Unfortunately, Sterling had tied me up pretty tightly, so there was little give, and I wasn't strong enough to break it.

That didn't mean I didn't try. My wrists were raw, but I had yet to break skin. Maybe if I did, I'd be able to slip out of his knots, thanks to my blood slickening my bonds.

We rode in silence, with Sterling only paying me occasional glances in the rearview mirror. I'd expected him to interrogate me the entire way to wherever we were going, but he appeared content to let me fidget. I think he was getting some perverse pleasure out of it. He was smiling like he was.

Eventually, we left the main roads and turned down a dark, forested path. The Mercedes bounced down the rough dirt road filled with potholes and the occasional large rock. As we bounced along a rather large rut, a low-hanging branch scraped alongside the car with an ear-splitting whine.

"That'll leave a mark," I muttered. It was petty, but at that point, I was going to take every win I could get.

"It'll get repaired," Sterling said, sounding just as unconcerned as his words implied. "I always fix everything."

"Is that what this is?" I asked, sagging back into my seat. It wasn't like I thought I could throw myself from the car and escape into the woods, even if I did break the twine. "A fix?"

"For my troubles? Yes, it is." He sighed. "I'm sorry it's come to this, Mrs. Denton, I really am. You seem decent enough, though I do wish you would have left well enough alone. Joe Danvers was definitely not worth all this trouble."

"He didn't hurt anyone," I said. "He didn't deserve to die."

"Maybe not," Sterling said. "But he was getting too close. I gave him as much leeway as I could, yet he insisted on looking for his wife."

"You mean your daughter."

Sterling's hands tightened on the steering wheel so much, I could hear it groan. "She should never have been born. Her mother made a mistake and she paid for it."

"With her life." I didn't know why I was egging him on, but I couldn't help it. This man had killed people. I didn't care how much money, how much power he had, he didn't deserve my respect.

"As I said, I fix things. When the Hemingways decided to go public, I had to silence them before they could make a mess of my career. It was unfortunate, but had to be done. Ah, here we are."

We turned down a gravel drive that seemed to vanish into trees and brush. Without his headlights, the darkness would have been absolute.

The driveway ended at a log cabin deep into the woods. A large, sparkling lake could be seen down a slight decline. It reflected the moon and surrounding trees with near perfect clarity. It would have been beautiful if it hadn't been so ominous. Sterling parked his Mercedes alongside the cabin and got out. He opened my door and grabbed me by the arm. His touch was surprisingly gentle.

"We're going to go inside for a little chat," he said. "Then, together, we'll make my troubles go away."

I glanced at the lake. "How many bodies are beneath those waters?"

Sterling smiled. "Enough."

I tensed, a brief thought of running flashing through my mind, but Sterling produced a gun from his pocket. I'm not sure where it had come from, but it was there now, and all hope of escape died for good.

"Don't try anything," he said. "I'd rather this not be messy."

I let him lead me into the cabin. Inside, it was clean and tidy, and looked well used. I didn't see a man like Sterling Wright as someone who would spend time fishing at the lake, but there were fishing poles in the corner that looked to have been recently used, as well as a pair of muddy rubber boots.

"It's not mine," he said, as if reading my thoughts. "Martin keeps this place because . . ." He glanced around the room with a grimace. "I don't know why. We've moved well beyond when this sort of life is necessary. Yet, I suppose I can't be too cross with him. I've used his hidey-hole quite often over the years."

He shoved me down onto the couch. I fell heavily onto my side, nearly wrenching my shoulder out of its socket since my hands were still bound. It took some work, but I managed to sit back upright. I fixed Sterling with a stare that would have killed a lesser man.

"What are you going to do with me?" I asked, somehow keeping my voice from trembling. I wanted to be sick, wanted to close my eyes and pretend none of this was happening.

But it was, and I refused to show weakness. A man like Sterling Wright would feed on it.

"We talk." Sterling snagged a chair from a dining nook and set it in front of me. He sat down and crossed one leg over the other. He rested the gun in his lap, pointed in my general direction. "Who knows about me?"

"No one," I said. "I didn't know until just before you showed up. I was on Martin's trail." And then, because if I was going to die, I wasn't going to go down without causing as much trouble for bad people as I could, I added, "He has a file on you. I think he's biding his time until he can use it against you."

"Does he now?" Sterling didn't seem too bothered by the idea. "Blackmail is it? Or do you think he'll go to the police?" He smiled. "Would it even matter?"

"You've been controlling them."

He waved the gun, dismissing my comment. My heart leapt into my throat as I watched the barrel wave in front of my face. Thankfully, it didn't go off.

"Nothing so dramatic," Sterling said, returning the gun to his lap. "I've distracted them, that's all. It's not difficult, you know? A meeting here, a new required training session there. And before you know it, the evidence against me is gone, the trouble has passed, and we all move on with our lives."

"Except for the people you've murdered."

"True." Sterling sighed and sat back, casual as you like. If it wasn't for the gun and my bound hands, you'd think we were having a pleasant evening chitchat. "But the rest of the world still moves on, does it not? People die all the time. And when it's in the name of progress, it's a nasty reality we can't avoid."

"I'm pretty sure not everyone kills people who get in their way."

"No, but they should. It's far easier to make a body disappear or an investigation fade away than it is to fight battles against those who feel they are owed something. And removing these irritants proves I deserve my place in the world."

"Or that you can't win fairly."

He laughed. "*Fair* rarely plays into my line of work."

My mind raced. There had to be a way out of this that didn't end up with me going for a long, deep swim. "I'm friends with the detective on the case, Detective Cavanaugh. He won't just drop Joe's murder. And if I vanish, he'll look even harder. How long do you think it will be before he puts it all together?"

"Maybe he will, maybe he won't," Sterling said. "The evidence against me is gone; I made sure of that. And even if the good detective suspects me of a crime, he won't ever find you. You'll have vanished, just like Christine did all those years ago. Someone will be framed for your murder, just like Joe was for his wife's. It'll all be nice and tidy and easily manipulated."

"You told Harry to lie about Joe. Are you going to have him make up a story about me too?"

"Perhaps, but I had no direct hand in his involvement. Martin was the one who brought Harry in. I wouldn't have chosen to do so, but by the time I realized what he was doing, it was too late. He does work as an effective scapegoat if it comes to it, however."

"Martin knows about Christine," I said. "He ran DNA tests. He knows about me too. Your little scheme has holes in it. If he talks, or decides things have gone too far, he's going to turn on you."

For the first time since we'd arrived, a look passed over Sterling's face that wasn't arrogant or confident. Was it fear? It was hard to tell with my own fear overriding everything.

"I take it you weren't entirely untruthful about Martin keeping a file on me," he said. "I suppose I'll have to deal with that after I'm finished with you." Sterling stood and stretched. For an older man, he seemed awfully limber. "You'd think he'd realize that he can't use anything he has against me without his own crimes coming to light."

"He killed someone." I knew it without needing to be told.

"At his practice. On purpose, no less. The man wasn't to his liking, if you understand my meaning. This was before *Doctor* Castor decided to limit his patients to those who fit his ideologies and lusts." The sneer reached his voice. "He did a good job making it look like an accident, but not good enough. It happened at an opportune time for me."

"You covered for him."

"I did."

"And in return, he'd run your DNA test for you,

would keep your secrets, and would help you kill innocent people?"

"It's a small price to pay considering the alternative, wouldn't you say?" Sterling checked his watch. "I suppose we should cut this short. I have an early meeting in the morning with your Detective Cavanaugh. I wouldn't want to show up to it too bleary-eyed." He flashed me a smile. "Sit tight. I'll be right back." He went to the door, opened it, and then vanished into the night.

As soon as he was gone, I started working at the twine. Panic was trying to well up inside me, but I kept it in check as best I could. If I panicked now, I might miss something that would help me. If I did that, then I wouldn't be leaving these woods.

I'll literally be swimming with the fishes. A giggle burst from my lips. I was on the edge of hysteria, and there wasn't a thing I could do about it but succumb.

"Mom!" The harsh whisper came from behind me.

"Amelia?" I stood, and very nearly tripped over my own two feet as I spun. "What are you doing here?"

"I followed you. The police are on their way." She hurried across the room and produced a pocket knife. "Turn around. I'll cut you free."

"Hurry," I said, turning my back to her. "He could be back at any moment. He has a gun."

She sliced through the twine like it was butter. "I know. I heard—and recorded—everything."

"Where were you hiding?" I asked, rubbing at my wrists. "And how did you get in?"

"The bathroom. The window was easy to open. We can get out that way."

Amelia led the way through the cabin, to a small bathroom. There was just enough room for a small sink, the toilet, and a standup shower. The window was next to the toilet, and was thankfully large enough so I wouldn't have to try to squeeze through like Play-Doh through a clenched fist.

As soon as we were inside the tiny room, I closed the door. It made the room feel even more claustrophobic.

Amelia motioned for me to precede her through the window, but I shook my head.

"No chance," I said. "You go. I'll follow."

"I can boost you up."

"I'll be fine. I'm not going to risk you getting caught."

"I don't want to leave you behind."

"Amelia." I put on my Mom voice. "Do as I say. If we keep arguing about it, he's going to come back and catch the both of us."

She made a frustrated sound and rolled her eyes, but she did as she was told for once.

Amelia used the toilet to boost herself up and through the window. When she jumped down, I could hear her land in the leaves outside. I sucked in a worried breath, but Sterling didn't call out or fire his gun at the sound.

"All right, Liz. Let's do this." I put a foot onto the toilet, and grabbed the windowsill. The seat shifted as I tested my weight, and a flash of fear shot through me. *What if I'm too heavy?* It was a stupid thought, but I couldn't help it. It would be just my luck to fall through the lid and get my foot stuck in the toilet.

The front door opened. Sterling had returned.

My muscles strained as I pulled myself up onto the toilet the rest of the way. The window wasn't *too* far off the ground, but it was far enough that I worried I wouldn't be fast enough.

"Mrs. Denton, this is pointless. You have nowhere to go."

Sterling's voice came from deeper in the cabin. It wouldn't be long before he checked the bathroom.

I hunkered down, coiling up like a cat might before a high leap. I checked my grip on the windowsill to make sure it was secure, took a deep breath, and then leapt.

At the same instant, the bathroom door flew open.

Adrenaline shot through me. On a normal day, I might have been able to pull myself up and through the window, and slide right down to the other side somewhat gently.

Instead, I flew through the window as if I'd been shot out of a cannon. My knee cracked the windowsill, upending me as I passed through the opening. By some grace of fate, I didn't land on my head, but continued to flip. I slammed hard into the ground, back-first.

"Geez, Mom!" Amelia hissed, just as Sterling shouted, "Get back here!"

Amelia met my eyes. Hers were nearly popping from her head.

"I'm okay," I gasped, barely about to get enough air to speak. "Go."

She helped me to my feet and we started to run.

"Car's this way," Amelia said, taking the lead.

We'd taken only a pair of steps in the direction of her car when a gunshot rang out. The bullet struck a tree about two feet in front of us.

Amelia screamed and veered off, into the trees. I followed after her. A spot between my shoulder blades itched, and I fully expected another shot to follow, but it didn't.

Instead, I could hear Sterling running behind us. He was already too close for comfort.

"He's gaining," I gasped. There was no way I was going to reach Amelia's car. My back was screaming, and I still had yet to regain my breath from having it knocked out of me during my fall. I was slowing her down.

I made a snap decision then. Without informing Amelia of my intentions, I darted around a tree and came to an abrupt halt. It was too dark to see much, but my foot hit something in the brush at my feet. I knelt and came up with a thick branch that felt half rotten.

It would have to do.

Footfalls neared. I reared back, anticipation making my hands slick. Every breath came out ragged, and I was positive Sterling would hear me long before he reached the spot I needed him to.

But Sterling Wright was an older man. And while he might be fitter than your average seventy-something, he was still getting up there in years. His own breathing was just as loud as mine.

Time seemed to slow down and speed up at the same time. His pant grew louder, as did his footfalls. I remained poised and ready.

The moment Sterling reached the tree behind which I was hiding, I put every last ounce of strength I had left into a swing.

The branch caught him square on the nose. It shattered in a spray of spongy bark in my hand, but it served its purpose.

Sterling's feet went out from under him, while his head came to an abrupt halt. He grunted and then landed hard onto his back. The gun in his hand went flying into the woods.

I raised the stub of branch I had left, ready to knock him back down with it if he tried to rise, but Sterling wasn't moving. He was still breathing, but he was out cold.

As I sagged to my knees, completely spent—both mentally and physically—sirens sounded in the distance. Before long, Martin Castor's fishing cabin was awash in strobe lights, and I was sitting in the back of an ambulance, hugging my daughter close, happy that we were both still alive.

28

"Are you sure you don't want a carrier?" I asked, limping only slightly as I followed Erik Deavers to the front door.

"No, I think we'll be okay, don't you?" He brought Sheamus up to his face.

Sheamus sneezed.

"I guess I deserved that," Erik said with a laugh. He wiped at his face with the back of his hand. "Thank you for everything, Liz."

"Of course." I ran a hand over my eyes, which were starting to tear up. "I'm glad you're taking Sheamus. I think your dad would be proud."

"I hope so." Erik sighed and set Sheamus down. The cat immediately headed toward Wheels, who was watching, but he couldn't go far; the Maine Coon was wearing a harness. "I wish I would have had the chance to meet him."

"Me too." I knelt and ran a hand over Sheamus's back. "What are you going to do now?"

"Go home," Erik said. "Get my place ready for this

guy." When he smiled at Sheamus, I could see the affection there. The Maine Coon was going to a good home. "I'll take some time to visit Mom's grave, let her know what happened. I'll have to come back to deal with Dad's estate, and when I do, I hope we can get together."

"I'd like that," I said. "You have my number."

Erik patted the pocket where he kept his phone. "I can't believe all of this happened because some guy was afraid people would find out he'd cheated on his wife."

"People do stupid things all of the time," I said. Apparently, Sterling Wright had been newly married at the time Christine was conceived, a fact I hadn't known until recently. His wife died over ten years ago, and I wondered if he'd assisted her along. I doubt I'll ever know for sure. "Not everyone has the power to make them go away."

Erik nodded, and then picked up Sheamus. "I'd best hit the road."

"Hey, did you ever find out who broke into your hotel room?"

"I did." Erik sounded relieved as he said it. "Turns out, one of the hotel employees is married to one of the cops on the force. Guess she thought I was guilty of murdering Dad, thanks to her husband, and decided to wreck my room for me."

"Wow." I didn't know what else to say.

"I decided not to press charges or anything. The woman was fired, as was the friend who'd helped her, and I figure that was punishment enough."

"That was big of you." I wasn't sure I could have left it at that.

"Maybe." He hugged Sheamus to his chest. "I can't say I won't be happy to get home."

"Well, safe travels. Be good, Sheamus."

The cat meowed at me as Erik opened the door and headed for his car.

I watched them go, a strange sense of melancholy washing over me. I was glad Sheamus had found a home, but I was going to miss him. I had a feeling Wheels felt the same. She joined me at the door and, together, we stood watching until Erik's car vanished down the road with a farewell honk.

"It's just us, I suppose," I told Wheels as I closed the door.

She rubbed up against my leg, and then sped away, chasing after something unseen.

"Or not." I smiled after her.

"Mom, have you seen my keys?" Ben bounded down the stairs, dressed in a pair of his dad's scrubs. Kittens playing with twine decorated the powder-blue material. "Never mind." He snatched the keys in question off the table.

"Aren't you getting the keys to your new place today?" I asked him.

"Yeah." He grinned. "Then it's off to work."

"So, you're going through with it?" I asked. "Working full-time."

"Yep. I'm a working man now. No more slacking off."

And no more helping me with the rescues. It was a bittersweet moment. I was glad he was moving on with his life, but at the same time, I was going to miss having him around all the time. "Well, have fun. Let me know if you need me for anything."

He kissed me on the cheek. "I will." A strange look came into his eyes then. "I guess I should tell you that I won't be living alone."

"Oh? A new girlfriend already?"

He laughed. "No, not quite. It's Jack. I told him if he lays off the drugs and booze, and if he tries to find a job, he can live with me. After a few months, I expect him to pay his share. If he can't . . ." He shrugged, his meaning obvious.

Pride made my chest swell and tears come to my eyes. "You're a good friend, Ben. He doesn't deserve you."

"Does anyone?" He winked, and then made for the door. "I'll see you tonight."

And then, like Erik, he was gone.

"All right, Mom, you're all set."

I turned to find Amelia entering the room. While I was bruised and sore, there wasn't a mark on her that said that five days ago, she'd run through the woods, a killer on her tail. She had a closed laptop tucked under her arm.

"She pass?"

"With flying colors." She leaned against the wall. "No history of, well, anything. Chico is going to be in good hands."

"That's great." I was still annoyed that the poor Chihuahua had gone through so much, but was happy he was going to a home where he'd be loved.

Two days ago, Stacy Hildebrand had shown up on my doorstep, Chico in hand, demanding I find the dog a new home. Apparently, she'd always planned on giving up the Chihuahua, and Courtney had used her to try to make me look bad. The whole story about a stolen dog was, as suspected, just one big show.

"I'm going to Maya's for a little bit. I might crash at her place, so don't wait up for me or anything."

"All right," I said. I crossed the room and kissed her on the cheek. Amelia made a face. "Are you going to Chester's later?" She'd taken the last few days off to recover from our near-death experience, and I was kind of worried the nightmarish event had put her off working as a PI for good.

"Not today. I think I'll head back into the office tomorrow. I deserve a little time off. I mean, I *did* help unmask a killer."

"That, you did." And I couldn't be prouder.

Amelia headed for the door. A moment later, I was alone in the house with Wheels.

The quiet wouldn't last for long.

Sterling Wright was behind bars, as were his accomplices, Martin Castor and Harry Davis. I didn't know what all would stick, but that was okay. There was no way they were going to talk their way out of some serious jail time, not with people dead. I only wished I knew why Christine had run without taking Joe with her. Sterling wasn't talking, but I hoped that Martin eventually would. The story needed to come out.

I was sure I was going to get reprimanded at some point, but so far, Detective Cavanaugh had yet to show up on my doorstep with handcuffs in hand. Maybe he'd forgive my illegal activities since it helped put a killer away. Besides, like Amelia, I deserved a break. It had been a rough week.

I rubbed at my lower back as I crossed the room to my phone. I was going to have to take some more pain pills soon. Nothing was broken, but I felt like I'd been beaten with a large stick for hours.

I picked up the phone and dialed. Everything had worked out. The killers were caught, Sheamus had found a home, and both my children were moving on with their lives. Before long, Manny and I would be able to move to that beach he'd talked about.

Today, however, was not that day.

"Hi, Duke," I said when the phone was answered. "Chico is good to go. I can pick you up in twenty, and I promise, this time, I'll leave the drama at home."

Connect with Us

Visit us online at
KensingtonBooks.com
to read more from your favorite authors, see books
by series, view reading group guides, and more.

Join us on social media

for sneak peeks, chances to win books and prize packs,
and to share your thoughts with other readers.

facebook.com/kensingtonpublishing
twitter.com/kensingtonbooks

Tell us what you think!

To share your thoughts, submit a review,
or sign up for our eNewsletters, please visit:
KensingtonBooks.com/TellUs.